Volume VII

Where to Now Jack?

Frank English

2QT Limited (Publishing)

First Edition published 2022

2QT Limited (Publishing)
Settle, North Yorkshire
BD24 9BZ

Cover design: Charlotte Mouncey
Cover images: main photographs supplied by ©Frank English
Additional images from iStockhoto.com

Printed in Great Britain by IngramSparks UK Ltd

A CIP catalogue record for this book is available
from the British Library
ISBN 978-1-914083-50-1

To my wife, Denise Anne English,
without whose support and encouragement
Jack's life would never have appeared in print

"Carry On Jack"
... end of last chapter

Jack wasn't used to being in bed by ten o'clock and, because his mind was still whirling with the day's events, he found difficulty in slipping into unconsciousness. He had never been a sound sleeper, finding early nights an anathema.

Finally drifting into a shallow doze, he was startled into stark reality by Jenny's shrill, stentorian voice. "Jack!" she gasped. "Come quick! Mum was making a gurgling noise a few moments ago, and now she's not breathing. Help, please?"

...and now the story continues...

Chapter 1

"**Q**uick! Jack!"

Jenny's panicky, hoarse whisper added urgency to Jack's legs.

He set to quickly to try to bring Flora Mae back to them. "Paramedics, Jen?" Jack suggested quietly, but very concerned. "Quickly! We're losing her!"

Jenny rushed out of the room to phone for an ambulance as Jack continued with his near futile efforts to revive Flora Mae.

"Come on, lass," he urged, quietly insistent, hoping she would respond. "Tha can't leave us now. Too much to do yet, and we haven't spent enough time together."

The door flew back on its hinges, letting in two burly lads dressed in green coveralls and carrying large equipment-filled bags.

"All right, sir," the larger one said in a broad Geordie accent. "I'll take over from here. Prepare the defibrillator, George," he threw over his shoulder to his mate. "Soon have things sorted."

"Will she be all right?" Jenny asked, tears streaming down her cheeks, once they had stopped after twenty minutes or so. "She's gone, hasn't she?"

"I'm afraid so," he replied softly. "There's no response at all, so I'm afraid … 1.22am, George."

"She's gone, Jack," Jenny said, her shoulders heaving in

utter sorrow as she buried her face in Jack's chest. He drew her closer, trying to console the inconsolable. "She's gone."

"We have to take her into the hospital," George the paramedic said quietly. "If you like, we can blues it through town, and you could follow in your car."

"OK," Jack replied, still trying to soothe his wife's convulsive sobs. "We'll do that."

The journey to hospital passed in a nightmarish blur. Jack felt the ambulance siren cutting into his consciousness, but Jenny felt nothing other than the grief that had overwhelmed her. She had loved her mother much more than any dutiful daughter would have done, partly because they had been through so much together and partly because of that tight unseen bond that only *they* shared and were aware of.

"We're here, my lovely," Jack said gently, as he drew to a halt in the hospital's car park. As they got out of the car, an unmissable orange sign reminded him that he would have to pay to park in *this* car park.

He slid his arm around Jenny's waist to help her limp and unresponsive body out of the car, leading her to her mum's final resting place on this earth. Although largely empty, the traditional hospital smell pervaded the building, drawing his mind back to the desperate times when he had had an association with similar places.

Once the usual formalities had been completed, including a brief chat with a police officer concerning the protocol surrounding post-mortems, they were directed to a sterile, comfortless holding area. This would allow hospital staff to lay out Flora Mae's body so that her daughter might spend some time with her.

"Mr and Mrs Ingles?" a quietly spoken lilt crept into their sheltered circle. "Come this way, please. Your mother is through here."

Walking into the screened area to be met by Flora

Mae's still and pale body, covered to her throat by a pristine white sheet, rocked Jack back on his heels. His mind flooded once again with images and memories of *his* own mam in that state. He fought back the emotions; although he had loved his 'surrogate' mum, his purpose here was to support his *wife* in *her* grief as she sat close to her mam's form with head bowed and sobs convulsing her body.

"Well, owd lass, this *is* a pretty pickle." His low, soft voice broke into the stifling silence as he started a conversation with his wife's dead mother, who was obviously still alive in his mind.

"No idea what Jim's going to say or do," he went on, drawing Jenny's unresisting body closer to him. "Very upset that he wasn't here to support you, I should imagine. Still, we'll all be together at some time in the future, no doubt. Don't worry. We'll look after him."

Jenny slipped her arm round his waist; wiping her face, she kissed his cheek. Only her Jack, eh?

"I'm sure you can recall many a good time together, Our Jen," Jack said with a smile, "and no doubt a few not so good."

"Yes, I can," Jenny replied with a deep sigh, as she tried to fight off the tears that were threatening once again.

"Any you'd particularly like to share?" he asked, trying to engage her positive thoughts. "Perhaps from before I came on the scene?"

"Well…" she started, her voice fading into the normal background noise in evidence at this time, early morning in a busy hospital.

Jack knew that his diversionary tactic was just that, something to take her mind away briefly from stark reality. He knew, too, that it would take time for her to come to terms with the loss of her beloved mother – he only had to think back to *his* own losses. All he could do, as a loving husband, was to be there, and to share and support. He knew only too well there would be many tearful occasions that he wouldn't be *able* to take away or assuage. He simply would need to be … there.

"You do realise, of course, that we will have the unenviable task of telling Jim," Jack said, dropping his voice to a whisper once a silence crept into their stalled conversation. "That's something I'm not looking forward to."

"Sooner rather than later, perhaps?" Jenny suggested quietly, wishing Flora Mae was here to ask her advice.

"Play it by ear, I think," he replied with a resigned shrug. "We're visiting this afternoon, aren't we? Not far off, bearing in mind it's around five hours that we've been here."

"Five?" she gasped. "What time is it?"

"Close on six," Jack replied, slowly pulling her towards him, very aware of the effect that snippet might have on his distraught wife, who had just lost the most important part of her life. This would take a long time to accept and to put into some sort of perspective. He, of all people, understood that from more than thirty-five years before.

"Shall we go?" Jenny asked limply, looking towards her husband to guide her as she usually did.

"Well, we do need to have a drink and stuff," he reassured her. "I think we ought to go back to your mum's – Jim's – place and just … sit for a while. It would be too far to go back to Leeds. We need to phone our Jess to break the bad news."

"OK," she replied, staggering to her feet, loath to let go of her mother's hand as she turned towards the exit. "Jack?"

He disengaged her hand, drawing her unresisting body gently to him. He wrapped his arms around her to reassure her that they would see this awful episode through together. Guiding her carefully outside the screens, he knew she didn't want to leave. He knew she was leaving her heart right there, and understanding fully how she felt cut *him* deeply.

-o-

"I can't believe she's gone," Jessie gasped, with tears streaming down her cheeks. "I just had to come."

"And little Millie Alice?" Jack asked.

"Joyce and Stick offered to look after her until I get back," she replied. "What's next? Are you going back to the hospital, you know, to…?"

"To see your nana?" Jack said. "No. They have to do a post-mortem because she hadn't been ill before she died. Officially, they have to decide that it was a natural death, you see."

"Natural—?" Jessie replied, not understanding what he meant.

"If she'd been ill, it would have been obvious at her age why she died," Jack explained. "Because she didn't suffer from long-term illnesses, legally they have to be sure."

"So—?" Jessie asked again.

"We need to see how your Grandpa Jim is before we break the news to him," Jack said, again with a resigned shrug. "Not looking forward to *that* one."

"Have you let our George William and—?" Jessie asked, her tremulous voice betraying her emotions.

"Haven't had time yet, really, Jess," Jack explained quite firmly. "We need to let Grandpa Jim know *first*. Only *then* will I inform all other interested parties."

"Just come off the phone to Val," Jenny said, backing into the lounge with a tray laden with tea and toast. "She's going to book the next flight over for her and Mike."

"Over?" Jessie's puzzled question shouldered its way into the conversation. "Where are they? Holidaying in

Southern Spain?"

"Try *living* in Southern Spain – permanently," Jack replied with a wry smile.

"Wow!" Jessie whistled. "All right for some."

"I've told her to come to our old house in Leeds when they get back, if that's all right," Jenny explained. "Don't forget that Val's finally got the husband that loves *her* and with whom she feels comfortable enough to spend the rest of her life."

"Once we've explained the awful situation to Jim, we'll need to alert the *whole* family – including William," Jack added. "He won't want to be involved, but he needs to be told. Then a funeral will have to be organised, and Jim won't be fit to do that. Unless you would like to do it yourself, Jenny?"

"More than happy to relinquish all responsibility," she replied with quivering lips and tears threatening to burst down her cheeks again.

"OK," he said quietly, recognising her deep upset, which wouldn't allow her to be in control of her emotions let alone any project. "I'll set that in motion when we've seen Jim. He needs to be told as soon as possible, and then I can get on with … stuff.

"We should have a family gathering – probably here – as soon as we can," he went on after a piece or two of toast and a spot of Yorkshire Tea to wesh it down wi'. White toast wasn't his favourite, but it was a case of needs must. In this case, it was either white toast or no toast.

-o-

"I know he's improving slowly, Sister," Jack said quietly, in a side room in the hospital. "Is he fit, though, to be told that he's just lost his wife?"

"Probably not," the ward sister replied quietly. "However, he will have to be told before he starts asking.

Probably a reasonable idea to tell him now – better coming from you than by accident."

"Hello, Lass," Jim said with a forced smile as his granddaughter sat close to his bed. "It's lovely to see you. Jenny, Jack."

"How are you feeling, Jim?" Jack asked, his usual fixed, photogenic smile hiding his true feelings.

"I'm all rayt in t'circumstances, si thi," Jim replied. "Could be better, though. Your mam not here, Jenny?"

Jenny cast a panicked look at Jack as he tried to calm her with raised eyebrows. "We lost her, Jim," she said slowly as her eyes began to fill.

"Lost her?" he replied, sensing all was not right. "How could she get lost in a place like this? For goodness' sake!"

"No, Jim, I mean we *lost* her," Jenny murmured as tears started to course down her cheeks.

"As in she's … *gone?*" he gasped, a look of abject horror gripping his face. "But she were all rayt befoower. How come?"

Jenny explained what had happened in halting detail, all the while tears underlining how distraught she was, as Jack held her to stop her collapsing in anguish.

Although sitting propped up, on hearing all this, Jim's chin slumped to his chest and tears gathered.

"She wor mi world, tha knows," he muttered, when Jenny's words had disappeared into silence. "What am I going to do now? We've onny bin together for a bit on a while." His face lifted to look at the only 'family' he had left, desperation and fear dancing in his sunken eyes.

"A couple of things, Jim," Jack said once emotions had settled a little.

"Onny a couple, Jack?" Jim replied, a slight glimmer of his old humour glinting beneath his heavy lids.

Jack smiled benignly as he replied, "Aye, old chap. When they release thee from thi prison, one of three things we could do. Either tha can come and stay with us, or we could come and stay wi' thee, or we could come through from Morecambe every weekend to see to thi needs."

"If it's all rayt wi' you two, I'd rather go to mi own home," Jim replied laboriously. "No offence, mind."

"We're still working," Jenny butted in, eyes finally dry – for now. "So, we'll come every Saturday to spend the day and tidy up. If that's all right, that is.

"Not sure about planes and stuff," Jenny added after a moment's quiet, "but Val will be back from Spain within the next day or two. Do you want her to visit you here?"

"Not really," Jim replied. "See now – today's Saturday, so I should be out of here by the middle of next week. It'd be better to have her visit next weekend, at home. All rayt?"

"By that time, we should have details of the funeral sorted out," Jack said.

"Jack!" Jenny hissed, casting a sharp glance at him.

"What?" he replied, eyebrows raised in open surprise. "Just saying."

"He's rayt," Jim agreed, nodding slowly. "It has to be done at some stage. Better to be prepared than not. I just can't believe she's gone."

Jessie had been quiet throughout but had registered physically her hurt and profound sadness at losing the nana she had loved and looked up to all her life. "I'm sorry about all of this, Grandpa Jim," she whispered finally, as she put her arms around him and kissed him on the cheek. "Can we come and see you again soon?"

"Aye, of course you can, Lass," he replied equally quietly. "Shall you be bringing little Alice to cheer us all up?"

"Would that be all right?" Jessie looked round at her mum for confirmation.

"Too rayt it would," Jim replied with a deep sigh after a brief nod from Jenny. "And now, would it be OK if you went and I had a bit of a sleep? I've suddenly become very tired."

-o-

"How did our George William react when you telephoned him?" Jenny asked, as they sat in Flora Mae and Jim's lounge.

"I could tell he was devastated," Jack replied with a wry smile. "He loved his nana and I've a feeling that out of all of 'em, he will be the most upset. He said he would pass it on to Joey, and he to Mary and Edward."

"Do you mind if I leave you now? Only I need to pick up Millie Alice from Joyce's," Jessie asked tentatively.

"Yes, love," Jenny answered her daughter as she hugged her. "We'll be staying here tonight because we have to arrange for the funeral director to take your nana to prepare her."

"Prepare her?" Jessie asked with a puzzled frown.

"Aye," Jack butted in seriously. "For t'oven."

"Jack!" Jenny's look warned him about his sense of humour.

"What?" he replied, wearing his innocent look. "She *is* to be cremated at some stage, isn't she?"

"You know what I mean," she replied, her eyes and lips pursed in warning.

"It's all right, Mam," Jessie added. "I'm used to his humour. There's always a clever bit to it – unless he's having a go at someone. Then the humour is accompanied by that identical smile every time."

"Can't get away wi' owt wi' you two," Jack muttered as a smile lurked, ready to throw them off guard.

Almost as soon as the click of the front door had sounded Jessie's departure, the ringing of Jenny's mobile

15

phone leapt into the room. Not having any idea who it might be, Jack and Jenny cast glances at each other wondering whether to answer.

"Hello," Jenny said, to be swamped by shushing and crackling. Nobody answered. "Hello?"

She was greeted by that deep, monotonously continuous hum that advised her to hang up. The moment she did so it spat into life again, desperate for someone – anyone – to answer it.

"Hello?" Jenny answered tentatively, ready to hang up again. "Hello … Florence May? This is a very clear line, and almost instant, too."

"That's because we're not in Australia, Mam," Jenny's daughter laughed. "We're here, in Manchester."

"For goodness' sake, why?" Jenny asked as she put Florence May on loudspeaker. "Is Billy there with you?"

"Where else would he be?" Florence May asked, puzzled at such an obvious question.

"We had no idea you were coming," Jenny said. "Can I assume you are here to visit us?"

"We are here on an impulse, Mother," Florence May replied. "We want you to be there with us when we get married."

"Married?" Jenny gasped. "When? Where? H—?"

"We know perfectly well that you can't afford to come over to us," her daughter explained. "So, we're here for a couple of weeks, and we want to marry here before we return to Oz so that Dad can give me away. It's what you want, isn't it?"

"It certainly is!" Jack replied earnestly. "Do you want me to come over to collect you?"

"Not now," Florence May urged. "We're staying the night at the Radisson. It's Sunday tomorrow, so a quick lift would be excellent."

"Tomorrow, then," Jack promised as he hung up.

"You didn't tell her," Jenny said quietly.

"Tomorrow will do, my Sweet Pea," he explained. "Let them enjoy their evening and night in yon posh hotel. Tomorrow will come soon enough."

"What about somewhere for them to stay?" Jenny asked, confused by the whole episode.

"Several choices, really," Jack said. "They can either stay in separate rooms in our house in Leeds with Jessie, or they can do the same with Joyce close by, or … Billy with his mam and Florence May with us and Jessie. Their choice."

Chapter 2

"Seems to be an age since we last saw you," Florence May said when they were in the car squeezing its way out of Manchester's Terminal 1.

"*We* are very excited that you are here, and that I get to stroll you down the aisle to your doom!" Jack replied, to Billy's chuckles from the back seat. "We obviously need to talk through the sort of wedding you—"

"Already done that, Daddy Jack," Florence May butted in. "We know what we want and where it's going to happen."

"How—?" Jenny said, quite startled that things had been taken out of *her* hands. The modern way these days, obviously.

"We researched what's on offer and made arrangements from over there to over here," Billy answered simply.

"But isn't that the hard way to do things?" Jenny asked. "I mean—"

"Easy as breathing," Florence May answered, a satisfied smile creasing her face. "You see, all we have to do is arrange it with our Brothers in Australia and they make … it … happen."

"Brothers?" Jack asked with a frown.

"We've become Witnesses," Florence May said with a contented sigh.

"As in…?" Jenny asked, still not understanding what

they were saying.

"Jehovah's Witnesses," Billy explained. "No brainer, really. Some friends where we live in Perth—"

"Perth?" Jack butted in. "Isn't that in Scotland?"

"Western Australia, Daddy Jack," Florence May added. "A fantastic place. They took us along to a meeting and we were immediately hooked. Talk about wonderful, thoughtful and compassionate people!"

"We are, of course, open-minded and believe folks will worship in whatever way they wish," Jack went on. "JWs, unfortunately, get a bad press in parts of this country. They are often open to antagonism and aggression and suffer from unjust aggravation."

"It's world-wide, Daddy Jack," Florence May observed with a deep sigh. "However, our movement is on the increase – about nineteen million followers, up to now."

"Are you happy doing what you are doing, Sweet Pea?" Jack asked.

"We are," they chorused. "Most definitely."

"Then that's all that matters," he replied.

"The Kingdom Hall that we are aiming to marry in is not far from Leeds's Outer Ring Road, down Stainbeck Road," Billy chipped in. "It's all arranged, so we need to pay a visit sometime soon, if that's all right?"

"Certainly is," Jack replied with a cheeky grin.

"Now a less positive piece of news," Jenny said after a few moments of quiet, tears beginning to fill her eyes.

"We lost your Nana Flora Mae two days ago," Jack cut in, recognising the precarious edge his wife's emotions were balancing on.

"Lost as in … permanently?" Florence May asked quietly, a look of sadness descending.

Jenny could no longer hold in her tears of sadness as she covered her face.

"Very sad," Florence May whispered, eyes downcast.

"Yet we *will* see her again."

Jack understood what she was saying but, although he shared her beliefs and feelings, he had no desire to enter into a theological argument or discussion. On the whole, human beings tended to be driven and governed by the here and now. Emotions stayed raw for a certain length of time and only lessened gradually.

"Can I take it then that we will be heading for our old house?" Jack asked after a quiet mile or two.

"And mi mam's place, Jack," Billy asked. "Don't forget that we weren't sleeping together before, and now it's even more important that we don't."

"Why even more so now?" Jenny asked. "We knew about your high morals before you went to Australia, but … now?"

"Our religion dictates that we should only sleep together if we are legally husband and wife," Florence May replied. "Being a Witness sort of reinforces our *personal* principles."

"OK, then," Jack said as they approached the motorway. "M62 here we come."

-o-

"Do I see two cars on the drive already?" Jack muttered, as they approached their old house. "One has to be Jessie's and the other must be—"

"It can only be Val and Mike's," Jenny suggested quickly. "We don't know anyone else who would be likely to drive a hire car. Do we?"

"It won't be Brother William," Jack said. "He wouldn't dare show his face. Drop off at your mam's, Billy?" he continued, knowing Billy would like to spend some time with them.

"Please, Jack," he replied with a grin. "Probably see you again tomorrow?"

"Cup of Yorkshire and a chinwag with your mam and dad this evening at ours?" Jack suggested as his new soon-to-be son-in-law got out of the car.

"Probably not," Billy replied, looking over at Florence May, whose smile and nod corroborated his decision. "Be rayt. See you tomorrow."

The slide back down the road to their house that Jessie now inhabited felt strange and alien to Jack and Jenny after the multitude of disparate locations they had lived in of late. Ostensibly it was no different from the last time they had lived there, but they didn't get that comfortable, warm feeling they had grown used to previously.

"I think we can squeeze enough space on the drive," Jack observed, as he pulled to a stop an inch from the rear bumper of the last car before the pavement.

"Val!" he shouted as he hugged his sister-in-law. "That's a tan and a half and no mistake. Not good for you too much sun, you know. It can make you look like … a foreigner, if you're not careful. And you know what English people feel about foreigners!"

"Envy, perhaps?" Val replied, sharp as ever.

"No Mike?" he went on, ignoring her comment.

"He's seeing his daughter and then I'll meet him at Weetwood Hall Hotel, Lawnswood," she replied with a smile. "We'll be staying there for the funeral because no doubt there are going to be many wanting to stay here."

"Breakfasting with the hoi polloi, then?" Jack said, pulling his face in mock seriousness. "Come here when you've finished?"

"Thank you, yes," Val agreed. "Do Joey, Mary and Edward know? I've not been able to contact them."

"George William will have told Joey, and he will have told Mary and Ed," Jenny added. "We'll make arrangements and involve them when appropriate. Should be sometime this week. The man from the Co-op is coming to see us tomorrow, and Grandpa Jim has left it to us as far as organisation and costs are concerned.”

“How’s he coping, Jen?” Val asked carefully.

“Just about,” her sister replied, face screwed into a concerned grimace. “We’ve suggested that when he’s out of hospital on Wednesday, we will do for him on Saturdays – stuff like washing, cleaning, shopping. He’s happy with that – for now.”

“I’ll get it,” Jack chipped in as the shrill jangle of the phone urged him to pry his backside from his warm, comfy chair.

“How is Spain, Val?” Jenny asked.

“Apart from warm, comfortable and relaxing, you mean?” Val replied with a self-satisfied grin.

“Point taken,” her sister said with an envious shrug.

“That was Joey on the phone,” Jack said as he came back into the room, followed by Jessie with a tray of mugs of Yorkshire Tea and digestive biscuits.

“No scones or buns today, I’m afraid,” Jessie apologised, interrupting Daddy Jack as she set the tray down on the coffee table.

“He’s told Mary about the situation, and he and George William have got time off work,” Jack went on unabashed. “They’ll be coming over late afternoon this coming Friday and going back the following Tuesday. Mary has told Joey she’ll be here on Sunday and going back to Harrogate on Tuesday, after Monday’s funeral.”

“Harrogate?” Val asked.

“That’s where her expanding business is based now, apparently,” Jack explained. “She has a big house just on the outskirts, according to Joey. Didn’t you know that, Val?”

“First I’ve heard,” his sister-in-law replied, a puzzled shrug showing her ignorance. “We’ve not communicated much recently. The times I’ve phoned from Spain, there’s been no answer."

"I'm just nipping up to see Billy's mam and dad, if that's all right," Florence May said as she headed for the door.

"I'll walk you up," Jack offered, following her into the hall.

"It's all—" she tried to insist, only to be stopped by her dad's raised hand.

"Come on," he said, holding out his arm for her to link. "Let's go."

-o-

"Florence May not come back with you?" Jenny asked Jack, as he locked the door behind himself twenty minutes later.

"They've decided that she would stay there," he replied with a non-committal shrug. "That will allow us to house all ours – Joey and George William in the twin-bedded room, and Mary in the other. Apparently Joey's wife, Izzy, and George William's Sandy won't be coming. Neither will Mary's husband, Jake."

"Family affair, then," Jessie added. "Sad, but it will be good to see them all again to touch base."

By this time Jessie had gone upstairs to read one of Jack's stories to her daughter then put her to bed, while Jack sat in the lounge with his wife and her sister. Silence gathered around them as the cosiness of a warm and busy summer's day, a cup of good Yorkshire Tea and a Hobnob lulled them into their innermost thoughts.

"Do you remember the first time we became friends at Woodhouse Junior School, Jenny?" Jack said, a faraway look in his eyes.

"Do you mean when we met over the playground's dividing gate?" she said with a nostalgic smile. "Boys separated from girls?"

"When you were looking into our yard to see what was

going on," he replied, "and what games we were playing."

"And you wanted to see if we did different things from you," she added, nodding slowly.

"I allus used to wonder what that twirling a lengthy rope was all about," he replied, with a look of mock shock crawling across his face. "Surely someone was about to get strangled!"

"I could never see the point of those big lads rushing about down yon sloping yard to the outside toilets and back again for no apparent reason, to do the same again moments later," Jenny said, shaking her head disbelievingly.

"The first time was March 4th," Jack reminisced. "It was a Wednesday, because straight after playtime it was PE in the Hall with Mr Hardwick."

"Not long after my birthday," Jenny replied. It was like looking into the past as if it were only yesterday. Trust her Jack to remember the day, the date *and* what lesson was next.

"I've always been gobsmacked that *our* birthdays fall on the same day of the week but not the same date," he added.

"We met at the dividing gate almost every morning playtime from being seven years old until we left to go to the grammar and high schools," Jenny pointed out. "Do you remember what you called those meetings, much to your mam's surprise and amusement?"

"We were having dates," he replied emphatically with a triumphant grin. "And it wasn't until much later that we did it properly."

"High school and university sort of got in the way somewhat," she added. "Much to my chagrin, because I didn't think you were bothered."

"On the contrary, you were ever in my thoughts," Jack assured her with a shrug. "You seemed to want to do your own thing that didn't include me."

Jessie came back into the lounge amidst the reminiscing and the deep thoughts about the whys and wherefores of their relationship in the early days. "Do you realise that if you had been together from the start," she pointed out, "Daddy Jack would have been my *real* father?"

"But I thought I was," Jack answered quickly, a mock hurt look resting in his eyes.

"You know what I mean," Jessie replied, shuffling a little uncomfortably. She changed the conversation slightly. "By the way, *my* Daddy Jack, Millie Alice really loves the stories you have written, as I did when you read them to me all those years ago."

"I remember not being able to pry them out of your hands when you were able to read them for yourself," Jenny said with a smile. "You were a quick learner."

"We didn't have our dates at lunchtime because you had school dinners and I went home, first to Scarborough Row and then to Garth Avenue when we moved," Jack butted in, recognising Jessie's discomfort. "When I got older, I used to climb over the school's back wooden gate to traipse across the field to mi grandma's to have dinner with her. I can always remember with a shudder the tales mi granddad used to tell about the huge mound of earth I clambered over that hid the unearthly, mysterious air-raid shelter underneath."

"I, of course, was never party to that one," Jenny added quickly. "Did you ever climb into it?"

"Onny ever once," Jack replied with a shudder. "It became a rite of passage when we were in our early teens. We dared each other – as only boys would – to climb in one end down a metal grating and make our way to the other end, some fifty yards away, in pitch blackness on our own."

"That would be easy, wouldn't it?" Val chipped in, mesmerised by the memories he and her sister shared.

"What you have to bear in mind, dear sister, is that there was all manner of debris down there, some of it entirely … disreputable and disgustingly filthy. Also, your 'mates' would shout and bang and throw things down at you from the other above-ground grids as you passed," Jack replied. "An unpleasant experience not to be repeated. Cup of tea and a nibble, anyone?"

-o-

"Why are Billy and Florence May back here?" Val asked over a cup of tea. "Visit or holiday? Run out of things to do in Australia?"

"Billy's secured an engineering job, and Florence May is studying towards an accountancy qualification," Jack explained between mouthfuls of his favourite drink. "She's interned with a firm of accountants in Perth, Western Australia."

"And they're here to get married," Jenny added.

"Married?" Val said. "Any reason why they couldn't have done that in Australia?"

"A couple of reasons, really," Jack explained. "One, they wanted us to be present, and that had cost and school holiday implications. Two, they have become Jehovah's Witnesses."

Silence.

"Not sure about the Witness association, Val?" Jack asked, looking at her over his mug.

"Why should I be unsure, Our Jack?" she replied after a moment's thought. "My Mike's a Witness and has been for years."

"That we *didn't* know," Jenny said, a little surprised.

"Why would you?" Val harrumphed. "It's nobody's business but his own. As far as I remember, we still have freedom of how to worship in this country. Don't we?"

"Too right we have!" Jack jumped back in. "Too much

fuss made by bigoted ignoramuses about people who simply want to share their truth, in my view."

"A group of more level-headed, compassionate, helpful and open-minded people you couldn't hope to meet," Val replied.

"How about you, Val?" Jack said simply. "Any chance you might join your husband?"

"I share their feelings and beliefs," she replied with a shrug. "But as yet I don't want the commitment, although I haven't ruled it out totally. We do know lots of Witnesses hereabouts from when we lived in this house prior to decamping to Southern Spain. If Florence May is to marry locally, it will probably be the Kingdom Hall down Stainbeck Road. I've dropped Mike off there many a time. In fact, some of the Brothers and Sisters down there are good friends of ours with whom we still keep in touch. When are they going?"

"Wednesday of next week, we think," Jack said.

"Is it all right for Mike and me to come back here tomorrow morning?" Val asked tentatively.

"Do you *need* to ask?" Jack harrumphed. "Don't forget '*Mi casa…*'"

"'…*es su casa*'," Val replied with a smile. "Don't forget, *mi cunado*, I live in Spain now, and I am learning Spanish … from the natives."

"*Cunado*?" Jenny asked, a non-linguist by design.

"Brother-in-law," Jack explained.

"It might be good for Florence May and Billy to have a chat with Mike, as he has been in the Truth for a good few years," Val replied.

"Do you remember *our* wedding, Val?" Jack asked.

"How could I ever forget!" she said with certainty.

"I don't understand," Jessie said. "Why so final?"

"Well," Jenny started to explain as the telephone's stridently insistent ring intruded. Jack took the call in the hall while Jenny explained the scenario to her daughter.

"…And Joyce and Stick's daughter, Valerie, saw her first light of day in the women's toilet in the Registry Office!" Jenny finished. "Consequently, the fact that she was delivered by midwife Val here, prompted them to name their offspring after her."

"Wonderful story, you two," Val said.

"That was Mike, Val," Jack explained. "Says he's already at the hotel and he's ordered dinner for an hour from now."

"OK," she replied. "If you'll move your car from behind mine, I'll be off. See you all tomorrow morning?" And with that, she was gone.

Chapter 3

"You don't need me to reinforce what you already know," Mike said to Florence May and Billy over coffee in Jack and Jenny's front room. "I'm sure no-one coerced you, and you would now like to marry with the full blessing and best wishes of all your Brothers and Sisters, both over here and in Perth."

"We have arranged already to go to Kingdom Hall to talk through the ceremony, which is set for Wednesday of next week," Billy explained.

"In that case, the visiting overseer who will take your service is a Brother called Ronnie Haygarth who lives in Morecambe," Mike said. "He's a good chap that works for his local council, and with whom you'll get along just fine. A very ebullient fellow with an enormous sense of humour. When did you say you were visiting Kingdom Hall for a pre-nuptial chat?"

"We didn't," Florence May replied. "But it's today. This afternoon."

"And is this our little girl that's talking about weddings and stuff?" Jenny asked Jack in the kitchen, as a tear threatened to expose itself. "Our little girl who was shy, despite all your efforts to bring her out, and now listen to her!"

"She always was a deep one," Jack agreed.

"Do you remember when you asked *me* to marry *you*,

My Man?" Jenny added, a bout of nostalgia threatening.

"I do that, Our Jenny," Jack replied enthusiastically. "I was all for nipping out almost immediately to get it done but you were a little more … circumspect, in that you needed to *plan*. The day itself was a cracker, sharing with those nearest and dearest to us."

"We need to be off to the Kingdom Hall now," Florence May said, as she shouldered her way into the kitchen. "Mike's coming with us, but Auntie Val is staying here with you."

Almost as soon as the click of the front door signalling their exit had just about stopped rattling, the doorbell took over.

"That'll be the funeral chap from the Co-op, I should imagine," Jenny said.

"Good afternoon, Mr Lancaster," Jack said to the tall, slim, dapper man wearing a sombre dark suit and shiny black top hat. "Please come in. Like the hat."

"My condolences on your sad loss," Mr Lancaster said in a deep, resonant voice. "Distressing that we should meet in these circumstances."

"Cup of tea, Mr Lancaster?" Jack added, leading him into the lounge, where a sad-faced mother and daughter sat, waiting for the inevitable planning for the disposal of mother and grandmother's remains.

"Thank you. That would be excellent," he replied as Jack swished into the kitchen, leaving his wife and daughter to start the final chapter by first setting the context and conditions of their discussion for this day.

"You realise, of course, Mr Lancaster, that what we discuss can only come to fruition with the tacit agreement of Jim Arkwright, my mother's husband," Jenny explained. "He is still in hospital following a near-fatal heart attack. He comes home on Wednesday."

"That is completely understood, Madam," Mr

Lancaster answered her. "Today we will discuss procedures and protocols—"

"And costs?" Jack butted in as he placed the tray on the coffee table beside the settee. "After all, Jim is a dyed-in-the-wool Yorkshireman, not given to non-necessities."

Mr Lancaster smiled, a Yorkshireman himself by birth, but with an unfortunate surname.

-o-

Jessie had long since dressed Millie Alice for a walk in the fresh air away from all talk of doom and stuff she didn't need to be party to – not for many years, at least. The day was bright and the sun was warm, ideal for a drive to and walk in Golden Acre Park near Bramhope. This was a beautiful park with an enormous amount of fresh, open space where she had enjoyed many a walk with her Daddy Jack.

Fortunately, the small car park wasn't overwhelmingly full, as was usually the case on a Tuesday afternoon in the long school holidays. Improvements had been made, allowing visitors to cross the busy A660 Otley Road *under* the carriageway, via a narrow path that kept company with a meandering, chuckling, clear stream that was often the gathering place for noisy mallards waiting for daily handouts from generous food-bearing visitors.

Millie Alice had been here before with her mum and she loved the trees, greenery and, usually, the café. Today was no exception. "Bread, ducks, Mammy," she said, as she toddled round the corner with busy traffic thundering above them.

"Come on then, love," Jessie said, leading her by the hand once the ducks had devoured all the bread. "Let's go—"

"So, it *is* you," a rough voice snarled as they walked into the sunlight.

Jessie turned to see a face she had hoped wouldn't darken her waking moments ever again. "Simon Ridley!" she hissed with utter disdain. "Nightmare face! How's your broken nose?"

"You, bitch, are the one that lost me my job," he snarled again, making a threatening move towards her.

She backed away, drawing her daughter close, a look of fear dancing in her eyes.

"And now—" he went on threateningly.

"You are going to back off, Pal," a deep rumbling male voice interrupted, as a large muscular frame stepped between Jessie and her attacker. "If you don't, this young lady is about to phone for the police and an ambulance. And if that doesn't make you think twice about your cowardly action, perhaps *this* will."

Clenching an enormous fist, the newcomer pushed Simon Ridley backwards with his other hand. This was too much for the coward; he turned on his heels and fled, looking only once over his shoulder.

"Are you all right?" the newcomer said to Jessie. "I'm sorry you had to be accosted by that … piece of work."

"I'm fine," Jessie replied, finding her voice once the original fear had dissipated. "Thank you for intervening and saving us."

"You have nothing to thank me for," he replied with a smile. "My name's Johnny, Johnny Grey, and it's a good job I was here. Did you know him, or was he an opportunist idiot?"

"Oh, I knew him all right!" she answered, carrying on to explain why and where. They continued to walk while she explained her situation.

His grin grew as her tale unfurled. "Then he deserved everything he got," Johnny said. "Broken nose, eh? From a beautiful young woman like you? I like it. May I offer you a cup of coffee, as we are within ten paces of yonder café?"

"You may, and I thank you for asking," Jessie agreed. "My daughter really likes it in that café."

"Then it would be my pleasure to treat *two* lovely young ladies to a drink," he added, turning towards Millie Alice. "May I guess that you are called Alice?"

She looked at him, then at her mammy and asked deliberately slowly, "How does man know my name, Mammy?"

Jessie turned towards him to explain, eyebrows raised quizzically.

"I noticed two letters on the backs of your shoes – A.I. – and I decided they might be initials," he explained. "I thought that the 'A' was for a first name, and I thought 'Alice' would be better than 'Agatha'. Are you called Agatha?"

"No," Millie Alice replied, eyes wide at his magician's explanation. "I'm called … Alice, and I am four."

–o–

"He was a nice man, wasn't he?" Jessie said to her daughter as she buckled her into her seat in the back of the car.

"Yes, Mammy," Millie Alice replied. "How did he know my name? Is he a maj … a maji … magic man? I been joyed the milky shake. Strawberry is my favourite."

"Probably a good guess, my lovely," Jessie replied with a laugh. "You *do* look like an Alice."

"I like this park, Goldin Hayker," Millie Alice said slowly as Jessie set off, a smile caressing her face at her daughter's mispronunciation.

Intrigued, Jessie wondered if Johnny might be there the following week, because she had let it slip accidentally in conversation that *she* might be visiting Golden Acre Park with her daughter the following Saturday.

She was very thankful that he had been there to see off that awful Simon Ridley. Daddy Jack would have approved of the action Johnny had taken. He had always said that his granddad, Jud Holmes, would have advised that a punch in the mouth would often be a good incentive.

The drive home round the back roads to King Lane and the Outer Ring Road was a quiet one, with less noise from fewer cars and no noise from Millie Alice behind her. *She* had fallen fast asleep.

When Jessie got back, the only car on the drive was Daddy Jack's. Auntie Val's was probably still at Stainbeck Road's Kingdom Hall with her new husband Mike, Florence May and Billy.

"Hello, Auntie Val," Jessie said, once inside. "I didn't expect to see you here. Mike still with Florence May and Billy?"

"Yes," Val replied, draining her latest cup of tea. "Your mam and dad are in the dining room finishing off the business the funeral man brought. He's gone, but there's paperwork to see to."

"Goodness me!" Jack said cheerfully as he brought tea and digestives into the lounge. "Look what our Alice has dragged in. Cup of tea, Jess? Val?"

"No, thank you," Val replied. "I'll float away if I have anymore, and no thank you – Mike and I won't be staying for dinner because we've already booked in at the hotel."

"I *was* about to suggest fish and chips," Jack retorted jokingly.

"But there's no fish and chip shop close by, I don't think," Jessie butted in.

"There's Bryan's," he went on with a grin.

"That's miles away, in Headingley," Jenny said, as she joined the throng. "Do you remember our first – and only – sortie to Bryan's fish and chip restaurant, Our Jack?" she went on, changing tack slightly.

"Could I ever forget?" he replied, a faraway look descending. "We had to choose whether to eat in or take away, didn't we?"

"We ate in because it had started to rain," she added quickly.

"Sharing one portion because we didn't have enough money for two, if memory serves," he said.

"Actually, you insisted on having a plate of chips because you weren't keen on fried fish," she corrected. "You insisted also that I had chips *and* fish. It occurred to me *later* that it had probably been a money issue."

"But I thought you lived in Normanton?" Jessie said, confused.

"We did, but we had decided to have a day out at Roundhay Park in Leeds, followed by a trip to see the college where I trained to become a teacher," Jack explained. "That was in Headingley, and Bryan's fish and chip restaurant was just down from college, off Otley Road."

"Long time ago, Daddy Jack," Jessie added. "Even I don't remember that."

"You were staying with your grandma Flora Mae at the time," Jack said. "So, it would have been a psychic bit of magic if you had."

They all laughed as Val made her goodbyes and went to the drive to wait for her husband. Mike and Val had a few personal things they needed to sort out within the area, so they would be busy. She was pleased she didn't have to do the sorting out for her mother's funeral; she had had enough of that when their biological father died. Upsetting times, but Mother would not have wanted *their* life to be put on hold.

A click of the front door turned their heads slowly, waiting for them to hear—

"Hello! We're back!" Florence May's voice set their minds at ease. Jack got up and ambled to the kitchen to put on the kettle for a fresh pot of Yorkshire Tea. It was likely they would be gasping for one of his usuals.

"All organised?" Jenny asked, curious to see whether their ceremony would be any different from the usual.

"Yep," Billy replied. "Easier than we thought. Just like any other wedding ceremony – whatever *that* is."

-o-

"Are you sure you're fit to leave this place, Jim?" Jenny asked, as she settled him into the back seat of their Mondeo. "We could always—"

"Nay, Lass," Jim replied, tears beginning to well in his sad eyes. "I have to do it sometime. I don't want to snuff it in yonder. Your mam and I allus promised each other to get on wi' our life if owt happened to t'other, and now … here … we … are. Niver thowt it would happen. Allus thowt it'd be me first."

"We'll take you back home then, Jim," Jack added, "and get some dinner on, eh?"

"Aye, lad," Jim replied, "but don't think tha's off to mek a 'abit on it. I'm perfectly able to cook missen, tha knows."

"We know that, Jim," Jenny said with an understanding, if sad, smile. "Just until we get you settled, eh?"

The journey from Pinderfields Hospital was completed in double-quick time … in silence. Jim looked out on the local, well-known countryside as if he were reliving many a past journey with the love of his life. It was now all he had left – memories that could no longer be shared.

"I'm off to miss her, tha knows," Jim said quietly as they drew into his driveway. "More than I can imagine or tell now. It hardly seems rayt travelling back 'ome wi'out her, leaving her in t'ospital all cold and on her own." He fell silent, head bent, chin resting on his chest, with an errant tear gathering.

"We know, Jim," Jack replied after a moment or two of silence. He couldn't imagine being in Jim's shoes at this moment, having to manage without *his* lovely lady, the pillar of *his* life. He knew all the platitudes about loss in this sort of a context, because he'd had them heaped upon his shoulders following his mam's death more than thirty years before. Yet he couldn't imagine staring down t'barrel of t'ultimate gun wi'out Jenny by his side.

"What are we going to do about tonight then, Jim?" Jenny asked, once they had settled inside Jim's bungalow.

"I don't understand what you're asking, Lass," Jim replied, a puzzled frown drawing down his brow.

"I *am* doing dinner tonight, aren't I?" Jenny's explanatory question brought a smile to her stepdad's face. "But would you like us to stay, you know…?"

"I think I'd rather be on mi own, if that's all rayt wi' you," he said hesitantly. "I need to say 'so long' to her in mi own way in our house. It'd be better as well if'n you two went 'ome pretty soon. I've 'ad enough to eat in yon 'ospital and won't need anymore today."

"You sure, Jim?" Jack interrupted, concerned that being alone might not be the best answer for him.

"Aye," Jim assured them. "When did you say t'funeral was?"

"Next Monday," Jack replied. "We're staying with Jessie in our old house in Leeds so it's convenient to get here rather than travelling from Morecambe."

"Morecambe you say?" Jim said, perking up somewhat. "Spent many a happy Scottish fortnight there in August. The town used to be deluged wi' folk from Scotland and t'West Riding. And a grand time was 'ad by all!"

"Scottish Fortnight and Bradford Wakes Week all in one, eh?" Jack repeated with surprise. "I thought West Riding folk would have spent more time on t'East Coast at Brid or Scarborough, or even Filey at a pinch."

"Morecambe had a very long prom, if memory serves me," Jim reminisced. "Those views across t'bay also were summat grand, I must say. I have been there also, it has to be said, when rough seas have been ower onto t'roads and into t'gardens. I remember one time when there had been so much water, the receding sea had left boats on the road and in gardens yards from t'promenade."

"You're joking!" Jenny gasped. "Best not buy property on the front, then!"

"It doesn't happen now, Jim, I'm told," Jack assured them. "They've built a wall defence and have put in fish tails and other boulder defences."

"Fish tails?" Jenny puzzled. "What are they?"

"Simply a huge pile of local limestone boulders fashioned in the shape of t'back end of a fish – hence 'fish tails'," Jack explained. "Built to stop flooding and to prevent the erosion of sand from the beach. Morecambe has probably two or three, which have been very effective, I believe."

Chapter 4

"I know he's a hard-nosed, dyed-in-the-wool Yorkshireman from Normanton, but I've no idea how he will cope without Mum to guide him," Jenny said quietly as they drove back to Leeds.

The setting sun hung low over the horizon towards Morecambe, way on in the west, the place that held on to its bountiful rays the longest. Summer was a wonderful time – light early and dark late, the sort of time Jenny loved, particularly if it was warm sunbathing weather. This was the sort of weather that had become anathema to her husband, though. He had always preferred the temperature to be at a level that obliged him to pull on a jersey to keep out early spring and late autumn chills, and to fasten up a light jerkin when the gales blew and the frosts began to bite. He was, after all, a Yorkshireman, and they didn't like fuss or come any hardier.

"We'll just have to keep an eye on him," Jack replied. "After all, he is part of the family, and he has nobody else save us. His son doesn't give a toss whether he lives or dies, but I suppose he'll be sniffing around when there's a Will to be read."

"Still, Jim looked after himself before he met Mum," Jenny added.

"Ah, but that's a year or two ago," Jack said, nodding sagely as he turned into the bottom of their avenue, feeling ready to get to grips with a lovely cup of Yorkshire Tea. "That's a foreign car on our – Jessie's – drive!"

"They all seem to be foreign these days," Jenny said, as she stretched to relieve her aching body.

"Not what I meant," he replied, a grin overtaking his face. "I meant 'somebody else's car that I didn't recognise' on the drive, apart from Our Jessie's."

"Hello!" Jenny called out as they snecked the front door behind them. "We're back! Whose car—?"

"It's Our Mary!" Jack enthused, as he bustled into the lounge to a serious hug from his niece. "Wow! Beautiful lady … and a beautiful motor on the drive to prove your worth. BMW, eh?"

"Well, Uncle Jack, you know a car shows success," Mary replied, a smile quickly spreading as she sat next to him on the settee, arm linked with his.

"Did I catch a rumour in the business world I frequent that you are about to take over Chanel?" he said, a twinkle in his eye.

"Not quite," she assured him, "but we're getting there."

"Jake and Alice surviving without you?" he added, straight-faced but pulling her leg. Her business was becoming so successful that Jake had become her manager and their daughter's minder. *She* was now four going on twenty-four, by all accounts. Jack wouldn't know because the last time he'd seen her they were at Jenny's Aunt Effie's place in Carnforth, and then Alice was two.

Bearing the same name as Jessie's Alice, the latter had now assumed her other first name as well, called Millie Alice to cause no confusion between the actions of two very different but similarly headstrong young ladies.

"Jake is the one that insisted I come on my own," Mary replied easily. "Funerals are no place for a four-year-old. Anyway, our business won't run on its own, funeral or no funeral."

"When are we going to be invited to that palace of yours in Harrogate?" Jack asked, a wicked smile forming, looking over both shoulders surreptitiously as if to check no-one else was listening as he dropped his voice to a whisper. "Word has it that the Queen spends bank holidays at yours."

Mary burst into a fit of giggles as she squeezed Jack's hand affectionately. "I have most definitely missed your jokes, Uncle Jack," she sighed. "I think we *must* make time to see you soon. I should like Alice to enjoy your company as much as I did growing up."

"Do you remember how you received my humour when you had just entered the holy ground of your teens?" he asked, knowing the answer.

"Well, it wasn't at all cool at thirteen to react to your uncle's jokes," Mary said with a giggle. "It's a different matter now."

"Daft question, but have you seen your dad lately?" he asked, taking a drink of his slowly cooling cup of Yorkshire Tea.

"It is five years, two months and six days since I last saw him," she snorted, a disdainful look leaping to her face. "He has more current and attractive 'business' to attend to, I hear."

"Current—?" Jack asked, puzzled by her words and the aggressive tone in her voice.

"He's never been near, and certainly hasn't wanted to meet his grandchild," she added. "I believe he has a new family to occupy his time."

"Family?" Jack said, a little taken aback. "I knew he had *one* child with his fancy piece, but … family?"

"Three children in four years, I have been told," Mary answered, dropping her voice to a sad whisper as a faraway look entered her face. "He didn't even answer my note to him to tell him about Alice's arrival."

Jack slid his arm around her shoulders and drew her head to his chest. She smiled, knowing that at least he cared and always had in many more ways than her father ever had. She didn't know how she would have achieved what she had without his invaluable and unconditional help over the years.

"Do you remember taking me to see my first workplace and flat down King Lane?" Mary asked, overcome by feelings of nostalgia.

"Your face was a picture when you realised what it meant once we had looked around," Jack said with a chuckle. "When Alan Cliff came in and went on about your plans, you could have picked your jaw off the floor."

"I will never forget what you have done for me … and our Joey," she said seriously, reaching up to kiss him on the cheek. "I wouldn't be where I am today without your help."

"I think you would, Mary," he assured her. "It might have taken you a bit longer, but talent will never be squashed for long. All I did was to fill in the little gaps to make things happen … sooner. Anyway," he continued, "I thought you were coming Sunday?"

"I was, but after giving it some thought – about five minutes, really – I decided I needed to be here as soon as poss," Mary said quietly. "Harrogate is only a stone's throw away anyway, so here I am."

The clicking of the front door pricked up their ears and the sound of *two* sets of feet on the hall floor had them guessing that it might be—

"George William!" Jenny said, getting up to hug her son as soon as she saw his sad face.

"Joey and Ed," Jack heralded as his nephews followed. "Lovely to see you both, but not in the present circumstances."

"Good to see you all," Joey said quietly, wringing his uncle's hand. "Seems like an age since we were last here.

Nothing brings folk together like a funeral."

"Not seen you for a while, Joey, but you are certainly picking up your Uncle Jack's cynicism," Jenny noted as she hugged the lad.

"Teas all round? Coffee?" Jack offered, once they were all seated. "Then sleeping arrangements."

"We'll be fine—" Joey started to say but was cut short by Jack's insistent voice.

"*Here,* for as long as you are aiming to stay," he insisted. "It'll give us a chance to catch up as well. You've all grown up since the last time and must have stories to tell."

Joey and Mary laughed at their uncle's sense of humour but Ed didn't understand it. Never had. Never would. That was something his brother always pulled his leg about mercilessly. He was growing more like his Uncle Jack, was Joey, much to his wife Izzy's amusement.

-o-

"Bit of a busy week next week, eh, lovely," Jack said to Jenny, once everyone was tucked up. "Can't believe that we've a doleful Monday to be followed by a joyful Wednesday. Will you be able to cope with opposite emotions on two very close days?"

"I think I'll manage," she replied with an unconvincing grimace. "At least, I *hope* I'll manage. If I don't—"

"I'll be there, my sweet," he answered, gently sliding his arm around her as he took in her gathering sadness. "I'll be there. Your mum would have loved to have been at her granddaughter's nuptials. It's sad she won't see any of them. Mind you, Our Florence May's is the only one *we* will have seen. Fingers crossed for George William, eh?"

"I think it's lovely that she has such a positive fix on things," Jenny said, a faraway look in her eyes.

"Something to be said for this Jehovah's Witness-ness perhaps," Jack replied with a smile. "There's still sadness, but that's tempered by a conviction that we'll all meet again in eternity when a New Order arrives."

"Hark at you!" Jenny said, her mood lifting. "Now an expert on the Coming of a New Kingdom!"

"Been looking stuff up," he explained. "Can't have my daughter one of 'em and not know what they're all on about. You know me, Our Jen."

According to his once-close friends in school, Jack had always been an order and knowledge freak. *They* had turned out to be not-such-close friends at the end of it all because they weren't real *friends*. Like Harry Bowles and his brother, John, for example, and a variety of others. They had only allowed him to tag along out of habit. When push came to shove, they had disappeared like spirits at an exorcism. That underlined Jack's conviction that he had always been a loner. Who needed ne'er-do-well 'friends' anyway?

"Steady, Our Jack," Jenny replied with a grin. "You'll be banging a tambourine yet, if you're not careful."

"Wrong group, Our Jen," Jack said amidst his own generated peals of laughter. "I think you might find that *that*—"

"Is the Salvation Army," she added. "Yes, I know. I was having you on."

"I know you know, you know," he said, making her laugh, too. "I just didn't know that you'd know I knew, and now—

"Enough!" Jenny gasped, throwing up her hands in submission and supplication.

"Day after tomorrow is going to be a very trying day for us all," Jack said quietly after a few minutes of what he always called 'hissing silence'. He blamed that on the sounds his ears experienced when no outside noise intruded. A hissing silence. "I'm not sure Jim will be able to cope so soon after coming out of hospital. You know as well as I do that he will be blaming himself, saying that it should have been him. Do you think he'll come?"

"Don't you?" she replied, puzzled at the question

"Not sure," he replied slowly, without conviction. "He loses, whatever he decides to do. Do you remember the first time you met mi mam?" he added, after a few moments of drifting off into his hissing silence.

"She was lovely, your mam," Jenny replied. "Unfortunately, I spent very little time in her company, particularly with her leaving us before her time. Probably four or five times in all?"

"Three times when we were at Woodhouse Junior, and another two or three times when you were busying yourself at uni while I was at teacher training college in Leeds," Jack added sadly.

"That was a sad time for both of us, wasn't it?" she said with a regretful grimace. "I was at a complete loss without my Jack by my side, pointing me in the right direction. I really missed you."

"It was the worst thing you could have told me, that you had agreed to marry Jessie's father," Jack admitted in a moment of candour. "Felt like a kick in the proverbials. I was *more* than ready to look after you both."

"Do you remember that first time we went for a coffee?" she asked, changing tack slightly.

"Coffee shop on Wakefield Road, a few doors down from Colin Heald's chippy," Jack said, a glimmer of a memory flitting across his face.

"That was the time I realised I really wanted to be with you," Jenny said quietly. "A time I will never forget. You took my hand in yours across the table, and I'd never felt such strength, such depth, in a simple touch before. It shocked me to my very core and I had no idea how to cope with it."

"I was convinced I had lost you when you went back

to uni just before you got pregnant – my Jenny, that I'd always wanted to be with, off to marry someone else," Jack whispered, tears welling in his eye corners as thoughts of that time flooded back from the little corner of his mind where he stored his sad memories.

She put her arms about him and, drawing his head to her breasts, she kissed his eyes, tasting those salty tears she had experienced only a couple of times in all the years she had known him. They had come a long way since those late teenage years, with some of their times not as memorable as others. Yet they were still here together, and always would be.

-o-

Although Sunday was a quietly relaxing time, with the house full as it often was in more productive times, a feeling of foreboding and sadness lay over them all. Everybody took breakfast according to their particular habit, getting in no-one else's way as thoughts and memories of better times sneaked into their mind as if to re-emphasise the gravity of their collective situation.

Tears were quietly shed over shared memories, which nothing would ever erase, of Flora Mae, the family's matriarch, in all her glory.

"Do you remember when we were at Filey with David and Irene?" Jenny asked. "Remember, we were at the—"

"White Lodge, and David and I were building sandcastles and giving piggy backs to our nippers," Jack butted in, a huge smile decorating his face.

"Isn't that the time we went with Joyce and Stick Walker?" Jenny asked, not quite sure of the time scale.

"That was the time after, when we *all* went," Jack replied. "A fantastic time was had by all, if my memory serves."

"You announced, to my utter shock and disbelief,

that Mum was 'seeing' someone, and I didn't believe you," Jenny said. "Hate to admit it, but you were right."

"Jim Arkwright," Jack agreed. "And didn't he turn out to be just the right man for her?"

Jenny fell silent, a faraway look taking over her eyes that glistened slightly as tears started to well. All those memories, all those lovely thoughts. Trust her Jack to be able to recount them all – verbatim.

The telephone interrupted their reminiscences. Jack took the call in the hall then wandered back into the lounge, a puzzled look on his face.

"Trouble, Uncle Jack?" Joey asked as he sat down, a steaming mug of tea to hand.

"Well, it seems that Grandpa Jim has decided to change the order of play at the funeral tomorrow," Jack replied. "He's decided he doesn't want Grandma to be cremated, but he wants her laid to rest in Methley churchyard where he has a plot he already owns."

"A bit short on notice, don't you think?" George William said.

"Apparently, it's all been sorted," Jack sighed, with a slight shake of his head. "Funeral cortège to St Oswald's Church in Methley for a short service, then burial in the churchyard, to be followed by afternoon tea at a local hostelry. We need to be at his bungalow by eleven o'clock tomorrow morning."

"Obviously feeling a bit perkier than he was when we took him home the other day," Jenny added with a slight smile. "I hope he keeps it up."

Chapter 5

"Not seen you in that suit for some time, Jack," Jenny observed as they readied themselves for the day's business. She was determined she wasn't going to break down, and accordingly had prepared a short eulogy. Val was happy for her to do that because she wasn't prepared to do the same. *She* would have liked the funeral to be over with as quickly as possible.

"It's my wedding/christening/funeral dark suit, and when was the last time we enjoyed any of the aforementioned?" Jack replied. "Twenty or so years ago, perhaps? I've onny been to two funerals in mi time – mi mam's and now your mam's. Missed mi granddad's and grandma's."

His last pronouncement was almost an aside, not really for anyone else's ears. "It's just occurred to me," he said to Jenny. "We've not told your brother Michael about your mam."

"Val let him know as soon as she found out," Jenny said. "They can't come because they are in Amsterdam with their twin girls. He said they would call when they were able. He was upset, to say the least, and I can understand why."

"He's not been on the scene that long," her husband replied. "So that's understandable. Cup of tea before we set forth? Anybody?"

"Yes, please."

"Milk and sugar."

"Any chance of a … coffee?"

"Chocolate digestive to go with it?"

"I fancy a piece of cake…"

"The odd scone or two would be…"

"Cup of tea and an arrowroot biscuit for all!" Jack announced, amidst groans and calls of 'Oh no!' and 'Not arrowroots!' "Don't forget we will be having afternoon tea soon after the business of the day, and I for one wouldn't want to miss that. Anyway, you've all onny just had breakfast."

"Time to go," Jenny said once the tea, coffee and scones had been polished off. "It'll take us an hour or so to get to Methley, so we need to get a move on. We can't keep Flora Mae waiting, can we?"

-o-

The highly polished silver-grey hearse and one stretch limo waited quietly by Jim and Flora Mae's tidy bungalow just off Pinfold Lane, only a short way from the rugby grounds that Jack had played on as an eighteen-year-old. A quarter-to-eleven arrival allowed them time to satisfy themselves that Jim was well enough to withstand the strain that such a day might place on his already fragile heart. Still, he had already said before his wife's passing that he wouldn't survive her for long. If he was of such a mind, his stepchildren could only do so much to enhance what quality of life he retained.

"Hello Jenny, Jack," Jim said as he hugged them. "Thank you for coming. I hope you don't mind the alterations to the schedule. You will still be able to say a few words about your mam, Jenny – and anyone else that wants to stand up, for that matter. I just had to have somewhere … tangible to visit once she is committed. A headstone and a few words imprinted about her is all I want. I know she won't be there, but it's a focal point so I can have a chat when I'm feeling lonely."

"You don't have to worry on our account, Jim," Jack answered him. "We onny wanted to save you the aggravation of making arrangements when you weren't feeling so good. Did Val phone you—?"

"Abaht Michael?" Jim said. "Aye, she did. I've no doubt he'll be paying her a visit when he gets back from Holland. He seemed like a reasonable sort."

Looking around his bungalow, he noticed that all of them were there as ought to be. "All rayt, everybody," he said as he headed for the front door, "she's waiting. Let's get this dratted business ower wi', shall we?"

A heavy drizzle had begun to gather, dampening everything in its path, dulling all gleaming surfaces as it closed in. Jenny gripped Jack's hand and arm, desperately hoping she would be able to hold her emotions in check, at least until she had delivered the few words she wanted to say about her mam.

A few neighbours shared the sadness of the occasion, standing by their front doors, suitably clad and umbrella-ed against the rain. That same feeling that Jack had experienced when he clambered into that black funeral car as a twenty-one-year-old gripped his throat again as he supported his wife in her growing distress.

He looked across at his daughter, Jessie, and her daughter, Millie Alice. Both had tears streaming down pale cheeks, but without any sound from tight, almost bloodless lips. Jack's sense of déjà vu was unnerving; he felt like he had been here only a short while before, whereas decades had slipped by almost unnoticed.

The church was almost full, which astounded Jack. He didn't know that Flora Mae had had so many friends and acquaintances. He recognised only a handful of the fifty or so that had turned out to pay their last respects. He looked at Jenny and squeezed her hand in support as she stood up to make her way to the front of the congregation to say *her* few words.

"I'm all right. Don't worry about me. You go and enjoy yourself," she began, making them believe she was trying to reassure *them* that *she* was OK. "This was Mam's outlook on life. Never one to moan about herself. Always grateful and satisfied with what she had.

"She liked a laugh and she loved a bit of fun – often at someone else's expense. Slapstick was her style. If somebody tripped or banged themselves, her shoulders would shake, and she would laugh quietly.

"She had three siblings that most people didn't know about: her sister, Effie, and brothers, Tommy and George. The boys were older by a year or two and Effie is, give or take, a similar age. Effie is still with us but couldn't be here today, but I don't know about Tommy and George.

"One time in their early teenage, Flora Mae and Effie met some lads on the way home from school. When the lads came knocking at the door for them later that day – when Tommy and George were out and Mother was at bingo – the girls were frightened of the consequences. They put flour on their faces and told the lads they were too ill to go out.

"She related many stories, particularly from earlier years when the family was together. She told of the time, one Saturday morning, when Tommy and George led Flora Mae and Effie blindfolded along the canal bank and down by the Ings in Altofts. She said they led them into the edge of the water and then had a good laugh, telling them that Jenny Greenteeth would have them if they weren't careful.

"Her early married years were a struggle, being left with two children while her husband worked shifts down the mines. No benefits then, of course; she had to work herself to make ends meet, and she often went without so that we didn't have to. She lived from shilling to shilling.

"Auntie Effie and her friends were Mam's lifeline during difficult times. Lots of photographs we looked at show her laughing with her sister and Molly Sandford – friends who could take her from the daily worry to a time of fun and laughter. She was a character. A one-off with an answer for everything. A simple, uncomplicated person who was happy and satisfied with what she had.

"She loved her grandchildren. Joined in and played games. Treated them and cared about them, and I am sure they have many stories of her times with them, too.

"Her life changed drastically when Dad died. Although she had had quite a difficult life up to that time, she had begun to love him – opinionated and difficult to live with though he was. It hit her hard until, of course, she met Jim Arkwright. *Then* she could start to live again and enjoy the life that Jim had brought to her.

"*My* bond with her was very special, and she was a pleasure to look after. In recent years, when things had become … difficult, she never complained, was always grateful, and her resolve was just to get on with it. Fortunately, she never ailed anything and rarely went to the doctor.

"Although her memory wasn't what it used to be, and daily tasks had become increasingly troublesome, her sense of humour remained, and her strong spirit shone through.

"I think her message to us might have been … 'Cherish your family'."

Throughout, tears rubbed shoulders happily with smiles, titters and deep sighs, bringing to the room the essence of what Flora Mae Arkwright had given to this world and to the people in it. She would be sorely missed.

"Well said and beautifully done, my lovely lady," Jack

said to Jenny as she joined him in the front pews. "I felt that I needed to give you a standing ovation. Flora Mae would have loved what you said."

"Was it all right?" Jenny asked her husband as he took hold of her hand.

"Spot on," he replied. "You only have to look at the faces around you to see the effect you've had. Happy, sad, amused. Tearful and joyful at the same time. A bit like her eightieth birthday party at the local Salvation Army Club she used to frequent in her later years. Remember?"

"I do," Jenny said quietly. "Do you remember the look of utter surprise and joy on her face as all the family and friends trooped in to enjoy the afternoon tea and cakes? Even your brother smiled – once."

"Not too sure about that," Jack muttered. "Must have been wind. Are you surprised he didn't show up today?"

"Not really," she said. "We didn't tell him. At least, I didn't. Did you?"

"No fear!" Jack insisted. "He's made his choice of family, and that's the way it will stay. I have given him no thought at all. The ones that *do* matter are the ones here now. I wouldn't have missed *their* company for the world. Jim is the one that surprised me. I couldn't believe it when I saw him get into the hearse with Mr Lancaster. I would have bet a tanner that he would shy away from the day."

"Jenny!" a familiar, softly spoken voice crept over her shoulder. "Can I thank you for your piece about your mam? It brought me – and all around me – to tears wi' sadness and joy, and you captured the essence of what Flora Mae was to me. I shall niver forget that eulogy as long as I live."

"It's what I felt, Jim," Jenny said, with a nod and a smile. "And there's a lot more I could have brought in, if I'd had the time and space."

"A lovely service all round, and now the hard bit," Jim said. His face told it all. He, for one, wasn't about to enjoy seeing his beloved wife consigned to a black hole in the ground. Neither was Jack. Still too raw, thinking back to his experience with *his* mam. Gripping Jenny's hand, he walked steadfastly with her to the plot that would house Jim also when *his* time came.

"We therefore commit this body to the ground … earth to earth; ashes to ashes; dust to dust; in sure and certain hope of the Resurrection to eternal life…"

As the casket was lowered slowly to its final resting place, a brilliant beam of sunshine burst through the clouds, casting its glorious light onto the shiny brass work on the casket's top, highlighting the name plate – Flora Mae Arkwright. *Requiescat in Pace.*

It was all Jack could do to keep his emotions under control as the sunlight followed the coffin into the depths of its plot. That gave Jenny the strength to grasp his hand tightly and to hold her head high as she cast her gaze skyward.

"That was hard work wasn't it, My Man?" Jenny said quietly, as they walked back to the funeral cars, ready for their afternoon tea at the local hostelry.

"How did you know?" he asked in return. "It wasn't that obvious, was it?"

"How long have we been together, Jack?" Jenny said with a fond smile. "I can usually tell. Don't forget that I'm psychic."

"True," he replied. "It brought back memories that I thought I had under control. I had – but only just. I'll miss her, Jenny. We shared a certain … something … that she didn't share with anyone else."

"You were always special to her, you see," Jenny began to explain. "She never had anyone treat her like you did."

"I think we'll walk round to the hotel," Jack said, once they had all gathered by the cars. "It's not far and I could do wi' getting some oxygen into mi body. Anyone else with me?"

"OK by me!"

"I'm up for it!"

"Race you all!"

"Let's go then. I'm starving!"

All of the same mind, Jenny and Jack, Jessie and Millie Alice, Mary and Joey and Ed, Florence May and George William, Stick and Joyce and Billy linked arms and sashayed around to the Union for a buffet afternoon tea on Jim. He had been taken by the funeral car and was standing in the doorway to greet his guests as they arrived.

Close family and about half of the rest of the congregation squeezed into the hotel's snug tearoom to round off a challenging and emotionally draining day that they all wished they could have shared, physically and intellectually, with their absent host, Flora Mae.

–o–

"Don't fuss, Mam," Florence May said quietly.

Jenny had rushed around very early in the morning, unable to sleep on this day that her daughter was to wed Jack's best friend's son. Joyce Walker had been Jack's closest friend for almost the whole of his life, and it had been a shock that Florence May and Billy had decided to spend the rest of *their* lives together. The unfortunate thing was that, after their nuptials, they would be taking this arm of the family back to the other side of the world. Jenny's fear, shared by Billy's mam, was that she wouldn't be there if grandchildren appeared on the scene. Flying to Australia was a very expensive luxury that Jack and Jenny could no longer afford.

"Just wanted to make sure everything is as it should be," Jenny replied with an unconvincing smile.

"Don't worry, it is," Florence May assured her with a hug. "Are *you* all right? Are those tears of happiness or …

sorrow?"

"Very happy for you and Billy, my little one," Jenny reassured her. "It's just that in about three hours' time you will no longer belong to our arm of the family. My little lass will belong to … someone … else."

"I will *always* be part of this family," Florence May insisted firmly. "How could anyone not want to have you as a mother and Daddy Jack as a father? I'm going to miss you all like crazy, but it's what we want to do. It may not be forever, but for now…"

"Well, if you two don't look a beautiful picture!" Jack sighed as mother and daughter came downstairs into the lounge. "Changing your name today, Sweet Pea? No longer to be called Ingles, eh?"

"Actually, Daddy Jack, not quite true," Florence May corrected him.

His eyes climbed slowly to mid-forehead height, leaving him with no answer to give.

"I have decided to become Florence May Walker-Ingles," she announced forcefully. "Not relinquishing the name I love and have had all my life."

"Well now, Milady," Jack replied, bowing with a flourish of his right arm across his body. "How posh is that!"

All present in the room laughed, pleased to be part of a new chapter in the Ingles' saga.

"You decided to stay on then, Our Mary?" Joey asked, as they prepared to leave for the cars to take them to the Kingdom Hall and a marriage ceremony that none of them had experienced before.

"Couldn't not," Mary said, smiling broadly. "Don't forget that I am my own boss. I love that double-barrelled idea of yours, Cousin. I may well adopt that idea myself. What about you? Uncle Eric not cracking the whip?"

"George William and I have complete freedom to

run our business to suit us. Don't forget that I am a full partner," Joey replied. "He leaves it to us so he can enjoy more of a sleeping partnership. We go back tomorrow, early. I love you all, but I am missing *my* family, too."

"Come on then, you lot!" Jack shouted as they reached the front door. "Buffet and a nice cup of tea await! And for those that can't finish it off, doggy bags are available."

Chapter 6

"Well, that was quick!" Jack said to Jenny as they walked slowly to the exit in the Kingdom Hall's foyer, to be greeted by the officiating elder.

"Thank you for coming to help celebrate the joining of our young brethren," he said, holding out his hand. "It's good to see you and to welcome more people into our midst. Would it be all right for one of our local brothers and sisters to call to welcome you into the area?"

"Indeed, Mr Haygarth," Jack replied, wringing his hand warmly. "The only problem is that we don't live here anymore."

"Do you know," the elder said quietly, looking round over both of his shoulders as if to make sure no-one was eavesdropping, "neither do I."

"Then we are destined never to meet again, alas," Jack replied shrugging his ample shoulders. "We've moved to Morecambe."

"I know it well," Mr Haygarth assured him. "Which part?"

"Grosvenor Park," was Jack's firm retort.

"Funnily enough, I live not far from there," Mr Haygarth added. "Do you know Morecambe Road?"

"I certainly do," Jack said incredulously. "It's just round the corner from us. We've not been there long."

"Well, it's not there," Mr Haygarth chortled, a wicked

glint in his eye. "We live down Thornbury Road."

"I know it well," Jack laughed. "Next to the police station? Love to have you drop in for a coffee, some home-made fruit cake and a chin wag."

"Aww! You had me at 'home-made fruit cake'! Now you've got me drooling!" Mr Haygarth gasped. "Name's Ronnie, by the way. Jack and Jenny, I believe?"

"Are you coming to the bunfight at Roundhay Park's Mansion Restaurant?" Jack offered, shaking hands once again. "Everybody else is. I'm sure we will be able to find you a tiny stool in a corner."

"Ooh, you are awful, but I like you!" Ronnie said in his best Dick Emery voice, pushing Jack playfully on the shoulder, drawing a belly laugh from Jack and a giggle from Jenny. "I'd love to, but I have business to attend to here, and then I have to spirit myself back to Morecambe for an early evening service. Perhaps next time."

He took his leave of the gathering with a promise to call on Jack and Jenny in a week or two, when the dust had settled.

"Nice chap," Jack said with a nod. "I like his sense of humour."

"Me too," Jenny added. "And I like his philosophy on life, although I believe *that* was born of his beliefs."

"Thinking of becoming a JW, my sweet?" he asked, interested but not surprised. "Go for it, my lovely. You always were a deep one."

"Don't know," she replied slowly, a thoughtful look invading her face. "I shall have to give it some further thought. Although I have already broached the question, you know me – can't reach a decision without a lot of thought. I hope they don't pester."

"They won't do that," Florence May interrupted. "If at any time you don't want them to call, you only have to tell them, and they'll do as you ask."

"Well, Mrs Florence May Walker-Ingles!" Jack said as he hugged and kissed his daughter. "Bit of a gob full, don't you think?"

Everyone present laughed. Trust Jack to speak his mind.

"Don't you like it, Daddy Jack?" she asked.

"I *love* it, my beautiful daughter," he replied, proud and glad she had married the man of her dreams. "Back home to Oz tomorrow?"

"You trying to get rid of us, Jack?" Billy Walker butted in. "It may well be a lengthy time until we meet again. We're off back on Sunday, so we've three more full days after this one."

"I'd like you to stay as long as you have a mind, Old Chap," Jack answered with a cheery grin. "I've onny one son-in-law now, so I need to mek t'most on 'im, si thi."

"You mun realise, Jack, that youngsters these days know nowt about t'owd dialeck, si thi," Joyce added. "Thee an' me are part o' t'owd school, tha knows. It's a foreign language to 'em. Dodos both on us, eh!"

Florence May and Billy looked at each other as if they were in the company of two aliens that had just dropped from the sky, and smiled indulgently. Parents, eh? 'Toad dial eck'? What was that all about?

-o-

"I would love to see our Florence May settling into happily married life in Oz," Jack mused, once they had settled back into Lancashire life in their new three-bedroomed detached house in Morecambe. Lovely house, but tiny compared with the one they'd had in Leeds. That one, of course, was spoken for for the foreseeable future because it provided a home for their daughter, Jessie, and their darling granddaughter, Millie Alice. This was the reason why Jack and Jenny could afford only a small place in 't'back o' beyond', as Granddad Jud would have called it.

'T'back o' beyond' had, at times, been the most popular holiday destination for West Riding folk for many generations, with still a reasonable influx of them making permanent homes. It had been said that there were more Yorkshire folk living in Morecambe than Lancashire people born and bred – a 'Far West Riding', Jack always supposed.

The only problem with this tiny three-bedroomed detached was that it was surrounded by much larger *four*-bedroomed detached! More rooms, more children. Although he loved working with them, he really enjoyed his down time – which included his holidays having a bit of peace and quiet from their bouncy caged trampolines. These had just started to become popular.

"Do you remember the one and only time I met our Jessie's biological father?" Jack reminisced over a cup of Yorkshire in their new lounge, with only a week of their summer holiday left to enjoy.

"How could I forget the look on his face when you physically threw him out of our little terraced house in Normanton's Queen Street?" Jenny answered with a giggle. "He didn't know whether he was coming or going."

"I can't understand for the life of me why he thought that, after he'd deserted you both, he could just step in and have you act as if nothing had happened," Jack said. "Who did he think he was? Clark Gable?"

"More like Peter Gable," she replied with a titter. "Remember him? Woodhouse, in Mr Hardwick's class?"

"I do that!" Jack said with a shudder. "Always had his finger up his nose and he—"

"Sucked it when he pulled it out—" she went on.

"Wi' a dangling bogie on t'end!" Jack gipped, almost sick at the thought. They both laughed at the picture this conjured up. "Ee, those were the days," he added, still hugging his tea mug to his chest, a glassy look in his eye.

"Wonder whatever happened to him?" Jenny said.

"He became a local councillor in Castleford, I believe," Jack replied. Trust him to know that! "Don't think he had a proper job last time I heard," he continued. "Poking his nose into other folks' business for a change."

"I wonder whatever happened to Carol Anne Haskey?" Jenny said. "Didn't all the lads in Class 2 like her?"

"Wow! What a memory you've got!" Jack gasped. "You're right, although I've no idea why. I sat next to her once and decided to find out where she lived. Not my type, really. Very pretty pretty."

"And where was that?" Jenny asked.

"In the classroom," he countered. "You know, top side of Mrs Gunn's classroom."

"No, daft ha'porth!" Jenny snorted. "Where did she *live*?"

"Prefabs, just off Dalefield Road," Jack chortled. "Behind the Huntsman pub. I used to pass her front door most days when I was at the grammar school."

"How come?" she asked, not quite sure where he meant.

"Every day I used to cut through the snicket at the bottom of our street to cross the fields between the stream and the prefabs on Potts Terrace," Jack explained. "It led across Dalefield Road, on to Firville Avenue and up to school."

"I never went down there in all the time I was in Normanton," Jenny replied.

"Not posh enough, my lovely," Jack chortled. "We were just common, you see. I remember, when I was seventeen going on eighteen, seeing a high-school lass walking up Firville Avenue to school when I was there. I plucked up courage to talk to her and after a time or two, I asked her out. Her mam and dad had a corner shop just down one of the side streets. She was called Linda – Linda Howarth. She was fourteen. We went out together for about six months, then she dumped me. Went for a younger lad who had a motorbike."

"Her loss," Jenny said with a smile. "My gain."

"I onny ever really had three girlfriends," Jack said. "Ruth McDonald when I was eleven, Margaret Chadwick when I was fifteen and she was seventeen – she dumped me after six months or so for an older chap because he had a car – and Linda."

"Aw, you poor thing!" Jenny said, stroking his hand in mock sympathy.

"I think all this reminiscing has emptied mi mug," Jack said, almost in panic. "I'm off to mek a pot o'—" Just as he was getting up, the doorbell sounded almost stridently, echoing in the tiny hallway. "After I've answered that," he added, making the four strides to the front door.

"Do you know, you can't have five minutes' peace!" he said with a grin as he strode back into the lounge on his way through to the kitchen. "Just look what's stumbled by."

"Joyce! Stick!" Jenny gasped, as she got up to hug them. "How lovely to see you both. Just passing?"

"You've been living with Jack too long, Our Jenny," Joyce laughed at her smart comment. "That's one of his. Actually, we *were* just passing," she added, with a clandestine wink at her husband.

"Yeah! Right!" Jack offered over the top of his tray of goodies. "Pull the other one."

"Truthfully?" Jenny asked, not quite understanding where they were going with this one. "How come?"

"Stick was getting fed up with the travelling from North to South Leeds every day," Joyce explained.

"Along with the mundane and excruciatingly boring admin stuff I had to do on a regular basis," Stick added.

"And so—"

"He saw this job advertised in … Silverdale," Joyce butted in. "And—"

"Put in for it, got it, and now we're looking for a house," Stick finished off. "We've already sold ours, so we are officially … homeless."

"When do you start?" Jack asked, knowing what the answer would be. "Homeless?"

"September ninth," Stick replied with a shrug. "Yep. Nowhere to go."

"Twenty-one days?" Jack gasped. "How come?"

"My school in Leeds was shrinking because of major house demolition around it," Stick explained. "I suspect the local authority needs to slough off the expenses of keeping highly paid staff that would become surplus to requirements. I applied for this new job, got it, and resigned from the present one. Boom boom! Job's a good un."

"Where are you staying?" Jenny asked, expecting some sort of rational response. "I assume you're not travelling every day…?"

"We're in a B&B," Joyce added. "I've resigned from my library job and now am … resting. Everything's packed and in store, except for what we stand up in and have in our suitcases back at the B&B."

"May I make a suggestion?" Jack said, looking across at a nodding Jenny, who *knew* what he was about to suggest. "We have a spare double bedroom and a single one. Ours is en suite, and there is one other bathroom. We also have a toilet downstairs. If you go back to your B&B and collect your stuff then come back here, you can stay until you have found somewhere else to live."

"We can't do—!" Joyce protested.

"Oh yes, you can!" Jenny and Jack chorused loudly.

"No arguments," Jack emphasised. "It's the only

sensible solution. We can always arrive at—"

"A reasonable price for B&B?" Stick butted in with a laugh.

"They know you too well, Our Jack," Jenny giggled. "Well? What do you say? It'll be fun."

"Besides," Jack added, "I know that the two secondary schools in this area are looking for librarians. And as this is a large housing estate, new phases are being released all the time, particularly down the next cul-de-sac to us."

Joyce got up and, with tears in her eyes, hugged their friends, sincerely grateful – and relieved – for their offer.

"How about if we collect your things and drop into Hodgson's Chippy in Lancaster on the way back?" Jack went on. "Best cod and chips in the Northern Hemisphere. We can dine in the car."

-o-

"Are you sure this is all right? I mean—" Joyce reiterated, once they had settled in the lounge after fish, chips and scraps in the car from Hodgson's Chippy on Prospect Street in Lancaster.

"Is there anything wrong with your room?" Jenny asked, pre-empting another 'are you sure we're not in the way?' moment from Joyce.

"Have you enough room for your bags and togs and stuff with the other bedroom next to you?" Jack asked. "If you like, I can put a camp bed up in there in case Stick is ever in the doghouse."

They all laughed at Jack's strange sense of humour and settled to a cup of Yorkshire Tea and home-made scones out of the freezer.

"You can stay here as long as you like," Jenny said. "We are genuinely glad to have you. This *is* Lancashire, after all!"

"This is a lovely large and comfy settee," Joyce said. "I

love the colours."

"Bought it in Doncaster when we worked there a year or two ago," Jack replied. "Had to put it into storage when we left Greystone School in Cumbria. I think the odd mouse had had a go at the webbing around the internal springs, but t'damage was minimal. No sign of the pesky little devils, either."

"Mice?" Stick gasped, a look of profound shock on his face as he shot to his feet, glancing around to where he had been sitting. "Where?"

"Keep up, Husband," Joyce laughed. "Which part of 'no sign' don't you understand? He doesn't like them," she went on after a slight pause. "Never has done. He's like a big girl's blouse when it comes to vermin."

"Do you remember those sugar-candy mice we bought on the trip to Llandudno with the top class just before we left to go to grammar and high schools?" Jack began to reminisce.

"I do indeed," Joyce replied with a smile. "How could we ever forget? You, Jack Ingles, put one in your mouth … whole."

"They were onny small," he protested. "Still, it took an age to reduce it to a pulp I could swallow."

"That was because you hadn't realised that its tail wasn't candy at all," Joyce explained. "It was—"

"Thin string," Jack went on. "How was I to know? I thought 'hand-made' meant it was *all* edible. I don't remember much else about the visit, except that I spent a lot of time in and around the gift shops looking for presents for mi mam and grandma."

"I found mi mam a nice little necklace," Joyce said.

"And I got *my* mam a brooch, and for mi grandma, a tea-caddy spoon," Jack added with a grimace.

"A tea-caddy—?" Stick asked, not really understanding what Jack had just said.

"It's a special decorative scoop you keep in your tea caddy to spoon your loose tea into the teapot," Jack explained. "It had a Llandudno image and name on its wide handle. No tea bags in our day."

"And did she like it?" Jenny asked. "I didn't go on that trip because Mum was poorly. Val and I had to stop at home to look after her because Dad was at work."

"I got a rayt earwigging from her," Jack said. "*She* said she would have preferred a brooch or a nice necklace. I don't remember anything about the Orms."

"Orms?" Jenny queried. "Some sort of zoo creature?"

"Great Orm and Little Orm," Joyce explained. "One big and one small lump of headland sticking out into the sea, I think. Jack?"

"Aye, summat like that, I should imagine," he agreed.

"That's probably the only trip I went on in junior and secondary schools, for that matter," Joyce said. "Mi dad usually couldn't afford it. I was allowed to do *this* one because it was the last before we left, and he had done overtime to get some extra money."

"It was the only one I'd been on when we were at Woodhouse, solely because mi fatha wouldn't fork out, and he kept mi mam so short o' brass that she couldn't afford it either," Jack agreed. "How about you Jenny? I know about this last one, but did you ever go on trips?"

"Similar sort of thing really," she said. "I wasn't overly bothered about school trips, preferring to spend time at school because I enjoyed it. I can't say that I ever wanted to travel anywhere away from home. Life could be strained at times with Dad because he was strict. He vetted everything we did and kept a close hold on everything. People thought we were well off living down Cambridge Street, but Mum found it hard to manage sometimes."

"The onny other trip I did was when I was in my first year at grammar school," Jack continued.

"La Baule les Pins, by any chance?" Stick piped up.

"It was," Jack replied with a bit of a frown. "How did you know about that?"

"I spent the first two full years at the grammar school, don't forget, before leaving to go to QEGS in Wakefield," Stick explained. "I was on that trip."

"*That* Stick Walker was *you?*" Jack gasped. "Well, blast mi britches and sizzle mi socks! I never did!"

"Do you remember the French songs we used to have to practise with Mr Halam?" Stick asked.

"'*It etait un petit navire,*'" Jack offered in his dulcet baritone voice. "'*Qui n'avais ja … ja … jamais navigue, Oh ey Oh ey! O ey oh eh matelot'.*"

"You learned it, then?" Stick gasped, overcome with admiration.

"Usually happens with me," Jack continued. "Stuff like that allus sticks, and that was when we were eleven. Ridiculous."

"Weren't you the one that got lost when we were walking from the beach?" Stick reminded him.

"Took the wrong turning and ended up at a rubbish tip," Jack laughed. "Got so badly sunburned that day that I had to have calamine lotion puthered onto mi thin body. Didn't we have individual bed spaces with curtains all round them? Remember?"

"Now you come to mention it," Stick replied with a grin, "no, I don't remember."

"Aye," Jack continued, ignoring his friend's attempt at humour. "T'curtains round my area were pale blue, and one on 'em had a small tear in the top right-hand corner."

"You can remember all that sort of detail?" Stick said incredulously.

"Yes, he can!" Jenny and Joyce chorused loudly.

"Don't forget, Husband, that we have known Our Jack almost since birth," Joyce said. "*That* is just such a thing he *would* remember."

"I remember t'toilets as well – French toilets," Jack continued. "Small lockable cubicle. No seat but a bar – that we called a 'thrusting bar' – across the inside of the door to hold to steady you when you hovered your backside over a hole in the floor. Slightly raised ceramic footprints to give you t'rayt spacing for your feet either side o' t'oyl so you could—"

"Jack!" Jenny interrupted sharply. "Enough!"

"What?" he replied slowly, eyebrows raised and a sly grin beginning to grow.

Chapter 7

Late August was always a joy in Morecambe. No extremes of weather, warm but not overly so. Afternoons sitting in a deckchair in the back garden often encouraged the Ingles to think about retirement and what that might hold.

Jenny and Jack had enjoyed working together at Heysham High School for a couple of years, but that had obviously been short-lived because of his impending move to Fleetwood. He *was* looking forward to the extra cash in travelling expenses – up to £500 a month tax free – but he wasn't looking forward to the travelling. Jenny, too, had become unsettled. She loved working with the twelve-year-old lad she had inherited, and with Kath, Mary and Anne. Sadly, though, it wasn't with Jack.

Stick and Joyce had viewed a number of houses in the Silverdale area reasonably close to his new school, but they were over-priced and over … there. They had had to rationalise and look closer to where Joyce might be able to get a job, which was inevitably nearer to what Jack called 'civilisation' in Morecambe. Fortunately, several new larger detached houses were half-way towards completion on Jack and Jenny's estate, which they were very interested in seeing. One of them backed onto their house.

"How convenient," Joyce said. "All we'd have to do is to cut a generous gate in the fence between us and we could have a cup of tea together."

"Oh no!" Jack laughed. "Think of all the devilish noise!"

"Better the devil you know, eh, Jack?" Stick replied quickly with a chortle.

Still, Jack was looking forward to having his lifelong best friend close by. They had been through many a joyful – and trying – time together, sharing not only friends but family, too. Jack and Joyce's brother, Eric, had always been a joy to be around, with his ebullience and generosity – for a bluff Yorkshireman. Seeing him and his lovely family again would have to be a priority.

So many of those Jack loved were scattered about the place, making it difficult to catch up with them and *their* families! Harrogate, Normanton, Spain, Australia?

Time was shifting by so quickly.

Get a move on, Jack! Where to next?

-o-

Jack didn't like change. Since he had become a teacher in the sixties, the educational marketplace had altered beyond recognition – and not for the better in most situations. The promotion stakes, for example, had shifted unbelievably. Promotion up the ladder used to mean deputy head by age forty, moving on to head teacher by forty-five to fifty. This meant that the pupils' parents were never older than you.

These days, youngsters in their late twenties were becoming deputy heads and moving to head by thirty-five. In Jack's view, whipper-snapper fly-by-nights were becoming heads well before they had learned how to lead teachers and children properly. This was one of the reasons why lots of schools were beginning to struggle. It seemed to have become a case of *who* you knew rather than *what* you knew. The position then became sacrosanct, with the top person sitting in an ivory tower.

In a rapidly changing educational world, these youngsters were finding it increasingly difficult to hold on to their high-powered jobs because they possessed neither the skills, the know-how nor the experience to function smartly and to grow. Jack's positions, unfortunately, had been a case of wrong place, wrong time and wrong manager above him. Consequently, after the last fiasco at Greystone, he had decided that he would go back to what he did best: teaching children.

The last two weeks of the summer term just gone had been OK at the secondary school in Fleetwood, and he had been able to forge a link with all the youngsters he would be working with permanently from the beginning of the autumn term. One fourteen-year-old young lady, who was very close to permanent exclusion, stood out in particular. Her name was Hannah.

"But why is she close to permanent exclusion?" Jack had asked the female deputy head, once he had met and talked to Hannah. "She seems pretty reasonable to me."

"Now there hangs a mystery," the deputy head had replied. "Something's happened to her since you've been here that's never happened before."

"And that is?" Jack had said, intrigued by this … mystery.

"She's started to behave reasonably well," the deputy had said, almost disbelievingly, as if she had discovered a magic potion. "I believe it began the day after you started here and it has continued. She hasn't missed a day, nor even a morning registration."

"Normal child behaviour," Jack had scoffed, shrugging it off. "So, what are you trying to say?"

"That there's more to you than meets the eye, Jack Ingles," she had said, wrinkling the skin around her eyes as if scrutinising him. "It will be interesting to see whether she is in school tomorrow on the last day of this summer term, and whether she's back to her old self come the new term in the autumn."

Of course, Jack wasn't able to see because he had a meeting at his district office in the morning and school closed at lunchtime.

It was at *that* meeting that he learned that his job for the coming year was as a 'fire fighter'. There had been significant problems with support staff organisation, and with their expectation for outcomes while working with problem youngsters. Jack had been redeployed to bring a degree of order to local organisation in situ.

It was a significant job considering the amount he was being paid. Still, there was £500 a month extra – tax free – in travel expenses, for driving forty-five miles through country lanes and back again.

Country lanes? Wasn't so bad, thank you very much. It sounded wonderfully soothing and relaxing, but that all depended on how often he became stuck behind a slow-moving tractor and trailer or was held up by a herd of cows crossing from one field to another, or a little old chap and his lady out for a country jaunt in their Robin Reliant at twenty-five miles per hour.

"Looking forward to your first day in a new year in your new school, My Man?" Jenny asked over porridge and fruit for breakfast.

"Be rayt," he replied, which was his usual answer when he wasn't sure. She could tell he wasn't too sure by the way he pursed his mouth and squinted his eyes. "School and kids are all right, I suppose," he went on after a moment's silence. "It's the travelling that will no doubt become a bore, particularly in the winter – and that's not far away."

"Five hundred pounds a month extra, though?" she said.

"To be honest, Jen, it's the only redeeming thing about the deal. If it wasn't for that, I wouldn't even have entertained it," Jack replied with a sigh. "Still, got to keep you in the manner to which you have grown a custard."

"A custard?" Jen puzzled.

"Oh, come on Jenny! How long have you been … *accustomed* … to my sense of humour?" he explained with a chortle.

"I should have known!" she muttered, eyes looking heavenwards.

"I would still have liked a proper shot at being my own boss," he said quietly, a distant look in his eyes. "Do you remember that headship interview I had in Bradford, when I was in Merton Grange in Leeds?" he asked, skipping deftly from the ridiculous to the even more ridiculous.

"Not really," she admitted. "You had quite a few and I failed to keep track, I'm afraid."

"There were five of us," he explained. "Four existing deputy heads from Bradford middle schools, and me, a head of year from the largest middle school in the country. We'd done the role-play part of our day's interview – don't ask – and had been called for the face-to-face grilling in a room at the top of the town hall in the centre of the city. Windows all around the room allowed panoramic views of the surrounding roof tops. Beautiful blue Welsh slate – in the centre of which all I could see were two copulating pigeons that didn't allow me to concentrate on the questions at hand."

Jenny laughed as a picture took shape in her mind of her Jack's attention locked on sex-mad feral pigeons. "I assume you didn't get the job, otherwise you wouldn't … be … here," she said as she wiped her eyes.

"Those pigeons did it for me," he sniggered. "No headship was about to follow that."

"Tomorrow it is, then," Jenny said, once breakfast was over and tidied away. "I'm going to miss you at school, My Man. We're *all* going to miss you."

"You too, lovely lady," Jack replied, kissing her hand. "You too."

-o-

"Can anyone tell me why I signed up to this?" Jack muttered, as he sat in his car in a country lane near to Aspley Farm close to Thurnham. He hadn't been travelling more than a quarter of an hour and here he was, well and truly stuck just outside Lancaster on his way to Fleetwood High School.

Surrounded by fields either side of the road, he was concerned that a wall of hefty heifers and bouncing bullocks, crossing the road from one field to another just inches from his front bumper, would take him with them. Most of them, he imagined, would have done this crossing many times, but some of them would likely not be doing it many times more – particularly the bullocks. Farmers had need usually for only *one* bull, and so bullocks would become surplus to requirements.

If anything could usher him towards vegetarianism, it was the thoughts cruising through his mind about the fate of these young, healthy, boisterous bullocks. He would have to take note of the times that this hold up was likely to happen in future – if that were possible.

Because these country lanes were usually fairly quiet, he would make up the time to arrive in school reasonable early. It wasn't necessary for him to do assembly, so he could spend time in the staff work area looking through his notes and planning. The busiest times were crossing the road bridge over the River Wyre estuary near to Poulton-le-Fylde and the run from there through umpteen roundabouts to the school. Ample free public car parking opposite the school obviated the daily trauma of trying to squeeze his rather large blue Rover 420 into a parking space wide enough only for a sputtering moped.

"Hello, Hannah," he said as he entered the school's main entrance, surprised to see the fourteen-year-old young lady he would be supporting in some classes that day. His first reaction was to question why she was there. Surely she couldn't have been misbehaving this early on the first day back after the summer break? "Had a rayt grand holiday, I hope?"

"It were rubbish," she almost spat out. "Done nowt. Bin nowhere. Scuffed around most of mi time on mi own. Glad to be back."

"Well, *I'm* glad to see you," he replied with a welcoming smile cheery enough to brighten her sour face. "Why are you here? Waiting for me, I hope?"

"Course I am!" she replied, a slight smile almost lighting up her scowling face. "I wouldn't be waiting for any of these t—"

"Then let's away to somewhere we can talk," he butted in very quickly.

"Goodish holiday overall?" he said, once they'd sat down in the meagre little room that had been designated an office.

"It was crap!" she blurted out unceremoniously. "Did nowt, spent nowt, bin nowhere. Mi dad were pissed for most o' t'time and mi mam did nowt but play bingo."

"Just one thing, Hannah?" he replied with a smile. "Do you think you could haul back on the profanities when we are talking?"

"Prof—?" she puzzled.

"Swearing and harsh words," he explained quietly and with good humour. "I'm not overly keen, and it's what gets you a bad name in school."

"I'm not—" she went on after a moment or two's thought.

"Bothered?" Jack smiled again and pulled a face, at which she laughed. "I know you are a lovely young human being with a great sense of humour, and I know you *are* bothered."

"OK," she agreed. "Fair dos. What's on today?"

"No idea," he replied with a grimace. "It might be RE, or it might even be history, both of which I know you adore."

She curled her lip, showing her distaste for both subjects, but said nothing further.

"I'll support you throughout, if that's what you want," Jack continued. "I should point out, though, that if we don't succeed *together*, the likelihood is that you will be excluded, and I may go back to what I was doing before. I will do whatever it takes to make sure you stay in school. Do we have a deal?"

She sat quietly, staring into space until Jack said, "Hannah?"

"OK, then. I'll do whatever you say, if I have to," she replied finally, with what could have been mistaken for a smile.

-o-

"You look tired," Jenny said, once she had taken her seat next to her husband. "I bet Friday couldn't come soon enough for you."

"Very true," he replied, a huge sigh showing how much he appreciated the mug of steaming Yorkshire Tea in his hands and the sit down in his comfortable little lounge. It was five-thirty on the Friday of his first week of travelling to school. "I just got to know today that both of my co-workers from the Pupil Referral Service are being moved somewhere else."

"Moved? Why?" she asked.

"Because they are the reason I was drafted into that godforsaken place in the first place," he growled. "Their inadequacies are the reason I was transferred here.

Inefficient and useless in the extreme, I'm afraid. Also, I've been told that we have a service meeting every Wednesday after school."

"In school?" she queried.

"No," he added, "in Thornton, in a little office place on the way home. Apart from that, things have gone well with Hannah."

"At least that's something!" Jenny harrumphed. "Things are never straightforward in this authority, eh?"

"Well, that's me done with talking about school now that I'm at home," Jack said with finality, setting down his empty mug. "No more until Monday. Two-and-a-bit days to take it easy."

The snick of the front door made them both turn their head to see who or what was stealing into their snug hallway.

"Hello, Stick, old chap," Jack said. "And Joyce! Have you both been travelling to and from Silverdale?"

"No, but we have some wonderful news," Joyce gushed as Stick sidled into the kitchen diner to make a fresh pot of tea. "*I've* got a job – and we've chosen our new house!"

"Wow!" Jack gasped. "Don't tell me – two-up and two-down terrace in Silverdale for nigh on two-hundred grand?"

"Way off beam, old man," Stick assured him as he set down a tray with four cups and some chocolate eclairs.

"Are we having a party?" Jack asked with a whoop of joy.

"To celebrate my new job in Morecambe Library," Joyce said, with a self-satisfied smirk.

"And our new house—" Stick started.

"Just behind *this* house!" Joyce finished off the tale.

"But there aren't any finished houses behind us!" Jenny replied, more than a little confused.

"Not yet there aren't, but there will be in three months,"

Stick added. "Four bedrooms – one with en suite – and a reasonably sized garden, all for a £175,000."

"This calls for a celebration," Jack whooped again. "Anyone fancy fish and chips and mushy peas from Hodgson's Chippy?"

"But they'd be cold by the time you got them back," Jenny warned him.

"Who said anything about bringing 'em back here?" he replied. "I vote we have them there, in the car. We load up wi' two flasks o tea, our four trays, and knives and forks."

"Way to go, Jack!" Stick agreed, punching the air in triumph. "Couldn't think of anything better."

"Forgot to mention bread and butter," Jack threw in quickly.

"Good old Jack!" Joyce cheered.

"Can't do wi'out bread and butter," Stick chipped in. "One of my favourites is a chip sandwich."

"I remember mi brother when he used to come home for weekend leave from the army when I was nine or so," Jack said. "*His* favourite meal was a plateful of home-made chips and – get this – six to eight slices of home-baked white bread. He would proceed to make what I thought was a significant pile of chip sandwiches."

"What they call 'chip butties' in Liverpool," Stick added.

"Not heard of that one before," Jenny butted in.

"Me neither," Jack agreed.

"Strange person, my husband," Joyce observed. "I don't know where he gets all this from."

"It's because I'm widely travelled," Stick said with a twinkle. "Man of mystery."

"Man with a good imagination, more like," Joyce said.

They all laughed as they headed for their gourmet evening meal in the blue Rover 420, a huge holdall to hand bearing four small trays, four sets of cutlery and mugs, what seemed like a whole loaf of buttered slices, two chequered tablecloths, plus two bazooka-sized thermos flasks.

How fantastic was this going to be!

Chapter 8

"When you were at Normanton Grammar, Stick, did you ever know a lad called Alan Golding?" Jack asked, once they were sitting down in the lounge after their gargantuan fish-and-chip fest in the car at Hodgson's Chippy.

"Name sounds familiar," Stick said, after a moment or two in thought. "Don't forget that I left in the third year to go to Queen Elizabeth's Grammar School in Wakefield. Didn't he come from the terrace up Dodsworth way on?"

"Aye, he did," Jack agreed. "Anyway, we became mates when we were in t' fourth form, and that went on until the end of GCE O-level year. I had no idea what happened at the time, but he disappeared from school and I didn't see him again. Rumour had it that he got two lasses pregnant."

"Crikey!" Stick gasped. "Busy lad."

"Aye," Jack winced. "It was a shame because we had done a lot of athletics and stuff in both summers – usually around throws and power stuff. His great passion in life was gambling on the horses."

"At that age?" Joyce replied disbelievingly. "He would be too young, wouldn't he?"

"Actually, if you remember, betting on horses and stuff was not legal and that's why a lot of bookies were clandestine. They were hiding in premises where only the punters knew where to find them," Jack explained. "I don't know whether anyone can remember, but after the row of shops that contained the Co-op and the Meadow grocery on Wakefield Road t'other side of Woodhouse Junior School, there was a stretch of grassed land with a string of cottages almost at right angles with Bailey Place. On the corner of that street there was a small, double-storeyed clothing factory. Next to that, skulking down a dingy snicket, was a hidden hut that turned out to be a bookies."

"How do you know that?" Jenny asked. "Were you a clandestine horse better?"

"Neigh! Neigh! Not on your nelly!" Jack insisted with a snorting whinny. "Whenever I met Sam on the way to the grammar school, he would nip in to place a bet. One-and-sixpenny cross-piece double, or some other such garbage."

"And who was Sam?" Joyce asked, now intrigued.

"That was the name we always called Alan Golding," Jack explained. "Don't ask me why because I have no idea."

"Did he ever win?" Stick asked eagerly.

"Not so far as I am aware," Jack replied. "But who knows? He never told me whether he did or not. As I believe he still lives in Normanton, I would guess … not."

"Do you keep in touch with any of your acquaintances from then?" Joyce asked.

"Just the one, Our Joyce," Jack replied quietly, fixing her with one of his serious looks. "And she means more than all the others put together."

She smiled, knowing full well that he meant the same to her, and always would.

"Talking of which," he added, "have you heard anything of our brother Eric lately?"

"I think the last time we saw him was … a year or so ago?" she replied, turning to Stick for confirmation, who shrugged his shoulders lamely. "But we've had the odd telephone conversation or two."

Jack noticed that Stick looked like he might benefit

from a cup of tea and a touch of the sweet stuff with it. He decided that he, too, was feeling a little thirsty and missing a modicum of pudding or something. He got up and wandered towards the kitchen door.

"Jack?" Jenny said. "Is it cup of tea time? I think you might find some buns in the tins in the cupboard. Not home baked, I'm afraid. Haven't had a lot of time lately. Joyce? Do you fancy doing a bit of baking tomorrow?"

"You bet ya I do!" Joyce replied quickly. "That would be excellent."

Once equilibrium had been restored with a mug of Yorkshire Tea and a nibble or two on a jam donut from the local ASDA, which was only a step or two from their front door, conversation returned to Joyce and Jack's brother, Eric.

"I hope he's all right," Joyce said. "He seemed to be a bit pensive the last time we spoke. How are George and Joey getting on these days?"

"The company is running well under them," Jack replied with pride. "Eric seems to be taking more of a back seat and is letting them get on with it. There was even talk of their becoming a public limited company, but I don't know much about that."

-o-

"I have to say, Jessie, that was a lovely, lovely meal," Johnny Grey said, as he sat back in the settee in her home in Leeds. "The best meal I've had for a long time. I love the times we've spent together, and Millie Alice is a delight to be near."

"You are very welcome," Jessie replied as she re-entered the front room after settling her daughter in her little bed upstairs. "She'll be off until early morning."

"Those children's books she has don't happen to have been written by a relative, do they?" he asked, quite intrigued by the author's name. "Jack Ingles?"

Jessie giggled as she linked her arm through his. "Jack Ingles just happens to be my Daddy Jack," she explained. "I've called him that ever since I was able to speak."

"Wow!" Johnny replied in genuine awe. "Your father a published author? Now I see where you get your smartness."

"Don't forget my mum," Jessie added quickly. "I have always looked up to her, although she wasn't as she is now in my very early years."

"How do you mean?" he asked, a puzzled look invading his face.

"It's no secret that mum had me when she was at uni," Jessie explained quietly. "My biological father wanted nothing to do with us, and although he and mum had married it was a sham and he walked away. She divorced him and we moved into a cramped terrace house in Normanton. When I was about four, Jack Ingles stepped back into my mother's life and that was when life began in earnest for Mum and me. He adopted me and has treated me as his own ever since. I love him to bits."

"Well, a wonderful story," Johnny said with a genuine smile. Kissing her on the cheek, he continued. "How would you feel about following in your mother and Daddy Jack's footsteps?"

"Following—?" Jessie replied, not sure what he meant.

"Well," he began to explain, pulling a small, maroon, domed box out of his pocket. "What if I were to offer you this and to say ... will you marry me, Jessie? And allow me to take your daughter as my own, too?"

She clicked open the box and her eyes widened in surprised awe to see a gold ring adorned by a large flashing pink diamond. "But—" she stammered, "you want to marry *me*?"

"That's the general idea," he reassured her. "I've loved

you from that first time I saw you in Golden Acre Park being harassed by that … creep. I've been plucking up courage to ask you for weeks. If I'd kept this ring in my pocket for much longer, it would have taken root!"

They laughed and kissed as she slipped the ring onto her finger.

"What do you say?" Johnny asked again. "It'll be—"

"Yes!" she blurted out. "Yes! Yes! Yes! Of course, I *will*!"

"And will you allow me to adopt your daughter as my own, please?" he asked seriously.

"Of course I will, but you'll need to ask Millie Alice that one," Jessie replied, eyeing the glorious ring on her finger.

"You said that Jack stepped back into your mum's life?" Johnny asked, intrigued as to why 'back'.

"Mum and Daddy Jack had been best friends since primary school," she started. "And by *that*, I mean very close friends. They never went anywhere much without each other until she went to uni, and then she went off the rails to some extent, leaving her best friend by the wayside. Their friendship fell by the wayside, too, when she had decided to marry my biological father, which apparently upset Jack very much. They met accidentally – in a cemetery of all places – a few years later. His wife had walked out on him with their son. Mum and Jack married and he became my Daddy Jack, which was the best thing that has happened to me. Until you came along, of course."

Johnny laughed, putting his arm around her and drawing her towards him. "I shall have to be off soon," he warned her. "I have an early start and another busy day in court."

"You've not—?" she said with a worried smile.

"No," he laughed again. "I've just been promoted to superintendent at Gillgarth nick, and I have several cases that I need to see through the courts."

"I had rather thought you might … stay tonight?" Jessie suggested. "We are to be married, after all."

"But we aren't just yet, Jessie," Johnny replied. "You know my morality, and I won't compromise *that*. I am looking forward very much to our sleeping together … when we are married. Would that be a problem for you?"

"Of course it wouldn't," she replied with a grin.

"Here's a thought for you," he went on, getting up to take his leave. "It would suit me down to the ground for us just to nip out and tie the knot quickly without all the arranging and organising that can elongate the process. Then we can – well, you know."

"That's all right by me," Jessie agreed. "We've had four weddings and a funeral in recent history. Folks will be getting fed up with them by now, I should think."

"How's about we keep it to ourselves and just nip out and … do it?" Johnny suggested. "I think also we need to look out for a decent-sized house in this locality – like this one that we both like – ready to move into. *My* flat in Headingly, I am assured, will sell like the proverbial hot cake."

"This house is owned by Mum and Daddy Jack," Jessie said, watching carefully to gauge his reaction. "And if I leave, they will want to sell it."

"Is there any reason why we wouldn't be able to negotiate with them to take it off their hands?" he replied. "I really like its size and position and the layout inside."

"I don't see why not," she replied.

"It's big enough if we decide we might like to give Millie Alice a brother or a … sister – or both," he added. "Don't you think?"

"Can't wait!" she gushed, as they kissed passionately by the front door. "See you tomorrow at five for tea?"

"Bring it on!" he said as he turned to go.

-o-

"Not a bad run today," Stick said, as he sat down in his favourite armchair after his trip back from Silverdale. "Twenty minutes is all it took, gate to—"

"Gate to—?" Joyce asked, offering him a mug of tea and a tart.

He bit into it absent-mindedly without any real thought, until the flavour woke up his taste buds. "To … door. Wow!" he gasped, looking across at his wife who was standing in front of him, hands on hips as if waiting. "This is gorgeous! What is it?"

"That one is a coconut and jam tart," she replied, a grin of satisfaction splitting her face. "When you've finished that one, I'd like you to try one of these." She placed a mini fruit pie in front of his eager face as he flicked his fingers in anticipation.

"I might have to have another one of those if I don't recognise what it is," he replied, drooling over pastries he'd never tasted the like of before.

"I feel sure you will," Joyce told him.

"I've allus loved this part of home baking, Old Chap," Jack laughed. He sat down near to his friend and started sniffing the air gently, nose so obviously in the air, and eyes almost closed. "You bite into it and I'll tell you what I think it is."

"You've been here longer than me, and you probably saw what was being done," Stick protested.

"Not been in," Jack assured him. "I'm as new to what they've done as you are."

"Close your eyes then, and we'll see if you're as good at guessing as you make out," Stick suggested. "Otherwise—"

"Eyes shut," Jack said once his lids were tight and his back was turned. "Bitten yet? Aww, yes! That would be one of my all-time favourites – a … mince pie."

"You peeped!" Stick complained.

"I think you'll find that he can smell a mince pie at

fifty paces," Jenny laughed along with Joyce.

"Anyway, you don't bake, Joyce," Stick insisted.

"I do now," she said. "Jenny and I have had a fantastic time … baking. We did so much that we couldn't find enough places to put it all. So—"

"So?" Stick and Jack chorused.

"Well then, you'll have to eat it all," Jenny replied with a guffaw.

"Anyway, why were you in school on a Saturday morning, Old Chap?" Jack asked, quite nonplussed.

"Training day, Jack," Stick replied. "Remember those?"

"Too right I do!" Jack said with more than a modicum of distaste. "Kenneth Baker brought 'em in, in 1988. Five useless days that achieved nothing, that were stolen from our annual holidays. They became 'Baker Days' or eventually B-days, a bit like the similarly named contraption in a foreign bathroom – and just as useless!"

"Stolen holidays?" Joyce queried. "How could that be?"

"Minister for Education, Kenneth Baker, decided it would be a rayt grand idea to take five days from teachers' holiday entitlement and impose them on schools as 'training days'," Jack replied. "T'children were still on holiday but we … weren't. This charade was foisted on to school managers who had no idea what to do with 'em. Iniquitous!"

"Nowadays, to safeguard the holidays-as-was, we are allowed to do evenings and Saturday mornings," Stick added. "Hence today."

-o-

Although conveniently situated 'twixt Lancaster and Morecambe, the Grosvenor Park new housing estate wasn't the best placed or most attractively set out area in which to live. It was a large, sprawling complex, bordered on three sides by busy roads. The fourth side nestled next to an overgrown, now derelict, former railway line and an industrial estate. The only greenery within its boundaries was a stretch – perhaps the size of half a football pitch – which was bisected by a chuckling stream where fish roamed amidst weeds and sparse reeds.

The estate had been built upon a stretch of marsh land, where munitions factories in the Second World War had grown according to need, and where loud and sometimes deadly accidents had become commonplace. Ostensibly not an easy place upon which to build, many of the houses were constructed on substantial, large, pre-cast concrete 'piles' that had been driven into the yieldingly soft earth – some of which had been pushed downwards to a depth of twenty metres. The idea of living in a house 'floating' on a concrete raft was intriguing for Jack, evoking visions of South Sea island beauties swishing around in grass skirts and hob-nailed flip-flops.

"Just got a letter through the front door to say our new house will be ready to move into in two weeks," Joyce announced. "Yay! As the house costs much less than we got for the one in Leeds, this means that we will be mortgage-free in just … two years!"

"Excellent!" Jack replied, quick as a flash. "*We'll* be able to sell up and come to live wi' you!"

Chapter 9

"I hope we're not intruding, Daddy Jack," Jessie said as she embraced her father.

"Jessie! Johnny! Millie Alice!" Jack gushed. "What an amazing surprise. If I'd known you were coming – we'd have been in Spain with your Aunt Val and Uncle Mike!"

"He *is* joking, of course," Jessie explained, turning to Johnny in case he didn't understand Jack's sense of humour. "You'll get to know him before long."

Johnny grinned sheepishly, not having been alerted to Jack's way-out and unexpected humour.

"My goodness! Is this young lady really *my* granddaughter?" Jack asked as he picked up Millie Alice. "How old are you, young lady? Twelve?"

"No, Ganpa, silly," she replied with her brows knitted. "I four. Down, Ganpa, pease."

"She's still not keen on being picked up," Jessie warned. "Mam not in?"

"She's just nipped round to see an ageing neighbour about something or other," he replied. "She shouldn't be—"

"Do we have visitors, Jack?" Jenny's voice ricocheted from the tiny hallway. "There's a foreign car at the front."

"In the kitchen, Jen," Jack replied. "And yes, we do have visitors. Three, to be exact."

"Three?" she queried. "Jessie! Millie Alice! And—?"

"Mam and Daddy Jack, I should like you to meet my husband, Johnny," Jessie announced.

"Husband?" Jenny said, a seriously puzzled frown appearing as she shot a quizzical look at *her* husband. "We don't even—"

"Very many congratulations, young man," Jack interrupted his wife, thinking she was about to put her foot in it as she usually did.

"We just wanted to tell you face-to-face," Johnny explained. "Sorry about not inviting you all, but we felt like we wanted to do it quickly. Unfortunately, twenty-eight days was the soonest we could make it officially – so here we are, newly married … yesterday."

"I don't understand," Jenny said with a deep sigh. "We knew you were 'stepping out together', as my mother used to say, but—"

"We love each other, Mam," Jessie began to explain, "and Johnny dotes on Millie Alice. So, we decided to nip out … and do it, just like you wanted to do, Daddy Jack. We wanted to live together, and the only way Johnny would do that was for us to get married first."

"Good on you!" Jack boomed, shaking Johnny's hand and hugging his daughter at the same time. "This calls for a celebration. Cup of Yorkshire Tea and a home-made bun or two all right? I like your style, Johnny, mi owd mate."

-o-

"I still can't get over it," Jenny gushed, over tea and a coconut tart. "My Jessie settled at last with the man she deserves. How's little Millie Alice taken it?"

"Well, you know how she is," Jessie replied. "She either loves or isn't too keen. But with Johnny, she can't get enough."

"I love your books, by the way, Jack," Johnny added after a refill, "and so does your granddaughter. She has her own mind, has that one, and she's not afraid to let you know."

"I wonder if there's anyone in this room she reminds me of?" Jenny said, a knowing smile growing as she fixed her eyes on her daughter.

"We do have some other news for you, too," Johnny began, filling an encroaching silence as buns were consumed and mugs refilled. A look of surprise filled Jenny's eyes and one of intrigue and interest crept up on Jack.

"And how are you going to spend your lottery win?" Jack quipped, to comments of 'I wish' and 'Yeah! Right!'.

"It *is* to do with property and finance," Jessie added.

"I can lend you £20, but I have to warn you that the interest rate *will* be unaffordable," Jack quipped.

"Seriously, Daddy Jack, Johnny has sold his two-bedroom flat in Headingley," she went on. "With the proceeds, we have bought a house in North Leeds."

"Is it big enough for us to come to stay on the odd occasion?" Jack enthused, seeing a way to spend more time with his daughter and granddaughter.

"It certainly is," Johnny assured him. "Four beds – one en suite – big kitchen, huge conservatory, and here's the cheque for it. We did take off ten per cent because there are one or two things we would like to do to it."

He handed over an envelope to Jenny, who showed a startling degree of confusion and uncertainty on her face. She looked hurriedly across at her husband, not understanding why he was grinning so hugely.

"Well, I'll be buggered!" Jack exclaimed, as he hugged and kissed his daughter and wrung the hand of his son-in-law again. "Do you realise, Jen, that they've onny gone and bought our house from us? Not sure whether to laugh or … to laugh even louder."

"We both love the house and its position, and, of

course, it's the only place that the little one knows," Johnny explained to a stunned Jenny and an ecstatic Jack.

"It took most of our money at the time, but it was a lovely home and a convenient safety net for Jess and Millie," Jack said quietly. "I can't thank you enough, Old Chap. All I have to do now is to clear the mortgage and bank the rest. Dinner is on us this evening. You are stopping ower, I trust – hope?"

"What about your friends? I take it they are not still here, otherwise the spare room might be a bit cramped," Jessie added with a grin.

"They moved into their new house just over the fence behind us four days ago. There'll be plenty of space for the three of you," Jack explained.

"Perhaps you can see where Jessie gets her humour from, Johnny?" Jenny laughed.

"Twenty or more years living with an intractably dour but witty Yorkshireman," Jessie added. "Yes, please, we'd love to."

"Everything's clean and fresh, and we have a bed somewhere that we can put up in the smaller bedroom for Millie Alice," Jack added. "The bathroom next to your room is for your use. We have a small en suite, and there is a loo by the front door – inside of course – in our palatial five-feet-by-three-feet hallway."

-o-

"We're not paupers after all, Jen," Jack said quietly to his wife once bedtime had drawn them in. "I'll need to sort the finances out early next week and then we can heave a contented sigh of relief, eh?"

"Finally, we've got some breathing space," Jenny agreed.

"Now that they're all settled, perhaps we should take early retirement and emigrate to Southern Spain to live our life in the sun," Jack said, to a quizzical look from Jenny. She still couldn't tell when he was being serious over matters that were contentious, to say the least.

"Now I *know* you're not being serious," she said. "Are you?"

"Course I am … not!" he laughed at her puzzled face. "But … we *can* afford to go abroad more frequently. What are we celebrating on the twenty-second of February next year, for example?"

She had to think for a moment or two before her face sank at the thought of her first large birthday milestone. "Don't rub it in!" she muttered soulfully.

"Two choices, then," he replied. "A long weekend in London, or a week in Benidorm? Although I am certain which you will choose, I have to give you the option. London?"

"On your bike!" she snorted.

"Benidorm it is then," he agreed immediately. "Hotel Calypso. Done."

"What are you on about – 'done'?" she sneered.

"It's already booked," he assured her. "I have the tickets. Don't forget that it will be February half term. I've booked to go out on Saturday the twentieth of February and come back the following Saturday. A week in the warm Spanish sun, to be fed and watered and looked after. Heaven, eh?"

"How—?" she replied, gobsmacked at her wonderful husband's ingenuity and kindness and … sneakiness.

"Ha-ha!" he chortled quietly, tapping the side of his nose with a smart finger. "I'll show it to you in the morning."

"It won't be the first time," she muttered with a suppressed giggle, kissing him quietly.

-o-

A week to go, and October half-term break couldn't come

quickly enough for Jack. Several things had come to pass in a very fast-moving educational environment. Although his working and organising at the high school in Fleetwood had been very successful, apparently the present system of the Pupil Referral Service hadn't followed suit. There were rumours among his fellow professionals in the field that its present, slow-moving, leviathan-esque progress couldn't, in all honesty, be sustained.

Lee McKee had taken early retirement because of ill-health, and the head of the service in the education authority had resigned to take up a post elsewhere. For Jack, after only twelve months in post, this was not a good omen. In effect, the organisation had become rudderless, and major areas of the ship were lacking in steam. Consequently, schools where behaviour support teachers with the PRS had taken up post might be asked to take them onto their payroll from the next educational year.

This highlighted a whole raft of problems that could occur. There was a likelihood that many teachers might leave the service before the plans came to fruition, leaving schools and their problem youngsters without the appropriate support on which they had come to rely.

"How is Lee?" Jack asked Josie Speak at their usual end-of-half-term meeting at their little office hut.

"Not good, I'm afraid," she replied. "She certainly won't be back. We thought it might be respite, but it seems to be more serious."

"Can we do anything? Have a whip round for some decent flowers or summat, perhaps?" he offered.

"Not really, I don't think," Josie said with an air of finality. "Not allowed."

"Then I'll send some missen," he harrumphed. "Don't thee worry thissen, because I'll find out from t'office in White Cross. If they say nay, I have one or two others as'll know. Do you have t'same response if I ask thee about t'future of this godforsaken organisation we serve?" he asked with some degree of irritation. "Closed book again, eh?"

"We've been told very little," she replied, a little flustered at Jack's attitude. "Don't worry. I—"

"Don't worry thissen," he interrupted with a disarming grin. "You've probably been sworn to t'Artificial Secrets Act. Any road, it's Friday and I have the best part of an hour's travelling at the busiest time of the week so I'm off 'ome – if there's nothing else?"

"Nice one, Jack," Peter Farbridge said, as they sought out their motors. "You never get to know owt in this organisation unless you ask forcefully – and then you'll be lucky."

"Aye. I like what I'm doing here, but I can't do wi' officious little upstarts as know nowt," Jack replied, tight-lipped. "I don't like being kept in the dark. Any road," he added as car doors opened and slammed shut and engines spat into life, "I'm off." He wound down the window of his Rover 420. "Si thi, Peter. Weekend, here I come!"

Within seconds, he was gone.

Friday's traffic from Fleetwood to Poulton-le-Fylde across the four roundabouts along Fleetwood Road, Amounderness Way and onto the Shard Road bridge over the River Wyre, was usually a pain. Every car seemed to carry one person who was desperate to get home early to enjoy that extra bit of his weekend. Still, Jack supposed, a fifteen-minute cup of tea at home had to be better than a quarter of an hour in the umpteen snarl-ups he encountered most weeks.

This day was different. There *was* traffic, but in no way did it match up to the usual. A few vehicles slowed him a little, but everyone seemed to be aware that he needed to get home urgently.

The day was warm, though not as sunny as it quite

often was at this time of year, and the scenery and countryside seemed to have taken on a magical vibrancy. He was astounded to see an enormous flock of curlews feeding on goodness knows what in the fields either side of Marsh Lane, literally spitting distance from the southernmost end of Morecambe Bay. He would have loved to stop but the road was too narrow, with no laybys or passing places.

"You'll never guess what I saw across the marshes on the way home today," Jack said to Jen, as they sat gratefully, blissfully, with a mug of freshly mashed tea and a toasted currant teacake.

"An enormous flock of curlews, by any vague chance?" she replied with a quiet self-satisfied smile as the steam from her mug licked around her face.

"I know you're intuitive and psychic, but that's ridiculous!" he gasped, not even able to hazard a guess as to how she knew that. "How on—?"

"It's just been on the early-evening local news," she explained. "It must have been a spectacular sight."

"Too right it was, and I couldn't stop to watch because the road is too narrow and there were lots of idiots pushing to pass," Jack said. "You are so … clever, Jenny Ingles."

"I know," she agreed with a giggle. "But I'm not clever enough to have foreseen what Mrs Riddler, the deputy head at school, has done."

"Now what?" Jack sighed, almost resigned to some calamitous concoction of a cock-up no doubt perpetrated in the name of progress.

"She's only gone and advertised our jobs without consulting *us*," Jenny started. "I know rumours are rife that the PRS is to shut down, and they want to save money by not reemploying Kath, Mary, Anne and me when the axe falls."

"She can't do that!" Jack insisted, his anger rising.

"She has," Jenny emphasised.

"I say again," Jack repeated, "she can't do that … legally. You must get me the name of your union rep and—"

"It's already done," she replied. "Kath's husband knows him, and he – the rep – wants to talk to us. I've suggested we can have that meeting here on Wednesday of next week – the week before half term."

"You don't let the *dents de lions* grow under your feet, do you, lass?" Jack replied, eyebrows raised in surprise. "You won't be needing me in another twenty years."

She laughed and said, "I think you'll find it's grass."

"And me wi'out a mower, eh," he replied quickly.

They both laughed at how they had grown to know what each other was about to say in any given situation. Jenny had always been able to read Jack's mind – well, nearly always. She was painfully surprised when her readings were inaccurately off-centre. Still, that was Jack for you. Sometimes he *allowed* you to believe you had him taped, to find later that you were way out with your assessment.

A real Yorkshireman, eh?

-o-

"Your deputy head has made a serious mistake," said Jeff Royd, union rep for Jenny and her colleagues. "Advertising someone's job without telling them their contract is up for grabs is definitely not something you can let her get away with."

"Next step then, Jeff?" Kath asked, as they all sat around the enormous circular table in Jack and Jenny's kitchen diner, steaming mugs of Yorkshire Tea and home-made Victoria sponge to hand.

"I've already made representations to the headteacher setting out our next steps towards an industrial tribunal," he explained. "If they would like to deal quietly with this grossly misjudged and unacceptable occurrence, without recourse to local authority involvement, they will accede to our demands. We will demand reasonable compensation and a guarantee of the continuation of existing contracts."

"Compensation?" Anne gasped. "How much?"

"Probably in the region of one to two thousand pounds," Jeff pointed out.

"So that would be about five hundred each?" Mary queried.

"Sorry, no," he replied. "One to two thousand pounds EACH."

"I'll have some of that!" Anne replied with a gasp. "That will allow me to study for my PGCE so I can become a teacher. Wow!"

"I think I can speak for us all when I say that we have become more than a little fed up with being side-lined and more and more isolated from the rest of the staff," Jenny said.

"Hear, hear", "Too true", "Completely fed up", they all chorused.

"I think we had all decided that there had to be something better out there at an appropriate time," Jenny continued. "Is now that time?"

"Leave it to me," Jeff reassured them. "Don't do anything about looking for other jobs, otherwise it might jeopardise whatever figure we arrive at."

"Well, I never did," Jack said to the group, once the rep had set off to his next appointment. "More tea, anyone?"

"I'm sure you must have," Kath replied with a mischievous twinkle in her eyes. "I, for one, would love more tea and another piece of that gorgeous cake."

Chapter 10

"Indian summer, eh?" Jack observed, as they sat in a comfy chair in Joyce and Stick's new garden on a newly laid stone patio just outside the dining room's French doors.

"Can't whack it!" Stick said, as he deposited a Jack-style tray of afternoon tea on an occasional table within reaching distance.

"Can't be!" Jack replied, eyeing the cakes and tarts and an enormous ceramic teapot decorated with a variety of British wildlife. "Tea bread and honey, and lemon sponge cake. Not had any of that for ever such a long time."

"And the tea bread not only has walnuts and dates in it, but dark muscovado sugar and … molasses," Joyce added with a self-satisfied smile. "I can see you drooling now, Our Jack."

"It's donkey's years since I had some of that," he replied. "Mi grandma used to make a semblance of it, but this sounds a lot richer and yummier."

"Is thy off to stop thi wailin', and 'ave a chew?" Stick laughed, as he bit into his doorstopper of a slice. Almost immediately, his eyes closed slowly, a look of extreme enjoyment covered his jowls and a groan of pure joy escaped his throat.

Jack followed almost immediately, not to be outdone by his close friend. "I 'ope tha's got a batch of this, Joyce," he said in between sucks and chomps and lip smacks. "It's absolutely – oh look! Somebody's tekken a piece out on mi slice."

"It's called your … mouth, that has taken it," Jenny and Joyce laughed at the picture before them.

"Believe it or not, I've got a large one of those secreted in ours," Jenny warned. "I'm not telling you where, and woe betide if you go searching!"

"Did you ever go to the roller drome at Wakefield, Stick?" Jack asked. "Just about the time rubber-wheeled roller skates came in?"

"I had some skates, but they were metal with metal ball bearings," Stick replied. "How quickly they wore out depended on how much you used them and where you skated. Mine were useless. Wore out in no time."

"And you had to buy new wheels," Jack added. "Waste of time … and money. I asked mi dad for money to buy some new rubber wheels, but I got a flat 'no'. It would have tekken me until I was twenty-one to save up my weekly tanner pocket money."

"A tanner!?" Jenny said incredulously. "I had 2/6d when I was twelve."

"Half a dollar?" Jack gasped. "To get that amount I would have needed two part-time jobs! I didn't start getting mi own money until I did pea picking in the summer I was sixteen."

"I got a tanner when I was five," Stick butted in.

"Pea picking?" Joyce said with a frown. "What did that involve?"

"T'pea-picking wagon would roll up to the bottom of Garth Avenue where it runs into Dalefield Road at about six in t'morning and take us to the pea-growing fields Castleford way on," Jack began. "We would then spend the whole day in these enormous fields pulling pea plants out of the ground to strip them of their full pea pods. To be paid 3/3d, we had to weigh in a one-hundredweight sack of pea pods – and nothing else. No stalks or leaves, just peas. Back-breaking work."

"Was there a café close by to get refreshment?" Jenny asked.

Once Jack had stopped laughing, he said, "Not really. We had to take a sandwich and a bottle of water to have during our half-hour break. Still, it was a sight better than being in school."

"Didn't you do it during school holidays in August?" Jenny puzzled. "I would have thought—"

"No fear!" Jack insisted. "It was a case of earning a bit o' brass working, or slouching about in school doing … nothing. School knew it was happening but turned a blind eye. As absolute novices, we were lucky to fill four bags a day – some older ladies could do six or seven. I would come away at the end of one week with £3 10s."

"Which would be in today's money—?" Joyce butted in.

"Three pounds fifty, which was good money in 1962. In today's money, it would be worth about forty pounds now," Stick added.

"I could do a lot with that," Jack replied. "Like save it towards my holidays in Brid or Scarborough, or going to Caton Bay wi' mi mate, Curfy Wood, and his mam and dad, younger brother, David, and his sister."

"Caton Bay?" Joyce asked. "Don't know that one."

"Wallis's Holiday Camp," Jack explained. "Caravans and chalets not far from the cliff top. You had to go down a steep slope and some steps to reach the sands. Not far from Scarborough and Filey."

"And how often did you do that?" Jenny asked.

"Twice," he replied. "The year before, when I was fifteen, I went for the first time with my pal, David Hartley, his mam and sister, Christine. We spent a lot of time on the beach shot putting and leaping about because we were both into athletics. He went on to play professional rugby league in later life for some class Yorkshire clubs. Memories, eh?"

"You mentioned Wakefield Roller Drome," Stick said, after another mashing of tea and another slab of date-and-walnut tea bread. "Did you ever go to watch the wrestling there?"

"Did I ever!" Jack replied with a look of sheer nostalgia. "You mean to watch Mal Kirk and Mick MacManus…?"

"And Bert Royal and Jackie Pallo," Stick added.

"And Johnny Black Kwango and Les Kellet," Jack butted in. "Along with Masambula and Billy Two Rivers, with his Mohawk hairstyle. I remember his Red Indian war dance when he was annoyed, and his signature knock-out Tomahawk Chop.

"Now here's one I bet you did know about or do," he added, touching the side of his nose and winking. "Before I left Normanton to go to teacher training college in Leeds, they introduced wrestling to Normanton baths."

"I bet that was a spectacle, threshing about in the deep end!" Stick mused to everyone's laughter at the thought.

"Daft bugger!" Jack grinned. "During t'winter off-season, when t'boards were down. Picture it. Wrestling ring in t'middle o' t'floor and chairs all round. Exciting. I onny saw one or two events before I wor off to t'next world as would envelop me."

"You're wrong there, Our Jack," Joyce chipped in. "I *did* go to t'wrestlin', tha knows. Mi dad took me a few times, and then I went on mi own when he couldn't get. Not many top names, as I recall, but I remember seeing Johnny Black Kwango and Bert Royal and his brother – what was his name?"

"Faulkner, I think," Jack replied hesitantly. "Not sure of his first name, though. Alan? Pete?"

"They're not wrestling names, are they?" Joyce said quietly, almost to herself. "Something sharp and snappy … got it! He was called Vic Faulkner."

"Ee-eck! 'Ark at you!" Jack said, clapping in triumph. "A female Kent Walton!"

"Who on earth was Ken Walton?" Jenny asked, showing her obvious ignorance of that era and that very popular British sporting television pastime.

"Ken*t* Walton, my dear Jenny, was the commentator in ITV's Saturday sports programme, *World of Sport*, aired in the 1960s, that included wrestling," Jack corrected. "He was born Kenneth Walton Beckett."

"I would have loved that, but we didn't watch such common stuff when I was that age," Jenny said with a cringeworthy shudder. "Mum didn't like such barbarity, and Dad wasn't overly keen. He preferred darts and cricket."

"Talking about the baths in the winter," Stick asked, changing tack slightly, "did any of you go to the Saturday dances?"

"Did we just!" both Joyce and Jack burst in.

"Why, Stick, didn't you?" Jack replied, more than as little surprised at his response.

"Went once or twice," Stick said. "Wasn't owerly keen, really."

"Loved it at fifteen and sixteen," Jack enthused. "Very early 1960s, when bopping was the rage. How did we ask a girl to dance, Joyce?"

"'You dancin'?'" Joyce said. "The lad would say."

"'You askin'?'" Jack replied. "The lass would answer."

"'I'm askin','" Joyce added. "Lad would reply."

"'Then I'm dancin','" Jack said. "The lass would agree."

"Then off they'd go," Joyce continued, a nostalgic smile decorating her face. "That lasted for only one dance unless the lad fancied her, then she *might* do it again depending on whether or not *she* fancied *him*."

"It allus got me that a group of lasses would dance around in a group with their handbags in a pile on the floor in the middle of the group," Jack remembered with a puzzled frown.

"And then we'd peel off when we got asked to dance with a lad we liked the look of," Joyce said with a giggle. "Unless it was somebody that was touchy-feely, or a clod-hopping lump or who … smelled."

They all joined in with a hearty nostalgic laugh.

"Sometimes it doesn't seem longer ago than yesterday," Joyce said with a sigh.

"And at other times, it could have been another lifetime," Jack added.

"Which indeed it was," Jenny added, a faraway look in her eyes.

"What made you want to become a teacher anyway, Jack?" Stick asked.

"A chap called Herbert Hardwick," Jack began to explain. "Remember him, Joyce? Jenny?"

"Certainly do," Joyce replied. "One of the nicest teachers I ever came across. Generally taught Classes 3 or 4 at Woodhouse."

"I came across him in Class 3 as my form teacher," Jack went on. "I liked his easy style from the start. If I remember right, Joyce, we sat together at the back of the classroom in one of those double-desk things – two tip-up wooden seats, two box desks, all fastened together by a cast-iron framework. They were heavy … and painful."

"Painful?" Stick queried.

"Aye," his friend explained. "Bang your knee on that frame and you knew about it for ages. My mate, Gordon Gittins, once banged his knee and pretended to limp all day, until Mr Hardwick threatened to give him something to really limp for. We all collapsed laughing."

"I remember that!" Joyce added with a snort. "We called him Limp-Along for quite a while. Do you remember Limp-Along Leslie in *The Wizard* comic?"

"My favourite comic and my favourite character. Late 1950s, I think," Jack gushed. "Wasn't he supposed to play for Darbury Rangers and have one leg a little shorter than the other so he couldn't run very fast?"

"But he was supposed to be a brilliantly skilful inside forward," Joyce went on.

"Wow!" her husband gasped. "How do you know all this? Football?"

"Like Jack, I loved the character," she replied. "It was mi brother's comic, but I always sneaked it away from his grasp when he had finished with it. Didn't he run a sheep farm for his widowed aunt, as well?"

"Indeed he did," Jack agreed. "He was a near-champion sheepdog handler as well. Low Dyke Farm, wasn't it?"

"In Peakshire, or now we know it as the Peak District," Joyce added. "Wasn't he supposed to be one of the first to be able to 'bend' the ball in flight?"

"'Ark at you!" Stick gasped again. "Lesley Welch, the Memory Woman!"

"Limp-Along Gordon, as opposed to Hopalong when he cracked his foot in the playground sometime later!" Jack guffawed. "The onny teachers I had time for when I got to fourteen and fifteen at the grammar school were the sports teachers, Alan Jubb and Chris Whale. The one I disliked most was a French and German teacher called Machin, which funnily enough is French for 'thingy what not'. We called him Maxie – but not to his face. He was rather harsh and something of a bully. I remember one time when we were fifteen, he brought us out of our class into his while he was teaching. He made us kneel on the wooden floor for a full hour's lesson, all for some minor misdemeanour or other. Not a pleasant man."

Unfortunately, sunny and warm October half-term breaks didn't last long; colder weather was snapping at the heels of such balmy and relaxing times. The run up to Christmas was enjoyable in a way, but not *so* wonderful when you had miles to travel through driving rain, the occasional deluge of snow, freezing fog and darker days.

For Jack, who was getting up in the dark and coming home in the dark, the days couldn't pass quickly enough. Never one for cold winters, wasn't Jack. Even as a nipper they weren't his favourite, especially when his one attempt at gliding majestically down a frozen slide on the long, sloping road outside his house on Garth Avenue at seven years of age had ended in abject disaster.

It had been sub-zero for several days, turning the inordinately wet surface into an ice rink. It hadn't mattered for the cars on the estate of 150 houses because the only car owner was Mr Garrett, three houses down from where Jack lived.

The lads on the estate had been working on the slide on the road for a day or two, turning a mildly slippery patch into a sheet of glassy ice around fifty yards long. This particular day was the ultimate test as six lads from age seven to twelve were to shoot down the ice, one after the other in quick succession.

Jack was fearful of the length and the incline, so he watched the others a time or two. Bolstered by their success and whoops of joy, he allowed himself to be persuaded that perhaps the joy outweighed the microscopic risk of injury.

Unfortunately, halfway along this exhilarating ride, little Joey Pilling skidded sideways and collapsed in a heap, two sliders in front of Jack. Unable to exit the slide before he collided with the pile of bodies in front of him, Jack had ploughed into them and fallen awkwardly to his right. Rolling over several times, he had caught his elbow a jarring crack on the raised concrete edge of the pavement, causing an eye-watering stab of pain to shoot up to his shoulder.

His walk up to his house had been slow and lopsided as he had tried to protect his painful elbow from further injury. Realising there was something not right, his mother could see through his tearless eyes that his arm was causing him severe pain. Mr Garrett, the owner of that only car on the estate, was also the only person to have a private phone – the nearest public one being the best part of a mile down the road, close to Dalefield Road opposite Howard Beckett's house. Mr Garrett had telephoned for an ambulance to take poor little Jack to Clayton Hospital in Wakefield, which was five miles or so away, to have his arm seen to.

Result? A pot to set his arm in a bent position. Why was that significant? Jack had broken the same elbow only eighteen months earlier when rushing across a pitted and seriously uneven field behind his grandma's house. Same journey … different ambulance.

This particular break was significantly more serious than the previous one. As Jack had chipped the tail end of the growing bone at his elbow's point, it could have had serious repercussions for future growth. Consequently, his bed had to be moved downstairs to the living room and his arm had to be monitored – by both his mother and father – for forty-eight hours to check for any discolouration.

-o-

The race to the festive season in schools was almost always a gay and exciting affair. Teenagers usually seemed to keep a check on their emotions, allowing only their dour side to be seen. However, it was impossible for experienced and seasoned teachers not to detect that almost hidden and clandestine frisson of excitement as the event neared.

As a child growing into adolescence, Jack had never wanted – nor would he have ever agreed – to take part in any celebration that would thrust him into the limelight of a public spectacle. He had always been prepared to watch, if folks insisted, but it was never his first choice.

One event had always stuck in his mind from when he was eighteen and a school prefect. He had always been able to relate to children younger than himself, who had problems adhering to behavioural norms. They always reciprocated his respect for them, so never caused him discomfort or displeasure.

Christmas 1963, just before his eighteenth birthday, during the week before breaking up for winter's fortnight celebration, the grammar school had decided to put on a show to celebrate the youngsters' talents and skills in certain areas – music, poetry, acting. Jack had been so mortified when he had seen the run through of the rude and unfunny play his fellow sixth formers were about to enact that he had refused pointedly not only to take part but even to be present on the night.

Morality thy name is, and always has been, Jack.

"Penny?" a recognisable voice sprung him out of his reverie as he trudged across to the school's main building. Being at the extreme western edge of the north of the country, Fleetwood was about as far away from *his* light of dawn as it was possible to get.

He turned round sharply. "Hannah!" he said cheerfully, glad to see the smiling face he had missed over the October break. "Good to see you. Would you stop calling me Penny?"

"You too," she said with a laugh, understanding his sense of humour, taking his arm into the warmth.

"Mum OK?" he asked as he took out his pen to sign in.

"So, so," she replied, her face betraying her disappointed

feelings. "Not a good holiday, I'm afraid. A few issues."

"Discuss 'em later?" he asked "Got to go up for the staff briefing. See you in a bit?"

"OK," she answered, loath to leave. She had grown to look forward to her interactions with this new supportive force in her life that had given her hope for *her* future. She was no academic, but she was a decent artist who Jack had so far encouraged to develop. The result? A greater liking for schooling where she would be able to develop and showcase her artistic skills, with who knows what in her armoury when she came to leave.

Chapter 11

"Good morning," a deeply gravelly voice accosted Jack from behind in the foyer to the staff room. "You're Jack Ingles, I believe."

Jack swung around quickly to see a tall, black-haired chap of about his own age who bore huge mutton-chop sideboards on his jaw line.

"Good morning," Jack replied with a grin. "I believe I am. I've seen you before – from a distance – and I have been told that you are Phil Woolcott, the Withdrawal Unit chap. Pleased to meet you."

"I am intrigued to meet *you* and look forward to having a lengthy chat," the newcomer said. "Can I take it that you are the specialist for youngsters with social and adjustment issues?"

"Indeed, you may," Jack replied. "I am attached to the local branch of the—"

"Pupil Referral Service which is going to—" Phil added.

"Cease to exist in the near future?" Jack butted in.

"How—?" Phil asked.

"Did I know what you were about to ask?" Jack added. "One of my major skills is that I can read minds. That is why I am so successful with youngsters."

Phil was silent for a short while, which didn't happen very often, bringing a smile to the lips of his lady assistant close by. "I like you," he went on suddenly, offering a welcoming hand. "How long have you been here? September, wasn't it?"

"It was," Jack agreed, warmly shaking his offered hand. "Unfortunately, I was assigned here by the powers that decide upon my direction to sort out a multitude of – how should I call them? – problems. Before we can move on or move out."

"You have to come soon to see us in our cocoon," Phil replied.

"And the beautiful young lady by your elbow?" Jack asked.

"My name is Zayley, Zayley Thomas," she replied, not waiting to be introduced. "And I don't just make the tea for my partner in crime here."

"I wouldn't have had the temerity to suggest such a thing," Jack protested. "Probably the other way round, perhaps?"

"Cup of tea today in our unit?" she offered.

"Indeed, yes," Jack said, accepting her offer graciously. "But where do I find it, and what magic words do I need to use to gain entry?"

"Out of this main building, turn right, and twenty-five paces will bring you to our lair," Zayley suggested. "Knock three times, whistle twice, and the door will open automatically. Bring your young friend along."

"My young—?" Jack queried. "Ah! Hannah! I will, if she wants to come. Thank you."

"All right, ladies and gentlemen," a deep male voice quietened the room. "Business of the day, please."

-o-

"Hannah had to go home, I'm afraid," Jack said, as he entered the holy of holies. "Not feeling very well. Probably something she ate."

"How do you mean?" Zayley asked.

"She doesn't eat the sort of stuff we eat," Jack replied. "So if she ingests anything 'normal' she can become unwell. I think she must have had a sausage roll or something at lunchtime. It takes only a short time for her to develop a reaction."

"Why were *you* brought here? I know there had been complaints of your predecessor's – 'inactivity', shall we call it?" Phil said, once cups of coffee and tea had been dispatched.

"Phil!" Zayley warned.

"It's all right," Jack reassured them both. "Lee McKee, my boss in Lancaster, caused a good deal of controversial comment locally when she said she was sending her best to sort out the inefficiencies here. You see, I had been there only a couple of years, which was a much shorter time than all the others. I've had an enormous amount of successful experience working with youngsters in residential schools, so it was a no-brainer that she would choose me to sort stuff out. I'm a no-nonsense Yorkshireman – say it as I see it –who tends to ruffle a few feathers while getting a job done. There seems to be much more than my twelve months of work to be done and, as my expenses do not attract a tax charge, I could well be recalled at the end of my stay."

"Lack of foresight on the authority's part as usual," Zayley observed.

"Is your husband a teacher, Zayley?" Jack asked.

"He is, but why do you ask?" she said.

"I was on a headship interview in Blackburn last year with a chap called Thomas – Ian Thomas," Jack explained. "I've noticed recently that this Ian Thomas has become headteacher at a local day school for pupils with emotional and behavioural difficulties."

"That's my husband," she replied quietly. "You must

be the Jack Ingles he mentioned. He was impressed by some of the stuff you were talking about at the time. Small world, eh?"

"Smaller than we realise sometimes," he agreed.

"Unfortunately, there are problems in his school that transcend children's behaviour and handling," she replied. "He had a significant difference of opinion with an inspector over how his school should be organised and developed. An inspector, I hasten to add, who had never run or even been *in* a day EBD school, let alone knew what he was talking about."

"Snap!" Jack said with a knowing sneer. "I was head of French and English at a residential school for lads with behaviour issues in 1993–4. Bear in mind that Ofsted had only just started inspecting that sort of special school. Believe it or not, they sent in three inspectors for three days who knew nothing about the whys and wherefores of this sort of educational establishment.

"The six lads in my group were in class sitting behind desks, working and doing stuff they had never done before – including sitting down in a classroom. The lead inspector – a young jump-up with little experience of life, let alone this sort of education – made one or two derisory remarks about what they would have, and should have, been doing had they been in mainstream. During our stand-up argument, he didn't appreciate my opinions and strongly expressed views on his ineptitude as an educator and inspector. He was trying to judge me and them by mainstream standards. I ordered him out of my classroom, after which I penned a serious complaint to the powers-that-be about his lack of professional expertise and seriously flawed educational judgement. The other two inspectors didn't come near."

"Bravo!" Zayley said. "At last, somebody prepared to stand up for his principles."

"Must be off," Jack said, realising he needed to be in class in five minutes. "Enjoyed the company, and thanks for the refreshment. Remember me to your husband, Zayley?"

-o-

Jack's drive home was unexpectedly wet. The skies had opened the minute he set foot out of the main door at the end of the day, obliging him to scurry to his Rover. This sort of weather did two things: it made him take much greater care, adding a further quarter of an hour to his journey time, and it made him appreciate the benefits of working closer to home.

Thoughts of past actions and mistakes flooded his already overactive mind. Could he have been more appreciative of the life he had with Jenny, knowing full well that he had done all that was humanly possible in his first marriage? Where was his son, Sam, now? Had Sam managed to escape from the cloying influence of his mother? Would Jack ever see him again? Would he ever *want* to see him again, to be reminded of the pain he'd had to endure?

Crossing the Glasson branch of the Lancaster Canal, the River Conder almost immediately upstream from its outflow into the Lune estuary reminded him sharply that home was only a hop and a skip away. For Jack, driving was automatic for the most part, part of conscious and subconscious life a bit like hearing, breathing and sight: inbuilt, safe and reliable.

The Pointer Roundabout in Lancaster, just above the infirmary, hove into view, reminding him as it always did at teatime that Hodgson's Chippy on Prospect Street was only a heartbeat away – a matter of five minutes around Dale Road and the street itself. How invitingly belly-filling would that be! Just a wee detour and— Perhaps

115

another time…

"I've given my notice in, Jack," Jenny informed him, as he managed to squeeze through the front door out of the unrelenting downpour.

"I love you too, Jenny," he said, his semi-sarcastic remark surprising her. "Let me get in and tek mi wet stuff off, have a cup of tea, and then tha can tell me thi business, eh?

"Nar then," he went on once washed and changed, a steaming mug of Yorkshire Tea nestled in his hands and buttered scone crumbs glued around his mouth. "What's this about notice?"

"I've – *we've* all resigned from our posts at school with effect from next week," Jenny said with a satisfied smile. "Not going to be messed about anymore."

"Oh aye?" he replied, somewhat taken aback. "Don't want to work anymore? What about the compensation yon union chap was talking about?"

"A cheque arrived in the post this morning," she explained, skipping around the room, wafting a piece of paper under his nose. "Fifteen hundred pounds!"

"Wow!" Jack grinned. "What do you intend doing with that?"

"Put it towards the Benidorm holiday," she replied.

"Oh no, you're not!" he insisted. "That's paid for. You must spend it on yourself, otherwise I'll send it back."

"Yeah! Right!" she scoffed. "I'll spend it how I like, then – probably on some more clothes. Don't forget that I've got nothing to wear."

"If you had," Jack replied, a huge grin growing, "I'd have a smile on my face all day long!"

"Don't concern yourself," she added. "About the job, I mean."

"Why should I be concerned, my lovely?" he asked, not understanding the reasoning behind her statement.

"Don't forget that that was one of the things my ex-wife couldn't stand about me – the inability to worry. So—"

"I have an interview tomorrow," Jenny told him, unable to contain her joy.

"Interview?" he gasped "To do what? Where? On a Saturday?"

"That's how they do it in these places, apparently. It's for a classroom assistant at the college," she replied. "It's only for ten hours per week in the first instance, but it's a start."

"But that's onny ower t'road … from t'end on our street!" Jack said, unable to comprehend how that could have fallen into her lap. "How jammy is that! What about the other girls? Are they in the same boat?"

"Anne's applying to do a teaching qualification, Mary's going somewhere else, and Kath I don't know about," Jenny explained. "We are all leaving at the same time to make a point. No doubt they will minimise our leaving, and make it seem as if we were never there."

"Come over here, please," Jack asked. "Something I want to show you."

"I've heard *that* one before!" she guffawed heartily.

"Some people do have mucky minds," he tutted as she sat next to him. Taking out a colourful piece of printed paper, he went on, "This is my payslip for October showing my travelling expenses for September. The figure you're looking at is under the 'Expenses' section."

She took the paper from him, and once she had found the section, a great gasp exploded from her lungs. "You're having me on!" she exclaimed. "£549.10? How come?"

"The expenses are paid a month in arrears," he began. "October's payslip pays for July and September travelling. November gives October's, and so on. What you have to remember is that these expenses are … tax free."

"Wow!" she gasped. "Nice little earner that we could

do with."

"This academic year will give us an extra £3,500 pounds," he announced grandly. "Less £440 or so for petrol. We gain just over £3,000. Not forgetting that, on the downside, every day gives me an extra two hours or more in travelling time as well."

-o-

Jack had accepted the reality of not being able to find as much time with his family as he would have liked. Ideally, a family gathering would have been a weekly affair barring unplanned and unavoidable issues that popped up through circumstance. Planning now had to be detailed and done significantly in advance because his loved ones had been dispersed to the four winds.

He accepted that Florence May and her Billy wouldn't be over from Australia for Christmas instead of sunbathing on a beach close to where they lived. Jessie was much nearer in distance, but she had Millie Alice and her new beau in tow in their new home in Leeds – which had once belonged to Jenny and Jack. Probably wouldn't be seeing *them*.

George William and Sandy were pregnant at last. Been trying for a while – *very* trying. They would likely be staying at home in Normanton to spend time with *her* parents.

Not heard from Joey and Izzy and their nippers. Ed was a different entity altogether. Jack was convinced often that he was from another planet. Would Jack see his favourite niece, Mary, in – or from – her magnificent pad in Harrogate over Christmas? Doubtful.

Jim, he knew, was away staying with his younger sister in Malton. She had recently lost her husband to prostate cancer and needed her children and her brother with her to lessen the loneliness that had been forced upon her.

Jack, therefore, was looking forward to a quiet Christmas with his lovely wife.

"Well?" he asked, as Jenny bounced through the door, closing it behind her with a sigh.

"Cup of tea, don't you think?" she said as she plonked her backside down on their comfy settee.

"Kettle's on," he replied. "And?"

"Well," she said slowly, with a smile, unable to keep her good news to herself any longer. "I got it!"

He plucked her from the settee to give her a congratulatory hug. He was pleased that things had finally turned the corner for her, taking her out of an organisation run by ne'er-do-wells and thoughtless individuals that didn't seem to know how to run a school.

"It's only ten hours a week, unfortunately, but it's a new place with scope," she added, jigging around her husband.

"No matter," he said. "At least you're going somewhere where you will be valued. I'll mash the tea and then you can tell me all about it and what you might be doing. When will you be starting?" he continued, to the rattle of teacups and plates and cake tins.

"Beginning of next term," she replied, joining him in their kitchen diner. "Nine o'clock sharp on the first Monday back, and that's only three weeks away."

"You could almost get up at half eight, breakfast, watch the news and get there with five minutes to spare," he jested, noticing Jenny's irrepressibly infectious grin. "Probably two hours a day, maybe? I suppose it could even be two full days? Umpteen possibilities to fill ten hours."

"Hey! Don't knock it," she said. "It may not be much, but every little helps."

"Too right it does," Jack replied to the click of the letterbox. "It's quite a large envelope addressed to us both," he said as he waltzed back into the lounge. "Here, you open it while I top up mi tea and examine those buns in yon tin."

"It's from Our Val," Jenny said slowly, a soundless whistle escaping her lips. "Look what she's sent."

"My God!" he gasped. "It's … it's a Britannia Airways aeroplane ticket to … Alicante in Southern Spain, along with an invitation to join them for two weeks over Christmas. How fantastic is that! You up for it, Our Jen?"

"Too right I am!" she replied, excited at the thought of two weeks in the warmth of the Mediterranean sun, relaxing away from all the stress of work and making ends meet. "When do we fly?"

"We finish school next Friday," he explained. "The flight out is very early on Saturday the nineteenth of December; come back on Saturday the second of January. Back in school for Monday – my birthday anniversary."

"What do you mean by 'early'?" she said with a minor frown.

"Try seven in the morning for size," he explained. "Means we would have to set off from here by three to get to Manchester Airport by half four."

"But the flight isn't until seven!" Jenny protested.

"Normally, you have to be there two hours before take-off to check in and be registered," Jack explained patiently. "So, three o'clock will be just right."

"And it's here we're off to sunny Spain!" Jenny burst into song.

"'Viva l'Espagna!'" Jack joined in.

Chapter 12

"This is exciting," Jenny eulogised on the hour or so's journey from Alicante's airport in Val's SEAT Aresa car. "Never done this sort of thing before – and look at the weather!"

"Eighteen degrees, and only just above freezing in Morecambe," Jack added. "Brilliant clear blue sky here but sharp frost in the UK when we left. I wonder why you decided to come to live here, Mike?"

"We can't thank you enough, Mike," Jenny said. "We couldn't have hoped to have done this if you hadn't invited us."

"You've both done so much for the family with Mary and Joey that it seemed the right thing to do," Mike replied. "Besides, we're now fully retired, and it will be good to see more of you both."

"Where are we going?" Jack asked. "We have no idea. I know this is the Costa Blanca, but that's quite a lengthy coast, I believe. Are we anywhere near Benidorm?"

"Why Benidorm?" Mike asked, a little surprised at the question.

"Because that's where we are going February half term after Christmas," Jenny explained, "to celebrate my birthday."

"It's roughly halfway between Alicante and Denia," Mike replied. "Not too far from where we are now, probably about ten miles or so."

The countryside was not at all what they had expected for a place that was generally much hotter than Morecambe by the sea. They had thought it would be dry and brown and scorched by the incessant sun, whereas there were places where it was remarkably green.

"Wow!" both Jenny and Jack gasped as Mike pulled into the wide driveway of a beautiful, traditionally white-painted villa overlooking the Mediterranean.

"A pool!" Jack chortled, rubbing his hands together. "Life don't get much better than this. And it's big enough to swim in!"

Val was already waiting for them at the door. The greeting from sister to sister was warm and tearful, bearing in mind the private time they had not spent together since their mother's passing.

"Jack," she said quietly as she embraced him. "Rock of *our* family. It's so good to see you."

"Now that's what I call a *real* hug," he replied. "We've missed you both since you decamped to come live wi' foreigners. No chance of you coming back then after all … this?" He swept his arms around the fabulous surroundings and the gobsmacking vista out to sea.

"No fear!" Val chortled. "Would you?"

"Too right I wouldn't," he assured her as they moved inside. "Mary?" His eyes narrowed and his brow drew down as he saw his niece sitting on the settee with six-year-old little Alice. "This is a joy!" he uttered in absolute shock. "Alice? How big she has grown!"

"Yes, Unca Jack," the little girl said, as he approached her carefully, mindful that the last time he had seen her she wasn't keen on being held. "You are right. *My* name *is* Alice." She stood up, put her arms out towards him and said, surprising everyone, "May I have a hug, please? I am very glad to see you."

He lifted her and sat her across his arm with her hands tightly clasped about his neck. She kissed his face twice then lifted her hands skyward, letting him know it was time to put her down. She crossed the room to regain her seat next to her mum on the settee.

"Well, that's a first," Mary said with a slight gasp but no real surprise in her voice. "You all right, Uncle Jack?" she said as Val brought through tea and a tray of goodies.

"I am now, Our Mary," he replied. "No Jake?"

She hesitated before saying, "Talk about that later when milady is in her bed?"

He nodded, wondering if the same thing had come to pass as with Jessie and *her* ex-husband, Brian. He hoped not, but young men these days didn't seem to know how to handle young lasses that knew their own mind and were well able to earn their own money that was quite often more than their men did. Ah, me!

"You staying here long?" Jack asked his niece.

"As long as Mam and Mike will have us, really," she replied with a hefty sigh. "I need time and space to breathe and think, away from … stuff … at home."

"And your business?" Jack asked tentatively.

"Is ticking over gently," Mary explained. "I have around six weeks' worth of orders in the pipeline that will be fulfilled automatically by staff. Once they get to the end of those, I will have decided my – our – future."

"Future?" he asked, not sure what she had in mind.

"Whether we stay over there or open up over here," Mary replied. "There's nothing I do over there that I can't do over here."

By this time Jenny and Val had taken Alice for a bath and to be made ready for bed.

"Things not working out—?" Jack asked, after kissing Alice goodnight.

"With Jake?" Mary ventured. "Not really. It's been

touch and go for some time now. We just don't seem to get on, and he was finding it difficult even to get along with his own daughter. I knew Alice would take to you, Uncle Jack, given time. Bit like I did, really, only earlier. How could anyone *not* take to you?"

"Try my ex-wife and my son," he replied after a brief moment's hesitation.

"Their loss," Mary assured him. "She must be either blind or barmy."

"Anyway, this holiday was made even better once I saw you here," Jack smiled. "I always wished you had been my daughter instead of my worthless brother's."

She leaned across and kissed his cheek, happy that he was there.

"Jessie was sailing a very similar unstable rocky tack to yours until …" Jack began, giving her the full story and its amazing ending. "We were a bit worried about her until she came to stay one weekend and brought her new … husband, who turns out to be a lovely chap. Not quite as good looking as me, of course—"

Mary laughed at his funny self-deprecation, knowing that he was certainly no narcissist, just a lovely man who had given her more than anyone else had or would ever know about. "There's hope and opportunity for me then … if I want to take it," she replied with a resigned smile.

"You'll get there, Mary. You're a lovely young woman who has a strong sense of who you are, and there is no reason on earth why you should be subservient to anyone else," Jack said earnestly. "Your forever young man is out there. We just need to find him … if you wish it. I think the next time you probably need to allow *me* to vet him."

"You may well be right, Uncle Jack," Mary agreed with a chuckle. "You may well be right."

-o-

"We don't celebrate Christmas and birthdays usually," Mike said, as they sat down for their late afternoon meal on Christmas Eve. "But we will be giving presents to Alice because she likes the pomp – and opening parcels."

"But how will you get around it not being 'real'?" Jack asked. "She is a *child*, and children of her age can be quite cute when it comes to the truth – if you'll pardon the unintentional pun."

"She'll be OK," Mary added. "It's never been much of a celebration in our house anyway. Jake was never *that* bothered about its meaning and what it offered in real terms, other than more expense. I was never bothered too much about what it cost because, as my business grew, we could afford whatever Alice wanted. It's strange because she never seemed to want much, apart from the usual toys, dolls and stuff you see here."

"How would she feel about not having stuff to open?" Jenny asked.

"She's been used to having odd things bought for her to open, so now it's no big deal," Mary replied. "She'll be fine."

"Have you ever thought about joining the Truth, Mary?" Val asked, not sure what sort of an answer she might get.

"Have *you*, Mum?" Mary replied smartly.

"Actually, I have thought about it, with no pressure from Mike," Val said after a moment's thought. "I love the idea of being among people who tell the truth and who care about other people, but I'm not entirely sure yet."

"How about you, Aunt Jenny?" Mary asked, throwing a king-sized cat among the pigeons. "Is it something you might consider?"

"I've met and talked to folks local to where we live, and I like their views and their friendship," Jenny said hesitantly. "And I'm almost there."

"Really?" Jack queried, a little surprised. "News to me. You can suit yourself *what* you do, I've always said so. After all, I'm not your keeper and will never try to dictate what you do or how you worship. What path you tread is entirely up to you, but … it would have been nice if you had shared your thoughts and feelings with me."

"I didn't quite know what your reaction might be," she answered rather lamely.

"You didn't know what your Jack's reaction might be?" Val said incredulously. "How long have you known him, for goodness' sake? He is the most uncontrolling man I have ever met, Sister, and you know as well as I do that all he would offer would be support and encouragement."

"I know," Jenny sighed quietly.

"Anybody fancy a stroll in the sun after such a lovely meal?" Jack said eagerly, trying to change the subject and the mood.

"A *sit* outside on the patio in the sun might be better," Mike offered. "I have no real desire to try to walk off that beautiful meal."

"I'd like mine to remain in my taste buds and my belly for a little while longer, too, if truth be known," Jack added with a laugh. "Besides, I don't think I could walk any more than half a dozen fairy steps just now. You coming outside, too, Alice?" he asked her.

"No thank you, Unca Jack," she replied firmly. "I need time to play with my things before bed. But thank you for offering."

It was hard for him to suppress a smile at her pert answer, which brought back memories of how her mother had reacted in similar circumstances. How Mary had evolved over the years he had known her, from the gauche and prickly early teenager to the ingenious young lady who needed help to embark on the entrepreneurial path to business success.

Why was it that personal attachments and relationships sometimes seemed to suffer at the hands of success? There weren't that many people like Jack who could see a need in a youngster and want to help feed and nurture it.

Way to go, Jack!

"This is a long way from my early days as a nipper, living at 206 Wakefield Road in Normanton," Jack said, looking around at this fabulous villa and its spectacular setting. "Two-up, two-down, with a scullery."

"This fascinates me," Mike added. "We lived in a three-bedroomed semi in Northallerton, a universe away from the coalfields of Yorkshire's West Riding. Tell me, did those sorts of houses *not* have a bathroom?"

"Jenny knows all that I am going to say because she's heard it all before," Jack answered. "So—"

"Not all of it, Jack," Jenny replied. "I know about the water supply and about the ablutions, but little else."

"No bathroom, no toilet, no running hot water," Jack began. "The front door opened onto the pavement beside a very busy road where a bus stop waved in at our front window. There were twenty-five terrace houses, all identical in spec, and only one passage through from front to back set in the middle of the row. They had been built in the late 1930s to accommodate colliery workers employed by one of the twelve pits surrounding the town and its outlying area.

"Next to the front door, a heavy cast-iron grid set in the pavement covered a chute down into the cellar where coal was tipped and stored. Because my father was a collier, he was allowed four free loads of coal a year – although he sold two of 'em illegally to pay for his beer.

"The front room was always shrouded in sheets and other covers and never used. It led into a large kitchen-diner with a coal-fired range and oven. There was another door that shared the wall where the front-room door was sited. This door was almost always locked and led down to the cellar where there lived a … bogeyman among the coals. I had been warned by my father. I never dared to explore, but every morning before I sat down for breakfast, I crept to that door gingerly and listened to see if I could hear … anything. There was often a cold draught blowing under the door, and sometimes I could hear a whoo-ing sound which I thought was—"

"The bogeyman?" Mary suggested in an awed whisper.

Jack's eyes opened wide in answer and Alice, who had just joined them with her doll, gripped her mother's hand tightly. The noise he had made sounded eerie and real, and the adults realised how spooky it must sound to a five-year-old.

"Of course, the sound and the draught came from the open-work grid above the cellar in the pavement outside," Jack started to explain in a hoarse whisper, looking over both shoulders slowly to see that no-one else was listening in. "Or did it?

"The tin bath hung on a six-inch nail on the wall, next to the black-leaded range, ready to set on the floor in front of the roaring fire," he went on.

"But I thought there was no running hot water," Val puzzled. "If that was so, how—?"

"Mi mam had two galvanised metal buckets which she filled with cold water from the scullery and placed in the oven to heat up for the bath," Jack explained. "Obviously not plastic for two reasons – plastic hadn't been invented and, if it had been, the bucket would have—"

"Melted!" Jenny and Mary chorused.

"And did your mother have to do that for each person's bath during the week?" Mike asked. "Wouldn't that have been a ridiculously heavy chore for her?"

"Not really, because she only filled it once every week," Jack pointed out.

"Once a week?" Val asked. "How come?"

"In the early days, all the family bathed on the same day with the father taking first dip, followed by the children in order of age," he replied with a grin. "The youngest was the last to bathe – in all the muck that was left by the ones who had gone before. Catch my meaning? Sometimes the baby was almost thrown out with the bath water."

"Yeww!" Mary gasped, screwing up her mouth and eyes, not really wanting to think about what might have been in the water.

"Fortunately for us, mi father was able to have a wash under the newly installed showers at the pit-head baths before he came home," Jack explained. "So we didn't have to bathe in all *his* muck. But even so, the concept was the same. The showers weren't all that good, so he had the first bath having washed the majority of the pit grime from his body before he dipped his toes in *our* bath water."

"I couldn't have done that!" Mary said, an involuntary shudder of disgust wracking her body.

"*Your* dad had to go through that in his younger days, don't forget," Jack added with a snort. "And don't forget that we didn't have a toilet in the house."

"You didn't do it in the … sink?" Mary asked, not really wanting to hear her uncle's potentially gross response. She knew him of old!

"We had outside toilets in rows of three, each with its own door," he went on, "probably twenty yards from our back door. Each toilet door had a hefty slice of wood taken from its bottom edge and, like as not, there might be two holes drilled in the door about eye level. Any ideas why, Mary?"

"I'm not sure I want to know," she replied in apprehensive disgust.

"For the person that wanted to use the toilet to check whether it was occupied or not," he sniggered.

"Not for them to … look in, surely?" she answered.

"Spot on," he said with a huge guffaw. "And as a last roll … toilet paper?"

"I wouldn't dream of asking," Mary said, brow wrinkled and her mouth drawn into a small circle.

"The wonderfully soft toilet tissues we have today hadn't been developed," Jack went on unabashed. "We had to make do with squares of newspaper fastened to a metal wire."

"You can't mean you bought a newspaper just to wipe your—!" she gipped.

"Mi dad actually read the newspaper first," Jack interrupted, to laughter from all those listening to this gruesome but engrossing story of his way into this modern world.

They should have known he wouldn't have spared them any of the grisly, gory details.

Chapter 13

"Will it be warm enough to paddle in the sea?" Jack asked, an excited jiggle in his step as they walked towards the beach. "It's been a while since I had a paddle, and then it was at Filey."

"It might be a bit chilly, but nothing like in the UK," Mike replied with a shrug. "Is this the first time you've been to Spain?"

"At this time of year, yes, but we've been before for a few days – funnily enough to Benidorm," Jenny said. "We didn't actually paddle because we only had a few days to fit in a lot of sunbathing. This stay is wonderfully relaxing, and I don't really want to go home even though we'll be back hereabouts in just over a month."

Jack sat down on the edge of the promenade and started to remove his sandals.

"What are you doing, Jack?" Jenny asked. "Going for a run into the sea?"

"I just like to feel the soft sand between mi toes, and then to swish them in the sea for a bit," he replied. "Going to join me?"

"No, thank you very much," Jenny said with a very emphatic shake of the head.

Jack turned towards Mary's daughter. Stretching out his hand towards her, he asked, "Would *you* like a paddle in the sea, Alice?"

"Mammy?" she asked as she jerked Mary's hand and stared up at her face intently, a hopeful look in her eyes.

"Go on then!" Mary said, seeing the expectant look on both faces. "Take your Unca Jack for a little paddle and then we'll go to the café for a drink and a bun. OK, Uncle Jack?"

"Will you make sure I get there safely, Alice?" Jack asked as he felt her hand grasp his.

"Course I will," she replied looking steadfastly up at him. "Don't worry, cos I will guide you. I've been here before, you see, and the sea is quite gentle today."

Jack smiled as they set off, Alice slightly in front, guiding her charge along the ribbed sands. It took him back to when *his* daughters were this age, taking their 'responsibilities' with their father as seriously as Alice was doing now with her Unca Jack.

"He is a natural with youngsters is your Jack," Val observed, as uncle and great-niece approached the quietly lapping waters. "Unfortunately, his brother never had the skill to handle his own children, let alone anyone else's. The difference is that Jack truly loves being with youngsters, that he always calls 'nippers'. I always trusted his judgement implicitly with my three – well, the two that understood the value of *his* opinions and actions."

"Mary and Joey?" Mike queried gently.

"Our Ed never got it," Mary added. "Never understood the value of Uncle Jack's input into any situation. The thing was that Uncle Jack never interfered, only offered solutions to problems when we were unable to see them for ourselves. Once we had involved him, he would go that extra ten miles and beyond to make sure no problem, however small, was left unsolved. Jessie and Florence May don't know how lucky they are, Aunt Jenny."

"Oh, I think they do, Our Mary," Jenny replied. "They have had their share of difficulties that they couldn't see their way out of. Who always came to the rescue and made everything right? Our knight in shining armour. Do you remember the time, Val, when, unbeknown to them, Jessie and her friend and cousin Jessie had been going out with the same lad – a twenty-three-year-old teacher of about the same age? He'd been stringing them both along until Jessie found out. She had punched him in the face and broke his nose, and he had threatened to sue her until Jack had sorted him out big style. Never one for tilting at windmills, Our Jack; always in at the sharp end, trouble-shooting."

"Don't tell me Jack went to … see him!" Val said, not quite sure what Jenny's answer might be.

"A good friend of Jack's was the lad's headteacher and employer," Jenny explained. "*He* warned him off, and eventually the lad became 'unemployable'. Needless to say, his threat to sue Jessie for assault evaporated like mist under a morning sun."

"Well?" Val said to her little granddaughter as she came back still clasping Jack's hand. "Did you have a lovely paddle?"

"Yes, Nanna Val, we did," Alice said quite firmly. "I guided and helped Unca Jack so as he didn't trip over the wavy water."

"We had a wonderful time, didn't we, my lovely?" Jack said as he lifted her into his arms.

She flung her arms about his neck, kissed him on the cheek and said, "Yes, Unca Jack, and now I really must go to the toilet. Please?"

He put her down gently and watched as she toddled off inside the villa, to the suppressed hilarity from the onlooking adults.

"You have another fan there, Old Chap," Mike observed. "She doesn't give her affections easily."

"How is she coping with the strain at home, Mary?"

Jenny asked. "I don't see any problems in Alice's behaviour."

"She doesn't get a lot of attention and affection from her father," Mary answered. "He's never been a demonstrative father, so she deals with people in an easy and usual – for her – sort of a way. She certainly isn't missing out now she's got a doting great uncle to relate to."

"Alice is an absolute delight," Jack interjected. "Very different from Jessie's Millie Alice. Lovely but … different."

"I know we've just done our normal thing over Christmas Day, but do the Spanish do the same as us in the UK?" Jenny asked.

"They celebrate at certain times within the period, but what they do is entirely different from us," Val said. "No Santa Claus, for a start."

"At all?" Jack asked. "I know they celebrate the Three Wise Men or Kings in France, and in Italy with the witch La Bafana arriving on her broomstick. Germans celebrate as we do on the twenty-fourth and twenty-fifth with Christmas trees, but Spain…?"

"Correct, Jack," Val agreed. "Presents from the Reyes Magos, the Magi. You are probably aware that the Spanish love fêtes and festivals throughout the year, and this time is no exception. Folks flock into the streets on January sixth, or Epiphany, when the Three Kings pass by on *cabalgatas* or floats and throw sweets to the crowds. It lasts most of the day. Christmas Eve and Epiphany see the same feast being enjoyed, with Iberian ham and seafood. The only difference is that at Epiphany they eat a piece of *turron* or King's Crown, which is a crown-like circle made from sweet brioche with pastry and cream topped with candied fruit."

"I like the sound of that!" Jack said, rubbing the palms of his hands together. "It can't compete with the spice cake we eat at home, though."

"Spice cake?" Mike asked. "Not heard of that one."

"It doesn't have spices galore in it, I can assure you, Mike," Jenny reassured him. "It's a normal fruit cake that the folks around Jack's area called 'spice' cake. Like you, I had never heard of it until I met him, even though I was born and lived my life there."

"Spice cake and cheese," Jack added. "It's much better to have home-made spice cake with Wensleydale or White Stilton. I'm sorry if I'm beginning to drool." He wiped away an imaginary dribble or two from his mouth corners.

By this time the sun had begun to dip towards the horizon and a fabulously colourful sunset greeted their eyes as they took in the unobstructed view across the bay. A huge sigh escaped Jenny's lips as she snuggled her head in her husband's shoulder, the sheer bliss of the place exacting a profound effect on her emotions. For some reason, her mam and Jack's mam had swum into her mind.

-o-

"You can't imagine how good this has been for us," Jenny said, as Mike dropped them off at Alicante Airport ready for their Britannia Airways flight back to the vagaries of English winter weather.

"We've loved having you, Sister, haven't we, Mike? And Mary and little Alice were over the moon that we had asked you to share our new life on the Costas, if only for a short while," Val replied as she hugged her sister and *her* man. "The door is always open to you two – any time."

"Any time you get fed up with this awful warmth and would like to experience what UK weather can be like, our door will always be shut fast to keep out the cold," Jack said, to a guffaw from Mike.

"Until the next time, we'll miss you both, and thank you again," Jenny added as they turned to seek the check-in desks.

"*Hasta luego!*" Jack shouted with a final wave as the automatic doors welcomed them into a very busy concourse.

A slow-moving tear began to find its way down Jenny's tanned face as she linked Jack's arm after check-in.

"I hope we'll meet again in the next couple of hours or so," he said with a smile.

"But we've only just left them!" Jenny puzzled. "Something you're not telling me?"

"I was talking about the suitcases, daft beggar," he chortled. "You never can tell with these places. *We* might end up in Manchester, and *they* might arrive in Minsk. You never know. Cup of tea time?"

"It won't be Yorkshire Tea, you realise," Jenny warned him. "You'll have to be prepared for 'foreign' tea."

"Tell you who we've not seen for a ridiculously long time – Irene and David," Jack threw out as they bought a cup of plastic tea and a crozzled bacon sandwich.

"What brought *them* to mind?" Jenny asked, surprised at the workings of his unpredictable mind.

"Been thinking about them a lot lately," he replied. "Don't know how or why we've grown apart. We don't even know how their two are getting on – Jessie and Imogen Rose. I think we should get back in touch. What do you think?"

-o-

Wrapped against the chill breeze, Jack and Jenny's daughter, Jessie, had decided that a short stroll in Roundhay Park with her husband, Johnny, was essential. They had been stuck inside for the best part of a week because of the typically inclement weather that Leeds was renowned for – a year's worth of everything in seven days, except for warm sun.

"Take it steady," Johnny said with a smile of concern,

his arm around Jessie's waist and the other one steadying her movements as they negotiated a patch of uneven ground. "We don't want to disturb Little Bump."

"I'm only a couple of weeks pregnant, Johnny," Jessie giggled. "I'll be all right for another six months at least, though I do love you for caring."

"I know, but I can't help it," he replied. "You two – and Millie Alice, of course – are all I've got in the world. I *have* to make sure you're all right."

"Can we stop a sec?" Jessie said quietly. "That woman over by the lake's edge, pushing the pram. See? I'm sure I know her. Quickly! Let's catch her up."

"Jessie?" Jessie called cautiously.

The young woman stopped, keeping a tight hold on her pram as she half turned.

"Jessie!" she replied with a whoop and a skip as she took hold of Jessie in a heart-felt hug, letting go of her pram as she did so. Johnny could see that they knew each other as he deftly caught hold of the baby carriage to make sure it didn't roll into the lake.

"Wow!" Johnny's Jessie gasped. "I thought you had emigrated or something."

"Bloomin' 'eck!" the other Jessie replied. "I can't imagine a better way to enjoy our walk out. Do you know, I had a feeling this morning when I woke up that something precious would happen today?"

"Where has all the time gone, and why haven't we seen each other the last year or two?" Jessie Grey-Ingles said softly.

"Wasn't it about the time we had the problems with Simon Ridley, and your dad sorted him out big style?" her cousin Jessie replied.

"I think you're right," Jessie agreed. "I'm sorry, Johnny, may I introduce you to my cousin and best friend from a thousand-million years ago – Jessie Aston."

"Pleased to meet you, Jessie Aston," Johnny said, shaking her hand. "I must say, you are wearing well for that number of years."

They all laughed as Cousin Jessie took hold of her baby carriage again. "It's Jessie Price-Aston now," she replied. "This little creature here is Poppy. She's six months old. Do you live around this neck of the woods?"

"Yes, we do," Jessie Grey said, as she explained where they were based.

"That's ridiculous!" the other Jessie gasped. "We live on the same estate, perhaps five minutes from your house. How bizarre is that?"

"No reason not to get together, then," Jessie Grey urged. "Your parents all right?"

"In the pink," she replied. "Still living in the same house in Beeston. Yours?"

"Very well, actually," Jessie said. "Now living in Morecambe."

"Morecambe?" Jessie gasped. "What's a Yorkshireman like your dad doing in foreign lands? Has he been captured and imprisoned in a little caravan there?"

"Your sense of humour!" Jack's Jessie laughed.

"Developed from the interactions between your dad and mine over many years," Jessie sighed. "They have a lot to answer for!"

"Got to go," Jessie Grey said. "Here's my phone number. Call me and we'll get together soon."

"Too right we will!" David Aston's Jessie agreed as she took her leave.

"Wow!" Johnny said as he heaved a giant gasp and took a deep breath. "Did you always converse at such speed? My head's spinning."

"Course we did," Jessie replied with a laugh. "So much to say and never enough time to say it in. Daddy Jack is Jessie's mam's cousin," she explained. "They go back a lot of years, although they only discovered each other when he was eighteen and she was twenty-one. Dad introduced her to her now husband, David Aston, when they taught at the same school. Events seem to have interrupted their relationship somewhat. Mum and Dad will be ever so pleased when I tell them."

-o-

"For goodness' sake, Jack, is that central heating not working?" Jenny asked, as they stepped back into their house after their rather wonderful time spent on Spain's Costa Blanca. "It's freezing in here!"

"Well, my Sweet Pea, it is after midnight and the timer will have turned itself off," he replied. "The delayed flight didn't help. Four hours is a heck of a long time to wait in any airport."

"Bedtime, don't you think?" she added. "We can unpack in the morning."

"You'll never guess who's left a message on the answer machine," Jack shouted to her upstairs as she was getting ready for bed.

"Surprise me!" she called back, through a mouthful of toothpaste. "The Prime Minister offering you a knighthood?"

"How did you guess?" he chortled on his way up after checking the house and setting the heating for morning. "Two messages," he went on. "One from our Jess to let us know she and Johnny had bumped into David and Irene's Jessie in Roundhay Park. She was wheeling an infant around. So, a cousin once removed for her, I believe."

"And the other?" Jenny asked through a yawn.

"Talk of the devil," he replied. "David Aston. How spooky is that?"

"We must phone them tomorrow," Jenny said slowly as she drifted off to sleep, soaking up the warmth that

Jack's body quickly created. Like a central heating radiator, he was.

Unable to drop off immediately because his mind took a while to settle into the notion that sleep was really important for the fatigued body not to become more … fatigued, their laxness concerning their lapsed relationship with David and Irene drifted into his head. Why had they allowed their close friends to drift out of their orbit when it wasn't necessary? What were some of the last things he had said for David not to forget? 'Don't forget that you're family, and family always has access.' He had allowed problems with work to intrude and to push their friendship very much into the background. *That* could not be allowed to continue, so he would…

-o-

"Fabulous holiday," Jack eulogised through his legendary porridge with the fruit and milk they had bought at the all-night store in Manchester Airport.

"Too right!" Jenny replied. "And so is this porridge…"

They were interrupted by the phone's plaintive warble.

"In demand already," Jack said.

"Going to answer it?" Jenny asked.

"If it's anybody important and/or offering me money, they'll leave a message," Jack chortled. "I'm finishing mi breakfast, so—"

"I know you're there, Jack and Jenny," a very familiar male voice drifted in from the lounge's telephone, "because your Jessie told my Jessie that you'd be back from your escape to the sun today. I should imagine that you'll be having your breakfast and are just about to decide to answer the phone. So, I'll hang up and speak to you later. Don't leave it too long though, because we are just about to go to our Imogen Rose's for lunch. Speak soon."

"That's ma man!" Jack guffawed. "I'll return the favour

when we're finished."

Almost immediately, the phone spat into life again. As the answer machine whirred into life, it said… "Mam? Are you there, Mam? Pick up, please." It was Jessie.

"Hello, sweetheart," Jenny said, plucking the handset from its cradle. "I'm here."

Realising who it was, Jack continued with his breakfast, mashing a fresh pot of tea for when Jenny returned.

"Toast?" she said to him, once she had returned to their breakfast table. "I'm just about to put a couple of slices under the grill."

"Go on then!" he replied with an encouraging smile. "Jessie? What did she want?"

"Oh, nothing much really," Jenny replied. "Just to let us know again that she had seen Cousin Jessie, that they won't be able to get over to see us for a while – oh, and that she is … pregnant."

Chapter 14

"Good morning, Josie," Jack said to his supervisor, as he entered the Area PRS office in Fleetwood. "How are you?"

"Two things, Jack," she replied. "Day before yesterday, Lee McKee passed away, and secondly, from January of next year, this service will cease to exist. *That* piece of information is *not* for public knowledge … yet, you understand. Before you ask, it was cancer."

"Will we be contributing to a floral offering?" Jack asked, knowing what he would prefer to do.

"Her husband has asked for no flowers, but for people to make a donation to the local cancer charity if they feel the need," Josie replied solemnly. "That is what most of us will be doing."

"Good show!" Jack replied. "Count me in on that one, please. Now, will I be doing school at all today?"

"They have a Baker training day, and we have a meeting here until eleven," she explained. "After that, you will be going home."

The rest of the team of support teachers consisted of four women whom he had met just once. He didn't know their names and wouldn't need to if the fate of the organisation were to be believed. There was also one man whom he had met. His two teaching assistants – Penny and Helen – were not obliged to attend these meetings, so they … didn't. For the amount of use this meeting served, he wished he could join them.

Fortunately, Jack had the sort of mind that could attend to several things at the same time, although physically he was unable to multi-task. He could listen to words and hot air discharged at useless and unproductive quasi-meetings while thinking about other, more important stuff, like what was going to happen in the best part of twelve months' time, and what Jenny had been up to in the college that was offering her work.

-o-

"You're early, Jack," Jenny said, startled by his sloping through the door at a ridiculously early time.

"Your fancy man had time to escape out the back door?" he said, with a mock air of seriousness.

"I beg your—!" she harrumphed, taken aback.

"Onny jokin'," he chortled. "I thought you knew me so well. Well?" he went on, once he had removed his coat. "What happened?"

"Happened?" she replied, getting her own back. "What do you mean 'happened'? Wi' mi fancy man?"

"Daft bugger!" he snorted, taking the few steps into the kitchen diner to put t'kettle on.

"It's a good job," she said, an air of nonchalance surrounding her like the proverbial bubble.

"A good job *what*?" he reiterated while stirring the full teapot deliberately slowly.

"The ten hours they offered initially is not ten hours at all," Jenny explained. "Lindsay, one of my bosses, told me that it would involve at least thirty hours a week, and more if I wanted it."

"What!" he exclaimed. "Is that what you want? I mean, is it – dare I say it? – too much?"

"Thirty is perfect," she replied. "It's more money than

I was getting for working in school. They laughed when I asked for travelling expenses."

"Now that's *funny*," he said, a great guffaw erupting from his chest. "When do you start your thirty hours?"

"Er, how does tomorrow grab you?" Jenny asked rhetorically.

"As you said – perfect," he added. "Set off at about quarter to nine – when I will just about have arrived at Fleetwood – and get back home at—?"

"Finish work generally at four," she replied.

"About three quarters of an hour to an hour before I land," he said. "Perfect. A pot of Yorkshire Tea on the mash. A bun or two next to mi mug, perhaps. An excellent start to every evening."

-o-

The work Jack was involved with in class was mostly mind-numbingly tedious. His role was to ensure that teachers were allowed to pursue their studies with their youngsters without outbursts from behaviourly disordered children. Consequently, his function was largely as a firefighter, minder or jailor. Fortunately, he had the sort of rapport with his youngsters that allowed reasonably stable and interruption-free classrooms to be the norm – when he was there. Unfortunately, he couldn't be in every room all the time, making his presence in multiple classrooms constantly in demand.

Often he found himself 'dragged' out of one quiet and productive classroom to settle bolshy and demanding youngsters in another. Some teachers had had the temerity to suggest he might set up a classroom where he could deal with these recalcitrant youths together at the same time.

Interesting concept though that was, the hierarchy in the school wouldn't hear of it, because it would have set a precedent whereby the 'naughties' would become more time-intensive than those that needed no input at all.

Jack often had to put straight the teachers who suggested youngsters would 'opt' into such a scheme because it would be the easy option for both youngsters – and teachers – to be with Jack. His response?

"All rayt, Lad," for it was almost always a male teacher, "do it. I'll guarantee young'uns will learn a darned sight more wi' me than wi' thee, *and* there'll be much less bother," he would say. "Does tha not realise they're trying to tell thee that they want to learn summat more appropriate than the bilge *thy's* forcing down their collective throat? Thy would have to provide significant amounts of work for 'em, as well."

It didn't make him many teacher friends, but it did shut 'em up, and, of course, the bosses in the school supported Jack's philosophy one hundred per cent.

Hannah was a different case altogether. She'd had a few problems at the hands of one or two ignorant teachers from Year 7 onwards, almost as soon as she had arrived in school from primary. Jack suspected that this had stemmed from the misinformation supplied by her primary-school teachers. The high-school teachers had unfortunately taken this as gospel and treated her accordingly.

Intellectually, she was a smart young lady with a deep artistic talent that wasn't being supported or developed at all – one of the many failings of high schools in general. High schools tended to be drawn towards academia, with not even a nod towards practical subjects for youngsters who had no academic leanings. There were many children in most schools who would have benefited from a practical education, and at the end of it would have become productive members of a society that benefited from them.

This education system and its educators didn't want

to know, unfortunately for the many children who would have profited from a slight adjustment in policy.

Often, when Jack got home from metaphorically banging his head against a system encased in cast iron, he needed a couple of mugs of Yorkshire Tea along with his new favourite biscuits – Hobnobs. It was said that you could dunk a Hobnob in your tea up to five time without it collapsing into a sludge at the bottom of the mug. Jack had not tried to prove *that* hypothesis because *he didn't dunk*. To have done that would have been heresy for him, as he insisted on a pristine biscuit with *unpolluted* tea.

Friday, at a quarter to five at the end of the first week back after Christmas, Jack was savouring his tea and Hobnob, eating and drinking each separate item slowly. The telephone rang. Mid-biscuit, he frowned, ignoring the stridently irritating ringing. He tried to continue ignoring it, but its insistence became so annoying that he reached over from his comfy chair and plucked the receiver from its cradle.

"Hello. Fire station," he spat down the phone.

"Now I know that voice, and it's never been anywhere near a fire station," a very familiar voice insisted. "Jack Ingles is either halfway through a mug of tea and a digestive biscuit, or you are an imposter."

"David!" Jack yelled joyfully. "I thought you had died, and I would have to wait until the next life to speak to you again. How are you, Old Man?"

"Under the usual stresses and strains, which I think are getting worse the closer retirement age approaches," David replied. "Can't stay on long, so I'll get to the point. What are you and your beautiful wife doing this weekend, because Irene and I would desperately *love* you to come spend the weekend with *us*."

"I don't even have to ask my boss's permission on that one," Jack replied. "We'd be delighted. Do you remember when we used to do that and call for a take-away curry en route for us all?”

“I do *that*,” David agreed. “But not tomorrow, if you don’t mind, Old Chap. Irene has prepared everything in the culinary line for the weekend. Eleven tomorrow morning all right, just in time for morning coffee?”

“Excellent!” Jack replied. “See you then.”

“Who was that?” Jenny asked as Jack finished his ever-so-slightly cooler mug of tea. “Anybody we know?”

“Try somebody we’ve not seen for an age, whom we used to spend time with regularly when we lived in Leeds,” Jack prompted her. “One of them—”

“David, by any chance?” Jenny offered.

“You’re too good for me – in more ways than one,” he replied quietly. “We’ve been invited to theirs for the weekend. Any good?”

“Erm,” she hesitated.

“No?” he queried with a frown. “OK. I’ll phone him back and—”

“Erm,” she continued after a pregnant pause. “Daft beggar! Just having you on. Of course it will be all right. Can’t wait.”

-o-

“Do you know,” David said as he greeted his friends at the front door, “we couldn’t have picked a worse weekend for weather, Old Chap.”

It had been snowing for a day or two, with significant drifts around every corner as Jack and Jenny had motored to their friends’ home where they had spent many a happy weekend in years gone by.

“No snow at all in Morecambe,” Jack replied, as they moved inside out of the raw northerly that threatened more of the nasty white stuff. People were right when they said the older you became, the colder it felt. “Full sun and twenty-degrees centigrade.”

“Don’t listen to him, David,” Jenny interrupted as she embraced her hosts. “There is no snow but it’s just as cold. If anything, it’s colder. Can’t wait to get back to the warmer times of holidays in Spain. Now, there it *is* twenty degrees.”

“I don’t know how you can afford it,” David said as they sat down to percolating coffee. “It’s all right for some.”

“*We* could afford it – only just – because we were invited over by Jenny’s sister, Val, who now lives over there with husband, Mike,” Jack added. “She sent us return air tickets to stay with them over Christmas in a fabulous three-bed villa near Denia on the Costa Blanca. Overlooking the Med, as well. Can you imagine what it would be like to live in a climate that rarely – *very* rarely – makes you feel cold?”

“And you didn’t have to waste your days in perpetual aggravation trying to run a school in an organisation that doesn’t understand what the word means?” David said with more than a little annoyance icing his words.

“Things not going as you would have wanted, David?” Jenny asked as she and Irene joined them.

“You could put it like that,” he replied. “Still, I don’t suppose I can grumble. We’ve got only a ‘counting down’ number of years left to retirement.”

“That would be three years, would it not?” Jack offered.

“And how did you know that one?” Jenny said, not really taking into account that he would have worked it out.

“David is four years older than me and I retire in 2006,” Jack explained. “As we are now at the start of 1999, it means just seven years for me, and 2002 for David. QED.”

“QED?” Jenny started to ask.

“*Quad erat demonstrandum*,” Jack explained. “Latin for

'which was demonstrated'."

"I've got some corking memories from your – our – time at Broughton, Jack," David said. "Do you remember that little eight-year-old that told another eight-year-old he'd never get away with anything with you because you had eyes in your arse?"

They all laughed at the scenario.

"And the time at Christmas that we got locked in school after hours because we'd had a glass or two of Scotch and had fallen asleep in the staff room?" Jack remembered. "Didn't we manage to get out of a loose-fitting window in the library?"

"One of those half-moon shaped ones," David agreed. "And that time just before parents' evening when we had Stan Awad on about some fault behind his display board in his classroom that he had taken days to put up—"

"And then had to take down all the display work because HMI Inspector of Walls – or some such person that *you* invented, David Aston – wanted to inspect his walls," Jack recounted. "What a hoot!"

"Do you remember Stan's ruined trousers?" David sniggered.

"Did you two ever get *any* work done?" Jenny asked, bemused by all these anecdotes. "A pair of overgrown pranksters, no less."

"Those last two were entirely Stan's fault," Jack explained. "He had been taking a class of six-year-olds for reading when he asked to listen to nervous little Lindsay—?"

"Buckle," Davis added quickly.

"To try to settle her nerves, he sat her on his lap," Jack went on, "and she peed on his best trousers."

The two men fell abouts in fits of laughter at the picture of Stan's face they conjured from their past.

"He had to go home to change," Jack said simply.

"In my scruffy blue tracksuit bottoms," David added, wiping his eyes.

"Not the most sartorially elegant we ever saw him," Jack agreed.

"Not that long after that episode from 'Stanley's Wardrobe Malfunctions', he bent over and split his trousers up the back," David remembered.

"And he had to change them again, in school this time, after hiding from Miss Page behind the staff room's laden bentwood coat and hat stand," Jack said. "This time his replacements were—"

"My blue tracky bottoms, which by then were even scruffier!" This had them both howling, with uncontrollable tears of mirth rolling down their face.

"This is just what they both needed. Don't you agree, Jenny?" Irene suggested, after the two had cleared away the dinner things and were washing up in the kitchen.

"Too right!" Jenny agreed. "Jack's had a tough time of it since he left here. Always blamed his misfortunes on the various jobs he has taken on, after his decision to leave his authority. Poor choices in jobs, he always says."

"Although David has been in his present position at this 'new' school since Jack left, there have been major issues throughout his time there," Irene said. "The problems always arose because of the gross inefficiency and ineptitude of those clueless high-ups in the Education Offices in Great George Street in Leeds, and David has always had to sort out *their* problems. It certainly hasn't been plain sailing. He is most definitely looking forward to retirement."

"Jack, likewise," Jenny agreed. "He is now travelling between Morecambe and Fleetwood every day – a matter of ninety miles round trip. Not ideal."

"One of the best memories I have is from when I was in my first year of teaching at the school in 1968," Jack started. "You have to bear in mind that I was one of the first half-dozen or so folks trained to teach French to eight-year-olds."

"I remember you on your first teaching practice here, shortly after you started your college course in Leeds," David added. "How different your lessons were from those delivered by the head, Mr Moore. The youngsters actually *enjoyed* your lessons."

"One day we had a group of thirty or so teachers, accompanied by two HMIs whom I knew," Jack went on. "They had come along as a group to see how teaching French to eight-year-olds was done. The group was so big that we had to take the lesson in the hall. Imagine, a probationary teacher showing two HMIs and thirty experienced teachers how to go about it!"

"If memory serves," David said, "you assigned each group of five teachers to work with a group of your youngsters. I've never seen so many cack-handed adults in my life! The HMIs just stood and smiled. *They* knew how good you were, and that's why they'd come."

"I enjoyed that lesson," Jack said with a huge grin. "With the likes of Kathryn Hill, Julie Thornton, Billy Naylor, Craig Fitchett and Tonia Nevin enjoying it, too. Ah, me! Times, eh?

Tonia was called Trumpton, following a really loud fart for such a petite young lady!"

"The most way out and funny thing I ever saw came at the end of Stanley Awad's production of *Scheherazade: 1001 Arabian Nights*," David said, a big grin on his face before he even started the tale. "The show had reached its climax very successfully, when the final curtain came down – literally."

"It was a good performance then?" Jenny ventured.

"In more ways than one!" Jack replied. "Because—"

"The winding mechanism for the makeshift curtain

had stuck. As the lad working it tugged sharply on the rope, the whole thing collapsed onto the stage and covered the entire cast," David added, as the girls carried in coffee, a snifter each of brandy in a traditional bowl big enough to hold a bouquet of flowers, and a platter of home-made truffles.

"May I ask one favour, Old Chap?" Jack suggested to David, once they had stopped laughing.

"Anything, Old Man, except for money," David promised. "Name it."

"That we won't allow time to get in the way of our arranging regular get-togethers or gets-together," Jack replied.

"You used that one once before, if memory serves," David said after a sip of the brandy Jack had brought with him.

"I did," Jack recalled. "Not long before I left Broughton. Well, is it a deal?"

"Indeed, it is," his friend replied.

"And Jenny and I will make sure of it," Irene reiterated firmly.

"Cheers!" Jack and David said as they saluted each other with chinking glasses. "Cheers!"

Chapter 15

Despite travelling every day for the following two weeks, their weekend with Irene and David had cemented a happy and memory-full smile on Jack's usually dour face. Their time together had brought many half-forgotten or hidden memories to the surface, making him relive some of the most exciting and remarkable times in his life.

Jack always purported to be a loner who needed only his wife and children to enliven and reinvigorate his existence, but there was a chosen and select bunch of human beings who always drew him out of the doldrums that occasionally ambushed his mind. David and Irene were the top two of that group.

Although he did his job to the best of his considerable ability, and always took that extra step or two to ensure success, his mind often time-travelled to that glorious event almost seven years in the future when schools would disappear from his horizon. Retirement would allow him to do those things that schools ushered out of sight to the depths of his mind.

If the service he worked for *were* to disappear, he wasn't sure what the future might hold or where he would peddle his wares and skills, but he would need to know sooner rather than later. He had thought that he might ask the deputy of *this* school to consider keeping him on, if only for *one* more year, but he was sure they wouldn't be able to pay him the extra cash he would need for travelling. There was no way he would travel for free!

The statue of Eros – an exact replica of the one in London – hove into view on Fleetwood's Broadwater roundabout, heralding his approach to the run into school. This statue had been presented to the town by the Lofthouse family, makers of Fisherman's Friend in the town, several years before. Knowing the association, this statue caused Jack to have a minor shudder – because he didn't like Fisherman's Friend lozenges! The very thought of popping one of *those* nightmarish things into his mouth made him want to retch and heave. He couldn't ever imagine ingesting them out of choice.

"They're lovely," his Granddad Jud used to say. "Tha dun't know what tha's missin. Don't be such a wet Nelly and get one dahn thissen."

But he would have said that, wouldn't he? He thought everything edible was lovely. How could any right-thinking person eat eyeballs, brains, udders, tripe and pigs' trotters? Jack remembered with fondness when his granddad asked him to fetch some pig's trotters from the butcher; when he said he was hungry, he would always ask for a pair of pig's trotters 'size eight'.

Jack shuddered at the mere thought, remembering also that one of Grandpa Jud's favourite foods of all time was … rabbit. Why was that? Not only did Jud love its texture and taste, he had a ready-made supply in the fields adjoining his allotments. Many's the time he would set traps in the deep grasses only yards from the edges of the Normanton Brick Works deep quarry, and rarely did he go home empty handed after a day's session in his greenhouses. Marion, his wife, would have had a fit if she'd known how close to the quarry's edge he set his traps.

Grandpa Jud's love of food was legendary. Grandma

put this down to the fact that he hadn't got much of it as a lad, not because he didn't like it but because his mother couldn't afford to buy it. They had migrated to the West Riding from the Stockton-on-Tees area of the north east when Jud was five in 1905 because of a shortage of work. When he was at Dodsworth Junior School, just up the hill from Scarborough Row where Jack was born, he was the only one who couldn't afford the bus fare when his class went to Wakefield swimming baths for their weekly session, a mere five miles away. The school set him off an hour earlier to run it, there and back.

It wasn't an easy life for Granddad Jud Holmes, but he had a heart of gold and lived for his family. The bottom fell out of his life somewhat when his only son was shot down and killed in his Lancaster bomber returning from a raid to Germany in 1942. He was twenty-two. Life was never the same from then on.

Jack wished he had been able to spend more time with his Granddad Jud and Grandma Marion. They had so much experience of life that he could have learned from and enjoyed. Unfortunately, the grind and unsought worries and concerns of real life do tend to intervene and interrupt the enjoyable and happy parts that *most* folks thrive upon.

His mind thrust itself back to the time they'd arrived at Jud and Marion's home to find it empty after his granddad was rushed into hospital. He was overcome still with sadness when he had realised that he wouldn't see Jud again. All those wonderful, magical times he had spent as a nipper wi' t'owd chap in his allotment flooded his mind, yearning to be visited again and again. His granddad had left him, but the fun Jack had had in his company remained as sharp as the day it took place.

How could he forget that first time Jud had taken him to visit his prized gardening space; that huge five-barred gate with the barrier of an horrendous stench of pig muck as proof against any alien invaders? The wide muddy pathway, marshalled by insurmountable, impenetrable hedges either side, jumped into his mind, to have that low black 'duck' shed imprinted upon it.

"A duck shed, Granddad?" Jack had marvelled. "Wi' ducks inside?"

"Nay, lad," Jud had replied. "T'door opening is so low thy 'as to duck so tha dun't bang thi 'ead on it."

All wonderfully evocative times that Jack now could share only with himself. He could bring back the first time he had heard a sky lark ower Goosehill fields way on, and the cuckoo, along wi' his granddad's tale as to its nesting habits. He wasn't sure about the truth of what Jud had said in those days, but now… Jack could still see his face as he talked about the cuckoo 'borrowing' somebody else's nest instead of going to the trouble of building her own.

"Penny?" Jenny would ask him.

"Would you stop calling me Penny?" Jack would reply, predictably. "Just thinking on mi granddad and grandma and the opportunities to spend time wi''em that I squandered."

"They knew you loved them, despite having your own life to lead," Jenny said.

"Not good enough, Jen," he would reply, saddened by the loss of the only adults – along with his mam – he was ever close to before he was fortunate enough to meet Jenny again in Normanton churchyard.

-o-

"For goodness' sake!" Jack gasped as he turned from laying flowers on his mam and grandma's graves. "Are my weary old eyes deceiving me?"

The target of his comments was another chap of about the same age and size, who was fulfilling a similar purpose.

The newcomer turned sharply with eyes narrowed and brow furrowed and asked, "Sorry, but do I know thee?"

"Perhaps not as well as if I'd bin nine again," Jack laughed, proffering his hand in friendly gesture. "Mi thinning thatch probably doesn't help. You used to live next to us on Scarborough Row, and when we moved to Garth Avenue … so did you!"

"I don't believe it!" the second man gasped. "It *is* thee! Jack kiss-mi-arse Ingles! Well, I'll be buggered!"

"Gordon Gittins – unless tha's changed thi name so as not to be recognised," Jack said with a snort. "Is this your dad's plot?"

"Nay," Gordon replied. "T'owd bugger's still wi' us – unfortunately. This is mi mam. Died in 1970 wi' breast cancer."

"Just three years after mine," Jack added quietly. "She wor a lovely woman, great friends wi' mi mam, as far as I could see."

"Aye. They were allus ready for a good confab wi' a cup o' tea," Gordon said, a far-away look clouding his eyes. "I can think on any number of folks as should have gone before 'em. You?"

"Too rayt!" Jack agreed. "But still…"

"How's your William these days?" Gordon asked, genuinely interested.

"Daft bugger couldn't keep it in his pants," Jack went on. "Had an affair wi' a bit on a 'arlot and lost his lovely wife accordingly. She's now wed to a grand chap, and they live in Southern Spain. Your brother'd know his ex-wife. How is Peter, by the way? Still with us? Didn't he lose *his* wife to cancer, or was it in childbirth?"

"T'latter," Gordon replied. "Mi relationship's on and off wi' Peter, I'm afraid. We've niver bin what you'd call bosom buddies. He's ten years older than me and we niver really spent brother time together – probably much like you and your William."

"Very true," Jack agreed. "William never had a lot
of common sense, and so hadn't a clue how to deal with
people in general, or the folks that he should have been
tight with – sons, daughter, wife."

"I've not seen thi abaht much at all, so thy obviously
dun't live around here, unless it's in a tent in Goosehill
Woods," Gordon observed as they laughed together. "Has
tha seen t'place lately? Bloody disgrace! There in't even
a path through any more by t'bottom field, tha knows,
where Farmer Borril's bull, Arthur, used to stretch 'is arse?"

"I was never sure about that," Jack replied. "Was he
really called Arthur?"

"'Course he was!" Gordon insisted. "Well, he *was* to
me!"

They both laughed at shared memories, fell silent for
a moment or two, and then chortled again.

"Ee, we could write a book about our shared times
at Woodhouse," Gordon continued. "Does tha remember
t'time I chucked mi pump bag at thi 'ed near t'front gates,
and it missed thee and nearly 'it Mr Tomlinson?"

"Too right I do!" Jack replied. "I killed missen laughing
when he beckoned you to him wi' a curl on his finger."

"I thowt I wor off to get a clout, but he could see
t'funny side on it," Gordon went on.

"He allus wor understanding and had a good sense of
humour," Jack observed. "We had a good set of teachers,
when you come to think about it."

"Even Mrs Crossley," Gordon added, which surprised
Jack, who always thought Gordon had held a basic dislike
for her.

"You're right, Gordon," Jack said.

"Which bit am I right about, Our Jack?" Gordon
asked, puzzled about the question.

"*I* don't live around here," Jack said with a snigger.

"Thy allus used to do that as well," Gordon replied. "Answering the last question but twenty! Used to annoy a lot of people, because they weren't able to keep up wi' thee."

Jack laughed. "I've allus been t'same," he explained. "It has been said that when I snuff it, I'll be answering t'question somebody asked me six months before."

"'As tha found somebody to tek thee on then, Jack?" Gordon asked. "Somebody as'll be able to cope wi' thi 'perfection'?"

"Aye, lad. She's called Jenny," he replied. "Used to be Jenny McDermot; sister to mi brother's first wife."

"I remember her!" Gordon exclaimed. "She wor rayt … posh."

"Smart, too," Jack said. "Is thy married?"

"Not married, but we've bin together thirty years," he replied. "Wi' six kids. She's called Jane Fearnley."

"She wor in our class!" Jack exclaimed. "She wor grand, and a good looker."

"Teks one to pick one up," Gordon bragged as Jack laughed.

"Yeah! Right!" Jack said, a disbelieving look on his face.

"Good to si thi agen, Jack," Gordon said finally. "If tha comes this way agen, tha can buy me a pint."

"Si thi, Gordon," Jack called as his school friend turned and walked out of the cemetery.

"Jack?" Jenny said as she joined him at the grave side. "Was that who I thought it was? Your old pal Gordon—?"

"Gittins," Jack added. "Six kids, would you believe? Should we make our way to visit Jim now?"

With one last look at his family's final resting place, he linked Jenny's arm, kissed her, and they set off to find the car.

-o-

"Didn't tell you, did I, that I had a telephone call from our George William the other day?" Jenny said, once they had started on the way to Methley and Jim's bungalow. Although his health had been deteriorating slowly, Jim was managing to look after himself, and was refusing all offers of help from Jenny and Jack to clean and tidy on a regular basis.

"For any particular reason?" Jack asked.

"He's discovered a new hobby that leads him up hills and mountains," Jenny explained.

"Hills and mountains?" Jack puzzled. "You don't mean he's become – dare I say it – a singer?"

"How do you make that one out?" she replied, more than a little mystified. "That bears no resemblance to a hill walker and mountain climber. Does it?"

"Well, Julie Andrews thought so," he snorted. "The hills *were* alive with the sound of music, weren't they?"

"Jack!" she laughed. "Sometimes you are impossible. He's discovered climbing and walking, and they're off to Skye when it gets warmer. He wants to climb in the Cuillins with a mate from school."

"They?" he queried.

"Sandy is going with him, along with her sister, Allie," Jenny replied.

"Are *they* climbers?" Jack gasped. "I didn't know young lasses did that sort of stuff."

"I've no idea, but they are going to relax while the lads are out climbing," she said. "Allie is married to Alan Smith, George's mate."

"Do you remember that time we climbed that mountain in Wales?" Jack asked, not expecting an answer from his wife.

"Cader Idris," she replied with a self-satisfied smile.

"Wow!" he whistled softly. "Didn't think you'd remember that one. School we went with?"

"National Children's Homes, called Crowthorn," she replied. "You were there only a couple of terms or so. School party – whole school? – to mid-Wales."

"I couldn't believe how tiring, cold and rainy it was climbing up that loose scree, and misty once we were at the top," Jack gasped, wiping the imaginary sweat from his forehead. "That walk across the narrow ridge at the top was unnerving, to say the least.

"I think it was called Foxes Pass, and you kept on looking for them," he explained after a moment's pause. "Much later I found out that it was the most difficult path of all, meant only for experienced climbers. And there we were, ten youngsters and three adults, all in inappropriate ordinary clothing and shoes, climbing up a heavily eroded scree slope – in heavy drizzle and mist."

"Didn't teacher Steve, our experienced climber-leader, have his dog with him?" Jenny remembered.

"You're right. He did," Jack said, flicking his fingers. "I'd forgotten that. Didn't the youngsters take turns to be pulled up the slopes by that dog?"

"And *we* never got a turn!" Jenny said. "Bummer!"

"What we did was dangerous in the extreme," Jack added, a look of deep concern etching his face. "The view on reaching the summit, Pen y Gadair, was supposed to have been breath-taking, but with the mist we saw—"

"Mist," Jenny butted in.

"If I remember rightly, it took us five hours to get to the bothy shelter at the top to have a rest and gather a modicum of warmth," Jack said. "That was where we should have had our non-existent refreshing sandwiches and a drink. Very badly prepared. All that day in the icy cold with no sustenance."

"Do you remember turning your ankle when we got back onto the flat?" Jenny said with a smile.

"Listen to you!" he chortled. "That's a stunning

memory you have there!"

"I enjoyed the private railway journey the day after, to goodness knows where, though," she added. "What was the little town called where we had our camping site?"

"Tywyn, I think it was," Jack said in a suspect Welsh accent, as they pulled up in Jim's drive. "Curtains still drawn?"

Jenny turned to Jack, a concerned look hovering around her eyes. Out of the car in a flash, she was pressing his doorbell quickly to gain access.

"No answer?" Jack asked, joining her. "You keep on pressing yon button and knocking, and I'll nip round the back. Have you brought his key?"

"In my bag, somewhere," she replied, her hand deep into its interior trying to find it.

"Curtains drawn at the back as well," Jack said as he returned to her. "Key?"

The bungalow interior was cold even for late January, with no sign of life anywhere. Separately, they looked carefully around each room so as not to disturb anything.

"Jen!" Jack called urgently. "In here. Bathroom."

"Oh my God!" Jenny gasped, covering the lower half of her face with a shocked hand. "Is he—?"

"Cold, and of course … dead," Jack replied slowly. "Been like it for some time, I should imagine."

"What do we do now?" she asked, tears welling.

"The usual, I suppose – ambulance and undertaker. We have his documents at home once we get back there. Rest easy, owd cock," Jack said, as he laid Jim out properly and covered him with a sheet. "Rest easy."

Chapter 16

"What a day to have a funeral, eh, Mam?" Jessie said, as they were ushered into the community hall for Jim's humanist ceremony. He'd never been much on religion, or 'religious paraphernalia', as he called it. Having somebody praying ower his earthly remains wouldn't have cut it for him.

"Aren't you supposed to be flying to Benidorm tomorrow?" Jessie went on. "Silly question, but will you still be going?"

"We're packed. Have been for a while, so what do *you* think?" Jenny replied. "Jim wouldn't have wanted us to do anything other than to carry on with our plans. So, that's what we are going to do. Jim's express wish was that we celebrate his life not his death, hence the reason your dad is wearing his pink Hawaiian shirt and white slacks."

"I *was* wondering about that," Jessie said with a quiet giggle.

"Jim didn't want his son to be notified because he hasn't been near his dad for more than thirty years," Jenny replied. "Some sort of a falling out that, according to Jim, was unnecessarily divisive. Consequently, we are his only family."

"All right?" Jack said quietly as he sat beside Jenny. The rest of the family trooped in, making a congregation of … ten, most of whom were dressed in bright, lively colours according to Jim's wishes. The only exception was Ed, who wasn't sure what day it was or why they had to be there at all. He hadn't been an active part of Grandpa Jim and Granny Flora Mae's life together, and was even less in evidence when his granny had died. A strange boy.

Mary and Joey had been completely different in that they had been around when their busy lives had allowed. Mary loved her grandparents, as did Jessie and Florence May. Val had brought Mike to the funeral, but Florence May and Billy lived too far away to make a casual visit, and Jim would have understood that. They had sent a beautiful wreath, however, all the way from … the florist in Castleford, to record that he was in their thoughts. They had said that they would maintain a vigil until the burial had been completed, even though they were seven hours ahead of GMT.

Val and Mike had jetted in from Denia in Southern Spain, to jet back with Jenny and Jack early the following day. Both couples were heading for the Costa Blanca – the one to live, and the other to holiday for a week.

The ceremony was short but powerful, again as Jim would have liked it had he been there to witness it. He had been a dour Yorkshireman who wouldn't tolerate cant and hypocrisy, preferring to call a spade a spade. He was, however, very generous in his dealings with those that meant anything to him. Contrary to popular belief, he wasn't tight with his money, but he did prefer to get value for his hard-earned cash.

Jim had arranged for a four-course meal for his 'family', once the funeral had been concluded satisfactorily, at the Strafford Arms in Wakefield, a place he and Flora Mae had frequented in their later years.

"Excuse me?" an unrecognised voice accosted Jack and Jenny as they emerged from the dimly lit hall interior onto a bright but decidedly chilly day.

"Yes?" Jack replied.

"I hear my father has died," the chap answered. "Jim Arkwright?"

"And who might you be?" Jack replied quickly.

"As I said, Jim Arkwright was my father," the man went on with a sardonic smile.

"And that has what relevance?" Jack replied in like vein.

"I simply wanted to know when the will was being read," the man replied, a little more forcefully. Wrong person to pick on!

"And how is that relevant to you?" Jack said, turning to face him. "If you are who you purport to be – and we have no way of corroborating that – isn't this about thirty years too late that you wish to reacquaint? It can't be about the money, because Jim left none. Now, bugger off and go pay to see a solicitor. You've a bloody cheek!"

Jack's slightly aggressive move towards the newcomer set the latter back on his heels somewhat, and he turned quickly and moved away towards the car park.

"Who was that, Jack?" Jenny asked as she turned back towards her husband.

"Young whippersnapper purporting to be Jim's son," he replied. "Wanting to know when the will was to be read."

"What did you tell him?" she asked.

"That Jim had left nowt and that *he* should bugger off," Jack said.

"Nice one, Jack," Mike butted in.

"You can always trust Our Jack to do and say the right thing in any situation," Val added as she put her arm around his waist.

"Similar situation when Jessie's biological father called to stake a claim when she was four," Jack said. "Remember?"

"Remember? Could I ever forget?" Jenny agreed firmly.

"Her biological father?" Val queried. "When you lived on Queen Street? But I thought you—?"

"Lived on my own?" Jenny interrupted, a broad grin re-emerging. "I did, theoretically, but Jack and I were very close to setting up shop together."

"What happened?" Val ventured. "Nothing untoward I hope?"

"Jessie's father tried to muscle his way in, but Jack was having none of it," Jenny explained. "He literally picked him up and threw him into the street with a warning not to darken my door again. We have seen neither hide nor hair of him since."

"Remind me never to cross you, Jack Ingles!" Val gasped, as the others laughed at the face she pulled.

-o-

Manchester Airport had been awash with folks eager to swap England's sunny but very chilly days for Spain's azure-blue skies and wrap-around warmth. February definitely was not the time to luxuriate in the low temperatures that a UK winter usually brought.

As soon as Jack and Jenny set foot on the top step of the stairway from the aeroplane to the tarmac, they were met by an intense wall of satisfying head-to-toe warmth that caused all the passengers to sigh or gasp at this unexpected welcome. Even now, Alicante was beginning to weave the magic that the Costa Blanca provided. Val and Mike joined in the collective sigh.

The two couples parted company at the check-out and baggage carousel, ready to meet up at a later date.

"Is Mary coming back to be with you?" Jenny asked her sister.

"Possibly in a few weeks," Val replied. "She wants to explore the possibility of relocating permanently to develop her business over here. She feels it will be beneficial for Alice growing up."

"If she needs a personal tutor for Alice, tell her to get in touch," Jack offered. "My rates are very competitive."

They all laughed as they separated, Val and Mike to collect their car, and Jenny and Jack to catch the coach to take them to their hotel in Benidorm. They were looking forward to spending a week enjoying their full-board package at the Calypso Hotel, just a few yards from the sea front.

"Do you realise that this is only the fourth time I have been abroad as an adult?" Jack said to Jenny halfway through their week's worth of luxury. "What do you think?"

"It's lovely," she replied. "And yes, I would come again. I know you like to get to know places before you move on, but I feel like I'd like to explore further afield."

"What, next week?" Jack quipped, raising a giggle from his wife.

"Yes, please!" she replied enthusiastically. "Now that we can afford holidays abroad on a regular basis – but not next week. This week so far has been so relaxing and restful."

"And the food's been excellent," Jack added. "Wouldn't recommend the calamari, though."

"Cally what?" Jenny puzzled.

"Squid," he replied with a yuk and a disgusted grimace. She laughed at what she saw and heard, knowing well that Jack wasn't an exotic food afficionado, or a lover of seafood in general. He always he said that he loved seafood only if it were either cod or haddock wearing a batter overcoat.

"Did you say you'd been abroad four times as an adult?" she asked. "Does that mean you went abroad when you were at school as well?"

"Aye," he said quietly. "When I was in my first summer at the grammar school in 1958. I was just twelve and they had decided to take a trip for a week to La Baule les Pins in Brittany. Seemed like a dream. Mi dad had refused to fund it – it was £20 – so mi granddad Jud paid instead and gave me some pocket money as well. We had a fantastic time, even though most of the other lads were older and wanted nowt to do wi' me. I had a great time on mi own and saw stuff I'd never seen before or since."

"Loner from an early age, eh, Jack?" Jenny said, feeling sorry for him.

"Hey! Don't feel sorry for *me*," he exclaimed, recognising *that* look in her face. "*They* were the ones to feel sorry for because they had no idea how to amuse themselves, other than being taken to places to do organised stuff. I didn't need all of that boring malarkey. I'd been used to being on mi own virtually since birth, so it was no big deal. Onny missen to rely on. Great!"

-o-

How is it that whenever you are enjoying something that you've anticipated for such a long time, it's usually gone in the flutter of an eyelash? It's almost as if it's never existed … almost.

Their memories of two holidays in the sun on the Costa Blanca – the White Coast because in the past many white almond blossoms could be seen along the coast – in Southern Spain would indeed stay with them forever, Jack would see to that. He had a wonderful knack of bringing back memories at any time of the night or day. What was it his granddad would say? 'Tha's like a tramp's owercoat – allus on!'

Jack's reminiscences were vaguely repetitive at times, but he could make memories bring past, *shared* experiences to life so they might be enjoyed time and again. He also had that credibility that allowed him to massage and manipulate slight inaccuracies to bring them into line with reality.

"You didn't know Harry Gamble, our first woodwork teacher," Jack said, as he and Jenny were having one of their usual afternoon cups of tea and home-made scones in their six-feet-square micro-conservatory. "He was at Merton Grange when I started. We both enjoyed wood turning at lunchtimes, but we ran into a significant shortage of wood."

"Wood turning?" she asked. "What's that? We can all turn over a piece of wood, can't we? Or isn't that quite what you are talking about?"

"This was about the time when blue plastic chairs were replacing wooden classroom ones," Jack explained. "The wonderful thing about the wooden ones was that the seats were made from reasonably thick elm – a beautifully grained piece of wood. Here's the thing. When a wooden chair broke – usually a leg or back – the whole chair was binned. We realised that the seat could be salvaged and turned on the lathe into a beautiful bowl or platter. This, of course, was the most wonderful sort of recycling you could have."

"And did all of those chairs break accidentally?" Jenny asked with a knowing smile and a nod.

"Of course they did," he replied with a grin and a twinkle in his eye. "They had been used and abused for many years and had come to the end of their useful life."

"How convenient you were on the spot when that unfortunate breakage occurred!" Jenny sniggered. "It was really lucky that you were able to reuse the wood."

"You know full well that I didn't get on with the hierarchy in that school, don't you?" Jack went on. "But there were those that I *did* like and got on with. Peter Shippleton and Chris Watters were two such chaps, along with Beardy Brian."

"Not heard of those two," Jenny replied.

"Peter took over from Harry Gamble, who had retired

because of ill health," Jack continued, "and he and Chris were mates. On occasion, we used to get together in Peter's workshop for a cup of tea – neither of them liked coffee – and a ten-minute chin wag on a lunchtime. An hour-and-a-half's break at lunchtime did seem rather long. Anyway, this day Peter was showing us the 'fancy dress' he had made for a function at home in Hebden Bridge, which he had stored in his lockable wood stockroom. You'll never believe what it was—"

"Fancy dress made out of wood?" Jenny gasped.

"It was a full-sized grandfather clock that he could fit inside of," Jack explained. "It had moving hands that disguised the holes for his eyes, and he had somehow fitted straps inside to fit over his shoulders so he could walk around 'wearing' it."

"Wow!" was all she could say.

"Well," Jack went on with a mischievous grin, "while we were congratulating him over this achievement, we heard the classroom outside door open and the deputy head's voice, 'Peter! Peter! You in there?'

"Mischievously, Peter whispered, 'Hide.'

"He got inside his clock suit, Chris hid in a cupboard, and I secreted missen behind a wall of spare wood. Our steaming mugs we had left on top of another cupboard, in full view.

"The deputy squeezed into the stockroom, had a scan around, said 'Peter?' tentatively, and wandered out. Once we had heard the outside door click shut, we collapsed in a fit of giggles when we emerged from our hiding places.

"'Bloody 'ell!' Peter said. 'He was so close to me in mi clock, if he'd looked around for the time, he would have seen mi eyeballs!'"

Jenny laughed at this tale. "Just like a group of naughty little lads! Did the deputy ever find out?"

"No," Jack replied with a wink. "And we never let on.

It was our secret. From that day on, we became The Three Musketeers."

"The Three Stooges, more like," she added with a snort.

"Well, we don't have long to go until the summer holidays," Jack said seriously. "That means going back to Lancaster to find something else to do."

"Something ... else?" Jenny puzzled. "And what does *that* mean? Another job?"

"In a manner of speaking," he replied with a shrug. "You know that the Pupil Referral Service will be folding before next September? Luckily for you, you have a good, productive and permanent job that you will continue to enjoy. I have no idea what is about to happen with mine after the the service I work for is disbanded. I know I won't be travelling to Fleetwood any more after July and will be spending time in a high school in the Morecambe area. I have no idea what will be happening after December."

Chapter 17

Jack's year at the high school in Fleetwood had been hard to rationalise, and it had moved him quickly to a place in his professional life he had experienced before. Unenviably, there were two equally uncomfortable situations he might find himself in once the new academic year had shouldered its way into his life. One could be a job that heralded his retirement, and the other no job at all. Neither option filled him with awe.

The last day of the summer term had always been his second-to-least favourite, paled into insignificance only by Christmas. As a child, Christmas had been his worst nightmare, and that feeling had always crept upon him slowly like a clandestine ambusher. Although the end of the summer term was never as claustrophobic as its winter counterpart, it still filled him with gloom.

"You all right, Jack?" Jenny asked him over tea on the last Friday before the first weekend of their six weeks together. "Jack?"

"Just rationalising what my new boss for the autumn term said to me today," he replied quietly.

"Your new—?" she said, not sure where this had come from.

"I spent the morning in Fleetwood, and the head of the school in Morecambe asked to see me this afternoon," Jack added. "Two o'clock was the time he had suggested and – you know me – I got there for ten to. He kept me waiting for forty-three minutes!"

"You're joking!" she gasped. "That's—!"

"Ridiculously bad-mannered?" he replied. "Just what I was thinking. The most astounding thing he asked me? To give him two reasons why he should take me on in September. I ask you!"

"You didn't!" she gasped when she saw the usual annoyed look that always descended on his face when he needed to put right some idiot's stupid statements.

"I told him straight that there were at least two reasons why he needed to employ me," Jack explained. "I let him know in no uncertain terms that I was the best at what his school needed at that point, and my experience and qualifications spoke for themselves. Then something completely unexpected happened."

"Knowing you in that frame of mind, nothing could have been unexpected," Jenny scoffed.

"No," he assured her. "The door burst open as the secretary urged the head to sort out a fight outside his door between two rather large sixteen-year-olds. He went out to sort them out, only to be dragged onto the floor by them. Although nobody else took any notice or action, I dived in as you would expect, grabbed their collars and tore them apart. I kept the one lad while the deputy took hold of the other. Talk about tag-team wrestling!"

"Wow!" Jenny whistled softly. "As you said, only to be expected."

"We resumed our talk, with the head saying that he could now see the other thing that should persuade him to take me on," Jack explained with a snort. "The upshot is that I start at the school on the second day of the autumn term. The first day is a training day that shouldn't involve me."

Jenny couldn't help but burst out laughing at the

picture he had just conjured in her head – Not-So-Big Daddy in his pale-cerise wrestling leotard rescuing his tag-team wrestling partner from two younger attackers. How majestic would that have been!

"That's just made my day!" she guffawed. "Nothing's ever simple or usual with you, Our Jack."

"Made my day, too," a very recognisable voice piped in from their undersized, couldn't-swing-a-cat hallway. "Just thought I would bring your front door key back to you."

"Joyce! Mi owd cock!" Jack shouted as he jumped up to give her a hug. "Long time no see!"

"Try twenty-three hours?" she laughed. "Long time for you sometimes, eh Jack?"

"Come in and sit down, and tell your husband to do likewise," Jack replied, noticing Stick trying to creep in unseen. "I'll go and put the kettle on."

"Keep the key, Joyce," Jenny said. "You never know when you might need it if Jack gets into any more 'wrestling' scrapes."

"Nothing ever *that* exciting at my school," Stick added. "I'm sorry to say. Lovely school, but a bit … sedentary."

"The worst problem I ever had in my part-time temporary job at our local library was when I had to remind an old chap not to be so loud in the reading room," Joyce said, to guffaws from Jack as he brought in his usual tray of goodies. "A look of horror covered his face as he picked up his man-bag and shambled as quickly as he could to the door, avoiding eye contact. One of the other librarians was sure she heard him whisper 'witch' as she passed him on her way in."

"In olden times hereabouts, witches were burned or hanged or cast into the rising River Lune for less," Jack said with a look of mock-seriousness. "An old pub called the Golden Lion in Lancaster is worth a look, I think."

"And why would we want to look at an old pub in

Lancaster?" Jenny asked, surprised at his choice of outing.

"Probably because it was the traditional place in the seventeenth and eighteenth centuries where people doomed to hang were taken for a last drink before they were measured for a noose," he explained. "It's also the place this facility was offered to the Pendle Witches before their doomsday of being hanged on the moor outside the town."

"Is that really a true story?" Joyce asked, knowing Jack's propensity for elaborating stories that took his fancy.

"The list is on the pub's outside wall," he assured her. "I kid you not. There is also the story that one unfortunate fellow refused the drink, so was taken away and dispatched. The story goes on to point out that if he had *accepted* the drink, he would have still been in the alehouse when his pardon came through, and he would not have been hanged."

"Ouch!" Stick gulped, to the giggles of his wife.

"The original pub was erected on the site in the sixteenth century but replaced by the present building in the eighteenth," Jack pointed out. "And one further point – there are two ghosts that have been seen from time to time – one of them a nun."

"And where is this gory edifice?" Jenny asked.

"On Moor Lane, a very short walk into the centre of the town, just across the road from a car park," he replied. "Anybody fancy a pint?"

The 'No fears!' and 'Not on your life's!' encouraged him to hotfoot it to put the kettle on again, even though it didn't suit him at all!

-o-

"Jack!" Jenny called from upstairs. "Jack! Where are you? I think there's somebody at the front door!"

"Here, Sweet Pea!" he shouted back, to the dulcet tone

of the flushing toilet.

"Where's 'here'?" she asked, not really sure that she wanted to know.

"Just coming out of the downstairs lavatory," he replied jovially. "You know – the one next to the front door that I am about to open. Hello," he went on, as he flung the door wide to a tall young woman of around thirty, and a smaller woman a year or two older than himself. "Can I do you for anything?"

The older woman started to giggle. Her shortish grey hair was becoming a little frizzy in the morning drizzle. "Is Jenny in?" she asked politely.

"Does she owe you money?" Jack answered with a disarming smile.

The younger woman's brow creased into a puzzled frown, but the older woman continued to giggle. "Not as far as we know," she assured him.

"Then who should I say requests the pleasure of her company?" he asked.

"My name is Marina," the older lady replied. "And this is Tracey."

"Jenny!" Jack shouted as he turned to the stairs. "T'Mafia's here!"

The women burst into fits of giggles as Jenny joined them and raised her eyes to the heavens. "Not asking them in?" she said.

"And be owerun wi' wimin?" he replied with a mock look of horror. "No fear!"

"Come in ladies, please," Jenny said to them. "Try to ignore my husband. He's a Yorkshireman."

"Wasn't there a puppetry children's programme on television many years ago with a character called Aqua Marina?" Jack said, as he put on his coat before going out to the car to head off to the local handyman superstore. "Was that you?"

He closed the front door quickly behind him to cackles of amusement from Tracey, the younger woman.

-o-

"*Stingray*," Jack announced baldly, as he snecked the front door behind him on his return.

"*Stingray* what?" Jenny replied, not understanding his reference.

"That's where Aqua Marina appeared as a puppet," Jack pointed out, satisfied with himself. "Couldn't have been modelled on a *real* woman, because *she* was unable to speak. Marina and Tracey gone?" he continued as he flicked on the kettle. "Cup of tea, methinks. You?"

"Go on then," she said with a smile. "Seeing as you need the practice."

Sitting at their large circular table in the small dining part of their kitchen-diner was an unusual occurrence lately. From there they could look through the French doors and beyond the tiny conservatory to the patch of mud they were hoping to call a garden at some stage in the relatively near future.

Fortunately, the garden was south facing so it would flourish, with no damp and dark corners where most plants would find it hard to survive. Unfortunately, because it was south facing and made entirely of glass, the six-feet-by-six-feet conservatory could function only as a greenhouse in the summer months but was heated by a Delonghi oil radiator in the winter. Nightmare!

"What is it with Aqua Marina and her sidekick?" Jack asked, matter of factly as he enjoyed the relaxation his enormous mug of tea provided – along with the jam-topped, buttered scone that matched it perfectly. "Have you decided to become a pukka fully paid-up Jehovah's Witness?"

"Well … yes, I think so," Jenny replied tentatively.

"Why do you ask?"

"Out of interest, actually," he said, steely-eyed. "I'm really … surprised."

"Surprised?" she cut in, a little on the back foot. "Why should you be surprised?"

"It's not that I object to your becoming a JW," Jack started to explain. "That's your business. It's just the nature of *how* you have decided to take that step. Don't get me wrong – I have no objection to whatever you decide to do with your life. It's just that … it would have been nice to have been informed sooner. Why didn't you let me, of all people, know what was in your mind?"

Jenny gazed through the open French doors in embarrassed silence, not knowing how to respond. After a few minutes, she said quietly, "I suppose I was a bit apprehensive at what you might say."

"How long have you known me, Jenny?" he asked, a hurt look gathering on his face. "Ten minutes? You *know* all I would have done would have been to support you in whatever endeavour you might choose. Always have. Always will. Never mind. I *won't* be joining you, of course. Not yet, anyway, but I will support you in your beliefs every step of the way."

"Thank you, my lovely man," Jenny said with an appreciative smile. "You'll get your reward in the next life."

"I was thinking more about teatime!" he insisted good-humouredly.

"Teatime?" she asked, not really sure where this was going.

"Aye," he explained quickly. "Fish and chips at Hodgson's Chippy. Celebration in t'owd jalopy."

"Can I assume that 'jalopy' is one of your words for 'car'?" she asked, not having heard the word before now.

"It is that!" Jack agreed with a laugh. "I've got a brochure in mi bag, as well, that I'd like you to have a look at. Nothing rude or suggestive, you understand, but summat I think you might tek to."

"I'm intrigued," she replied with a giggle. "Now I know it's not a skimpy negligée."

"Well actually, it's a couple of brochures," Jack added. "Same end, different approaches. And that's all I'm saying – for now. Dinner time?"

"By that I suppose you mean 'lunch'?" she said tentatively.

-o-

"You know when we were doing your favourite camping under canvas at Tywyn in Wales with Crowthorn School?" Jack said as they relaxed in their very warm conservatory box.

"My worst nightmare!" she gasped. "Having to put on my makeup and hotbrush my hair in a tent where I couldn't either stand up or look into a mirror – how could I ever forget?"

"Do you remember what we did as a complete group when it threw it down all day?" Jack asked, feeling smug.

"Didn't we go to a cinema or something?" she replied, not too sure.

"Good guess," he agreed, "but what was the film?"

"Ah," she sighed after a moment or two of quiet but unproductive thought. "Don't tell me! Let me think on it. No clues, if you please. I remember the young male care worker who used to wear a white dress shirt, maroon dickie bow and evening jacket, along with khaki shorts and flip flops, every evening for the barbecues at the camp site," Jenny dredged from the depths of her memories.

"One of the reasons why I don't like barbecues now," Jack muttered.

"What, his dress?" Jenny puzzled.

"No, sausage and burgers every night for the whole

179

week," he replied. "Black sausage and charcoal burgers! The sight and sound of them spitting on a flaming grill are enough to make me want to retch."

"*Dances with Wolves*, with Kevin Costner!" Jenny blurted out. "Good film."

"But a bit long at just ower three hours, don't you think?"

"The kids were quiet and attentive for the whole film, *I* thought," Jenny added.

"Talking about sausages," Jack carried on, the spark of a long-sleeping memory lighting his eyes. "Do you remember the incident with the half-pound of raw sausage and that unmarried older female teacher?"

"Tell me about it!" Jenny giggled at the thought. "Jeanie Spence, wasn't it? Late fifties? Didn't Russell Smith secrete those raw sausages in her sleeping bag? I can still hear her screams of anguish shortly after we retired for the night once the sausages had begun to crawl up her legs! At least, I *thought* it was anguish."

Jack burst out laughing as all those dormant memories awoke to cast images into his conscious thoughts.

Chapter 18

Although enjoying their time together generally, Jenny's mood occasionally allowed her sadness at losing Flora Mae to encroach and take over. During these times, day or night, Jack was always there to soothe and settle her, allowing himself to flow with her despair, providing a supporting and ever-available shoulder for her to lean and cry upon.

These episodes were becoming fewer and further between, but when they broke into Jenny's conscious, and semi-conscious states, they caused the dam to burst and could only be assuaged naturally and slowly. During these episodes, Jack drew on his deep well of patience and understanding to ensure she didn't drown in her negative thoughts.

"I don't know what I would have done without you and your understanding, my Jack," she would say as she snuggled up to him either on the settee or in bed.

"That's what I'm here for," he would reply. "It's a natural process that has to take its course. Our emotions will always take over, but they settle eventually. We learn to accept and adapt, but we *never* forget. We must always celebrate your mam's time with us."

Reminiscences of what they had done with Flora Mae and Jim regularly flowed to the surface, generated by some unsought happening that might have been unrelated, but still plucked a strand of consciousness that encouraged memories to be shared and enjoyed.

"I wonder if folks that we know – our nippers and *their* nippers – will remember the things *we* shared, and reminisce as we do about *our* parents?" Jack said after one particularly poignant session concerning Jenny's mam and dad's son, whom they had given up for adoption when they were sixteen.

"They certainly will," Jenny assured him. "How could our Jessie, Florence May, George William, and Val's Mary and Joey *not* remember the stuff we did with and for them? Mary and Joey, for example, wouldn't be where they are today had it not been for your support and help. I hate to think of what 'warm' feelings their father's inaction and ineptitude might generate!"

"I suppose," Jack replied, a faraway look invading his eyes. "And you, my lovely? What might your thoughts be?"

"Absolute devastation!" Jenny croaked, a haunted look overtaking *her* face. "Shall we not dwell, please? How's about thinking instead about doing something *this* holiday that smacks of opulence and luxury and … warmth?"

"Like a holiday in Tenerife, for example?" he threw in, catching her off-balance. "Good food, being looked after and, above all, rest, relaxation and warm … sunshine each and every day."

"Ooh, that sounds right up my street!" she replied with a deep sigh as her eyes narrowed and a contented smile crossed her lips. "Don't tell me you've—"

"No, Sweet Pea, I haven't booked," he reassured her. "But I have just the place ready to have a booking finalised for the week after next. All we have to do is to nip into the Thompson Travel Shop in Lancaster, and then—"

-o-

"So, what is this Thompson Gold thing, anyway?" Jack

asked the young lady in the travel agency. "Does it mean we get showered with gold doubloons the minute we step inside the door?"

"Not … physically," the young lady laughed. "Metaphorically speaking. It's adults only – so no screaming children causing a fuss and haring about the place. Top-class service and rooms, an Atlantic Ocean view, food to die for, and two weeks sheer bliss away from the vagaries of English summer weather."

"Sold!" Jenny drooled. "Jack?"

"To whom should I mek mi cheque out?" he replied with a grin. "Cost?"

"In total, £1,100," the young lady replied.

"That's not bad," Jack eulogised, pen poised ower t'cheque book.

"Each," she added with a smile.

"'Ow much?" he gasped. "Does tha think ahm med o brass?"

The young lady's face began to fall slightly at his brusque response.

"Don't take any notice, love," Jenny assured her. "He's a Yorkshireman."

"Aw, that's all rayt then," Young Lady replied, her winning smile resurfacing. "So am I."

"Well now, that's a rayt good price," Jack said. "Is there 'appen a bit on a discount, one Yorkshire lass to one Yorkshire lad from Normanton?"

"There is now," Young Lady replied. "I'm from Castleford. 'Ow does five per cent grab thi?"

"Like t'sound o' that!" he chuckled. "Total cost £2090 then? As far as it goes…?"

"Don't push thi luck, owd cock!" Young Lass said with a smile, as she took his cheque and handed over the holiday documents. "Tha's gor a rayt grand deal theeyer. 'Ave a rayt good time. Si thi."

"You do realise that all of that is probably built in, Our Jack," Jenny said as they headed for the coffee shop on Sun Street. "All those discounts and stuff."

"It is," Jack agreed. "I should think they can't go beyond certain parameters. But it wor a grand way to negotiate, even if it wor pre-determined. Castleford, eh? Clandestine invasion under way."

"And has been for many a year, I should imagine," she replied. "Before long there will be more Yorkshire folk in Lancashire than born-and-bred Lancastrians."

"Already there," he said. "Already there."

"For goodness' sake!" Jack gasped as they pushed their way into a bustling café. "Can't get rid o' you two at any price."

"Ay up, Jenny and Jack," Joyce replied. "Fancy meeting you two here. Fate, eh?"

"No Stick today?" Jenny asked.

"He's none too well," Joyce explained, as she relished her Danish pastry and percolated coffee. "He's doing a bit of painting that needs seeing to in t'bathroom. Should take him all of ten minutes, I imagine. You're looking pleased with yourself, Our Jack. Booked a 'oliday or summat?"

"You know me so well, Our Joyce," Jack said not taking his eye off the enormous flapjack that had just been placed in front of his drooling face.

"Just booked to do a fortnight in Tenerife at the Los Gigantes hotel in … Los Gigantes," Jenny replied. "Week after next, Saturday to Saturday."

"Snap!" Joyce giggled. "£2,087 for t'fortnight for two."

"Ay up!" Jack exclaimed with a start. "That's three quid less than ours! I shall 'ave to nip back and complain. Did you go to the agency in Market Square?"

"New-fangled … telephone, Jack," Joyce laughed. "It's easy. You should try it sometime. Three pounds is three pounds."

"Time of *your* flight? Jack asked, scarcely able to breathe.

"Same time as yours presumably, as there's onny one each day," Joyce replied. "We might be sitting next to you."

"Oh no!" Jack moaned in mock shock, head in hands. "Not that! Castle Secure car park just outside Manchester airport?" he continued, after ordering another pot of tea and another flapjack.

"I think so," she said. "Sounds familiar. I left that one – the only thing, I hasten to add – to Stick to organise."

"I'm not comparing on that one," Jack said, holding up his hands in surrender. "You've probably got the cost down to thripence less than me."

"Well, I'm off now," Joyce said, once she had drained the dregs of her cup. "Packing to finish off."

"To finish off?" Jack gasped. "We've not even started yet. Have we, Jenny?"

"Try looking in the little bedroom, Jack," Jenny said with a self-satisfied smile. "We're not all last minuters."

"Can't believe it!" Jack exclaimed with a soft whistle once Joyce had vacated her seat. "We're about to have a fortnight's holiday in t'Canaries wi' our best friends. How good's that?"

"You couldn't have written the script," Jenny agreed. "That alone will be five weeks away this year."

"And all of them in twenty-five to thirty degrees centigrade all-ower warmth," he said. "Just as *you* like it."

-o-

"Bloomin' ummer!" Jack gasped as he set his right foot on the top step of the stairway down from the plane door to the tarmac in Tenerife airport. "Now, that's warm."

The extreme heat had taken him completely by surprise. It was much hotter than he had felt in Southern Spain the last couple of times he'd had to endure such weather that was alien to his metabolism. As a child, he had always considered summers to be extreme when he had to carry a large glass bottle of cold water with him wherever he went. *This*, however, put him on a different planet that he wasn't too sure he would be able to endure.

The low, single-decker bus, which was about to carry all passengers from where the plane had come to rest on the tarmac beside the runway, was little better. Unfortunately the anticipated air conditioning wasn't working – or the driver had forgotten to push money into its meter to turn it on.

The coach waiting dutifully in the coach rank to transport them to their hotel was slightly cooler, and hopefully the air conditioning would spit into life once it was on the road. Fortunately, the full coach was destined for their hotel alone at Los Gigantes, with no intermediate stops.

Jack couldn't believe the banana plantations they motored through and the glimmer of the sea to their left almost all the way through their hour-long journey north from the airport. What really astounded him, though, was the hotel's position on a promontory into the Atlantic Ocean, with the third-highest sea cliffs in the world to its northern edge. Spectacular in the extreme. Boy, was he looking forward to settling into their room with its sea views and its air conditioning!

"Dinner will begin its service in an hour at six o'clock, Ladies and Gentlemen," the tiny female rep, who smacked of recent school leaver, announced over the coach's tannoy as they were about to disembark. "All you will need to gain access to the dining room is the ID your hotel reps will give you. Hope you enjoy your stay and don't forget the UK is only fourteen nights away."

"Smart arse!" Stick muttered as they trooped into the hotel's traditionally carved, wooden-ceilinged reception lounge, with its comfortably aged settees and air conditioning that was so severe it all but froze the sweat droplets to exposed skin. Heaven or what?

Tired in the extreme from their early morning start, they couldn't wait for dinner to be followed by an early evening night cap and bed. Unpacking could wait until morning, unless Jeeves, their manservant, was prepared to do it now – noiselessly.

-o-

For Stick and Jack, the first five days passed in a blur of sunbed snoozing under a shady parasol, interspersed with copious amounts of food and drink brought to them by staff driving buggies.

"I could cope with this for the whole time here," Jack often said, as he brushed the food crumbs from his mouth before tackling an ice-cream cone and a cold can of something resembling local cola.

"Please wake me up a week on Friday," Stick would reply, as he settled for another snooze before cooling off in the salt-water swimming pool for a little while, until the need for sleep warned him he should regain his snooze bed before he fell asleep in the pool.

Joyce and Jenny laughed quietly at their husbands as *they* sought something to do other than lazing about in the sun all day. Five days was quite enough for them.

"Do you fancy joining in with the games they play here at about this time every day?" Jenny asked quietly, not wishing to disturb her husband.

"What sort of games?" Joyce replied. "Board games?"

"'Stop-you-getting-bored games', more like," Jenny said with a shrug, causing them both to burst into a fit of quiet giggles. "I've seen adverts around the place for boules, darts, pool, hoopla. Do you want to have a look what might be on and what's involved?"

187

"Too right!" Joyce agreed. "And maybe our sleepy heads might want to join in before we go home."

"Don't hold your breath," Jenny advised. "My Jack's not a games' enthusiast. But we'll see."

-o-

Jack had experienced neither four-course meals, nor such warm balmy evenings before. The glorious, red setting sun created such a captivating out-of-this-world display through tall, silhouetted palm trees. He had never been given to standing and simply … watching such emotionally eye-watering events that he could not touch, either physically or intellectually.

"I tell you what," Stick said, after filling his belly to bursting point at dinner, "I heard on the news before we came here that tonight there is going to be a significant meteor shower in the western sky. I was wondering if any of you might be interested in staying up to see it? Jack?"

"Count me in, Old Chap," his friend replied. "Do we need to go for a run around the pool twenty times to run off these bellies we seem to be developing?"

"Joyce? Jenny?" Stick asked, turning to the girls. "Jack and I could always fetch a blanket and a pillow or two, if you'd prefer."

"Why?" Jenny gasped. "When will it be starting?"

"God's not sent down stone tablets yet to tell us the programme time, I'm afraid," Jack scoffed. "Probably about eleven?"

"Between eleven and one, I think," Stick said with a shrug. "At home that's usually been about right. I've witnessed several ower this last couple of years."

"It's ten o'clock already," Jack added. "A couple of blankets and the odd pillow?"

"If we have to," Joyce muttered.

"I'll go for the bedding if you set out the moon beds

188

down yonder by the pond, facing west," Jack offered.

Everything was straightforward, apart from the odd stare from couples making their way to the lifts to regain their rooms to retire for the night. Fortunately, the friends were only on the third floor so Jack was quick, even though he stopped to have a peek from their room balcony to see how Stick was getting on.

"Two spare pillows and a couple of spare blankets," he muttered to himself as he hoiked them out of the wardrobe cupboard. Should he take a cup of tea down for everyone? No; it would be cold by the time he got there. Have to wait until they had witnessed this wonderful display. By now, Jack wasn't so sure that it was such a good idea. How long were they prepared to wait if it didn't happen to time?

"Here we are," he said quietly as he joined his clan. "Are we warm enough?"

"It's Tenerife!" Stick scoffed. "In the summer! Of course we're warm enough. Well, I am, anyway."

By this time, the outside entertainment area and the stage had ceased to function, although the bar was still technically open and serving a few hardy drinkers with their night-time tipples and snacks.

"Ha, ha!" Stick chortled as he pointed skywards. "Shooting star! Now the fun starts."

Unfortunately, by midnight that glorious celestial display had been the only one.

"Well," Jack said, giving Jenny a gentle nudge back to consciousness. "I'm off to bed. Jenny's tired."

"And I'm cold," Joyce added. "Need to reclaim mi warm comfy bed."

"Did I miss anything?" Jenny asked, as she tried to de-stiffen her cramped body and open her eyes, which wanted to stay closed.

"Just the one," Jack said.

"Shower?" Jenny asked.

"Shooting star," Jack replied. "There might be some tomorrow night, but I shan't be stopping up on the off-chance."

"Me neither!" Joyce and Stick chorused.

-o-

"We're off to the harbour to take a boat ride out to see the whales and dolphins," Jack announced as they ate their very appealing breakfast the following morning. "Any takers?"

"Count me in," Joyce replied enthusiastically. "I've allus had a yen to see them and be up close with 'em in the wild."

"Not too sure about that," Stick said warily. "We don't have to be too near, do we? I mean, in t'water wi''em?"

"Don't be so soft!" Joyce scoffed.

"Not allowed to be in t'water within six hundred metres, Stick, I'm afraid," Jack replied with a grin. "All this, you realise, is not because I have my finger on the world's pulse but because I've read the occasional pamphlet or three in reception. Ten o'clock all right?"

Chapter 19

The hotel had been built on a small promontory of land where the designers and builders must have had vision by the shovelful because there was nothing else thereabouts – no houses, no roads, no means whereby guests might access the building except by boat. This was the ultimate in peace and seclusion for those that wanted – needed – to cut themselves off from the rest of humanity, to spend two weeks in splendid luxurious isolation.

Now a small village had grown steadily around the edifice, which had maintained its original shape from those early days forty or so years before.

Boutique shops, small *supermercados* and fashion outlets catered for all needs, from the necessities to maintain and sustain life in general to those that tickled the tastes of a well-heeled clientele that wanted for nothing. A plethora of bars and restaurants and snacking places dared passing potential customers to dip in to try a wide range of exotic foods not available on more northerly European tables.

Quite frankly, all these sorts of foods brought tears to Jack's eyes and a rising nausea to his throat. He would rather have eaten his own toenails than allow squid, octopus, crab, mussels or any other Iberian delicacy within even a yard of *his* tastebuds. The promise of a more recognisable menu was what had elbowed him towards *this* hotel that catered mainly for British tastes in food.

"Look at the temperature!" Stick gasped, pointing out a large digital display that grew magnificently atop a twenty-foot pole out of a little island in the middle of a busy road. This road carried coaches down the hill to the harbour/marina to allow hordes of holidaymakers from outlying towns and villages to board a growing fleet of pleasure boats that promised whale and dolphin watching trips, with a snack lunch thrown in for good measure.

"Twenty-five degrees centigrade! Already?" Joyce cried incredulously. "But it's onny half past ten – in the morning! Can't wait to get on yon boat for a hint of fresh air in mi face."

"And a dip in a bay out yonder, just shy of the cliffs, before a lunch of chicken salad in the sun," Jack piped in.

"How on earth do you know that?" Jenny asked, her question edged with more than a little scepticism.

"Read it on the board that we just passed at the crest of the hill that we are about to descend!" he chuckled. "Not sure I'm looking forward to the return journey, mind you. Talk about heart-attack hill! It'll tek us a couple of days to get back up that one, I should imagine."

"Hello. Good morning," an English voice drew Jack's attention to an open shop front. He turned sharply to see a lovely young lady dressed in tight-fitting shorts and a loose, floaty top.

"I recognise that accent," Jack said. "Which part of Yorkshire do you come from? Dewsbury? Huddersfield?"

"The latter," she replied. "How did you guess that?"

"T'wasn't a guess, my lovely," he assured her.

"He's a Yorkshireman, Lass," Joyce butted in, "and we can tell our own. We're all from t'West Riding, not far from your place."

"*This* is my place now," she replied with a satisfied smile.

"Doesn't matter where folks hang their coyts, they niver

lose their Yorkshire accent," Joyce explained, "especially with Jack here on hand. He could virtually pinpoint the street you lived on."

"Any road, we'd love a boat ride, if you please," Jack added. "Where do we purchase such a thing, wi' these 'ere Yourose?"

The young lady sold them the tickets and directed them to the far side of the marina. What a sight met their unsuspecting eyes as they negotiated a last, steeper part of the road downwards! Gift and confectionary shops greeted them, intent on seducing them to enter and look at what they had to offer. Surely there would be *something* eye-catchingly attractive for them not to be able to live without?

Then the full vista of the marina dragged their thoughts away from all that minor, unnecessary bric-a-brac. It was at least two hundred yards square of calm water, sheltered by mountainous parapeted outer walls that exuded menace *and* safety. The walkway, a yard below the parapet, had been fenced off because several strollers of late had missed their footing and fallen to the dockside two yards below, resulting in broken bones and other nasty injuries.

The glistening water was divided by four long pontoons that allowed moorings for a large variety of pleasure boats, small put-puts and luxury stop-over yachts, around the bottom of which swished myriad shoals of many-sized mullet. Stingrays and turtles had been known to nestle in the sand beneath, with crabs snapping in and out of the man-made piles of rocks and concrete blocks. The gigantic Los Gigantes cliffs glowered above and beyond, cutting out the sun entirely at certain times during most of these idyllic days.

"I think I could live here," Joyce said, as they made their way to the pleasure craft moored at the other side of this 'inland sea'.

"Unfortunately, my lovely, you are not old enough," Stick replied with a shrug and a heartfelt sigh. "Unless I snuff it and you claim on mi life insurance."

"Don't put ideas into her head, Old Chap," Jack added to the conversation with a hearty chuckle." Let's see what this jaunt brings, shall we?"

"*Hola mis amigos!*" a gravelly voice welcomed them. "Are you eer for zee treep out to sea to say *hola* to zee dolfeenz in our leetle yot?"

"*Si, muchacho,*" Jack replied. "*Vamos quando?*"

"You speek Spaneesh, senor?" the man said.

"*Un poquito,*" Jack said. "And I would imagine you speak much better English than that stuff you are trotting out."

"Jack!" Jenny remonstrated with her husband. "You can't say that. It's—"

"Very true," the man agreed in impeccable English. "Your husband is correct."

"Then why not use the excellent English you have?" Jack asked. "Do you think we are naïve enough to believe and accept? That accent sounds very Mancunian, by the way. Spent much time in Manchester?"

"You are very astute, *mi amigo,*" the man said with a sheepish grin. "Spent a lot of years there with … a girl I knew when I was much … younger. My name's Lukie, by the way, and I belong to this glorious boat here in front of us, *The Nashira Uno.* We're due to set off in the not-too-distant future, so on you go and choose your place. I would suggest the front, in the seats just below the window."

The sedate dawdle around the other boats to the staggered exit out to sea was a disappointment for Jack. He thought it might have been full throttle from start to exit. He did not know, of course, that the marina authority, in keeping with all others in Spain, had imposed a limit of four miles per hour to obviate bow waves that might cause damage.

Jack wasn't disappointed for long. As soon as their boat had crawled around the last corner, full throttle thrust his head and body back into his seat, forcing the air out of his lungs and turning his mouth into a wide uncontrollable grimace. Now that *was* better!

"Jack? Jack!" Jenny's voice forced its way back into his consciousness. "You all right? You look a little—"

"Sickly?" Joyce added with a modicum of concern.

"Just enjoying the speed, really," Jack replied. "Not been *that* fast on water before. I'm pretty sure the rowing boats in Peasholm Park in Scarborough, or on Waterloo Lake in Roundhay Park in Leeds, didn't have that effect on me. Did you know that in the late nineteenth and early twentieth century, there used to be a steamer that plied its trade on that *very* lake? When it was too old to carry on chugging about, they sank it. Another one – battery-operated, I believe – took ower until it finished service in 1923."

"Well, I never did," Joyce said with a twinkle. "Not a lot of people know that." Her Michael Caine impersonation didn't cut the mustard at all, although her husband laughed out of politeness.

"What would we do without you and your knowledge, eh, Jack?" Joyce went on after a little pause, genuinely amazed at the depth of useless information floating around aimlessly in his head. All it ever took was one almost insignificant snippet to stir some almost equally insignificant piece of obscure information to ease its way into the light of day. Even Jack had no idea where it all came from; 'the original sponge' his granddad Jud always used to say.

Lukie's voice cut into their conversations to announce that a group of slow-breaching pilot whales had just arrived. At the same time, a pod of Atlantic dolphins shot through the area not twenty yards from them. Jack was stunned into silence as the others gasped in amazement.

"Never seen anything like it," Jack marvelled at the unbelievable display they had witnessed. The onny thing to start to rival that was a dose of chicken salad and crisps.

They had edged into a largish, sheltered bay a mile or two up the coast, where the water was deep but crystal clear, with a myriad of iridescently coloured fish chasing each other through and around weeds and sunken rocks. Once the boat had anchored, Lukie announced that folks could swim for a while before lunch was ready.

"Anybody for a dip?" Stick ventured.

"Looks a bit chilly to me," Joyce said with a bit of a shiver. "I might just dip mi toes for a bit."

"I think I might join you," Jenny agreed.

Jack said nothing. He simply ambled to the deck's edge and launched himself into the invitingly blue water among the multi-coloured fish. They were having none of it, scattering quickly, wondering what lump of a living creature had just disturbed *their* world.

-o-

"Did we enjoy that little excursion, my dear friends?" Jack asked, once they had regained terra firma.

"The trip was lovely," Joyce replied.

"Couldn't have been better," Stick agreed. "Except for—"

"Dinner!" Jenny and Jack chorused.

"Could have been hotter," Jenny said.

"And there needed to be more of it," Jack grumbled. Trust Jack to state the obvious! "I do believe I can see a caff just down the harbour from where we came in. I wonder— Yes! They do!"

"Do what?" Jenny asked, puzzled by his obtuse answer.

Sometimes she just couldn't understand his logic at all.

"Look at what that chap at that table close to the edge is eating," Jack pointed out.

"Yes, please!" Stick exclaimed with an excited grin. "A chip butty – in a tea cake. I'm having one of those!"

"*Dos butties de fritas para mi, por favor,* senorita," Jack said to the waitress, much to his friend Stick's amusement.

"Two chip butties just for you? All rayt, luv," she replied in her best West Riding accent. "In tea cakes all rayt?"

"Two for me as well," Stick added quickly before she left, "and one each for the ladies, please."

"That'll be six in all, then? Would that be six mugs of tea as well to go wi''em?" she asked, noting it all down on a scrap of paper she had fished out of her pinny pocket.

"If you please," Jack said. "That's a grand West Riding accent you have there. Wakefield?"

"Aye, Lad. Spot on. Sharlston," she replied.

"Gerraway!" Jack gasped. "We're all from Normanton, just dahn t'road from you. Mi dad and granddad worked dahn Sharlston pit all their working lives. Small world."

"Too rayt," she said with a smile. "There'll be extra chips and tomato sauce for compatriots as well – on me."

-o-

"I'm not really sure that I needed that chip butty," Joyce gasped, patting her belly as they struggled up heart-attack hill back to their hotel.

"Me neither," Jenny agreed. "I think I need a lie down before dinner."

"Gerraway!" Stick and Jack chorused, smacking their lips in glee at feeling the enjoyment of the wonderful day they had just shared.

"They were a grand finale to a fab day," Jack said, slapping his friend on the back. "In fact, I think we could—"

"Eat 'em again!" they both exclaimed, punching the air.

"Ruby!" A loud squawk interrupted them as they passed a restaurant on a bend about halfway up the hill. Grateful for an excuse to have a breather, they gathered outside the open doors, inside of which they could just about make out a spacious meshed cage. Its occupant seemed to be a large green-and-blue iridescent parrot, perpetually dancing along an oversized perch.

"Now then," Jack said as he approached the cage carefully so as not to scare the bird and its companion grey parrot. "What's *your* name?"

"Ruby!" the bird screeched loudly after a moment of examining Jack's face. "Ruby! My name … Ruby!"

"I know you can connect with most people, Our Jack, but this is ridiculous," Jenny gasped, causing Joyce to giggle and Stick to guffaw loudly.

"Too noisy! Too noisy!" the green parrot screeched. "Silly bugger! Silly bugger!"

"Woah!" Jenny exclaimed. "Listen to that naughty bird! Hello, naughty bird."

"Hello. Ruby!" the bird screeched in reply, and then in a much deeper voice it said, "*Hola!*"

They all laughed at its pert response. As Jenny put her hand slowly to the mesh, Ruby nipped her little finger gently. "Ouch!" Jenny gasped with a giggle. "Naughty bird!"

Just as they turned to leave, the green parrot stretched its wings, caught its grey companion and received a nip in return, to which *it* screeched, "Ouch!"

"One smart bird," Jack exclaimed with a laugh, to be joined by his companions as they reached the hotel. "Don't know about you, but I'm ready for a sit down wi' a cup of tea."

"How are you going to manage wi' this Spanish rubbish, Our Jack?" Joyce asked with a bit of a concerned frown. "Take to drinking coffee, which, incidentally, is just as bad?"

"I'm not, Joyce," he replied with a grin. "I brought mi own Yorkshire Tea bags from 'ome."

"Home from home then, eh Jack?" Joyce asked, pretty sure what his answer might be.

"Actually … not really," he replied. "The two main features that decide that? This place has got space and it's … warm for most of the year. I think I *could* … live here. Music to your ears, eh, Jenny?"

"Do you know," Jenny said, surprised to hear his assessment, "I might try to get you to relocate at some stage when we are retired from this dire rat race that we seem to have become entrenched in."

-o-

The choice of food at *this* hotel was breath-taking. Jack had never seen such a wide range of succulent foods before – apart from the unacceptable Spanish rubbish like prawns, crab, octopus, squid and all other seafoods that weren't battered cod and haddock. Seafood was something he *would* eat only if there was *really* nothing else other than vomit left in the world.

"Did you ever miss your time at Normanton Grammar, Stick, Old Chap?" Jack asked his friend over a glass of Lumumba in the lounge after dinner.

"Don't remember much about it," his friend replied, "seeing as I left round about Year 3."

"Things keep dropping into my mind on a regular basis these days," Jack said. "They always arrive in great detail at inconvenient times when I'm not able to record them – middle of the night, or when I'm in class, or when I'm on—"

"Jack!" Jenny interrupted. "We don't really wish to know all that, thank you."

"With writing a story or planning lessons, I *was* going to say," he added, pulling his tongue out at her.

Joyce and Stick laughed, knowing Jack of old.

"Although the time in the sixth form was tedious and had become anathema to me big style, there *were* funny times," Jack went on. "I'm sure you might be able to relate to these reminiscences where *you* ended up, Stick."

"Too rayt, Owd Cock," Stick assured him.

"As prefects in 1963 to 1964 we had a special – small – room just for us at the end of the school on Church Lane," Jack went on. "December, it was. Snow on the ground. Cold as hell."

"Since when was hell supposed to be cold?" Jenny scoffed.

"Figure of speech," he said, discarding her interruption with a brief wave. "Anyway, it was getting on for the end of dinner time when the outside door was flung open, and someone lobbed a rather large snowball in among us and scarpered real quick. I recognised Geoff Bullock and Mick Carey's giggles straight away. I nodded to Pierre Gwillow and Brian Flynn, and we three set off in pursuit. They weren't expecting any comeback, so they took off like bats out of hell. Mick Carey disappeared, but Geoff Bullock headed swiftly into main school through the middle doors overlooking a large grassy knoll next to the longer stretch of Church Lane. When we got inside, he was nowhere to be seen.

"'Where's he gone?' Pierre asked, puzzled because the main corridor was long and had many doors dotted along its length.

"'I think he's nipped into our Year Six form room,' I said, pointing at the little alcove leading to the room's door.

"We opened the door carefully, to see Bullock at the bottom end of the room, close to where a large overhang gave access to an almost hidden window. I winked at Pierre Gwillow and, as Bullock started to climb up the wall shelving to reach the platform overhang near to the window, I said, 'Stay there, Pierre, and I'll climb up after him and throw him down to you.'

"He wasn't a large lad wasn't Geoff Bullock, so he took what I – a rather large First-Fifteen prop forward – had said very seriously. He picked up a large plank of wood that must have been loose and used it to smash the window," Jack went on.

"But why?" Joyce asked, a bit nonplussed by the story.

"Presumably because he believed Our Jack's word," Stick explained. "He wouldn't have carried out his threat, though. Would you, Jack?"

Jack paused for a moment or two before saying, "Who knows? Maybe not, or even … maybe."

"So, what happened then?" Jenny asked, gobsmacked by the unexpected story.

"Pierre and I returned to the prefects' room, chortling as we went," Jack said. "Served the bugger right. He shouldn't have chucked that fateful snowball. He didn't do anything like that again. As the window hadn't been smashed through and not left any broken glass on the stretch of garden outside, Bullock clandestinely brought in a piece of glass and some putty early the next day and mended it."

"How did you know that?" Jenny asked.

"Because it was our form room," Jack explained. "I got in early next day and climbed up the wall shelving to inspect the damage that he had almost finished repairing before my eyes. He'd made a good job of it, too."

"Lads, eh, Joyce," Jenny said with a sigh. "Can you imagine doing anything like that?"

"Too right I could!" Joyce exclaimed forcefully. "I wouldn't have let anybody get one over on me, either!"

Chapter 20

The enormous problem with wonderfully enjoyable holidays, lazing in the sun and doing something or nothing at all, was that those warm days were not endless.

"I could get used to this sort of life," Jack said at breakfast, four or so days before they were due to be repatriated.

"Have you ever thought about relocating, or even buying a holiday pad?" Stick asked through a mouthful of avocado and kiwi fruit.

"Would love to," Jack replied enthusiastically. "I would have a problem with not being able to afford food or shelter at this stage in our life, however. Not old enough to retire yet, and I don't see anyone forming a queue to offer me a golden handshake to allow us not to have to traipse to work five days a week."

"What do you fancy doing today? Anybody?" Jenny asked.

"Well," Jack offered, "when we were down at the marina yesterday, I noticed a fantastic-looking bright yellow speedboat called *The Ocean Warrior* tied up to the quay, near to where we had our chip butties. I also noticed that it costs ten euros to have a ride – a speedy ride – out to see the whales – guaranteed. They also have started to offer 'parascending'."

"Para-whating?" Jenny gasped. "Never heard of it."

"It's summat to do with parachutes, I think," Jack tried to explain. "But going up instead of coming down. Anyway, we could find out today. Stick? Joyce? Jenny?"

"Go on, then!" Jenny agreed. "Joyce?"

"I'm game," she replied. "Stick? I know you're not too – what shall we say? – enthralled by such stuff, but—"

"Love to," Stick added quickly. "We can onny give it a try."

"Excellent!" Jack enthused. "We need to be down there for ten-ish to set off at around half past. All rayt?"

-o-

"*Buenos dias*, senorita," Jack said to the young woman close to the berth of the *Ocean Warrior*. She was petite, slim, wore a baseball cap, reflective sunglasses, and was attired for a day in the hot sun.

"Hi, there," she replied with an obvious American accent. "Would you like to ride the waves in our new *Warrior*? That was a figure of speech, actually, because today it is flat calm out there. Anyway…"

"Sure would," Jack replied in a very poor attempt at a similar accent.

"Sorry about my husband's obvious Yorkshire attempt to replicate your wonderfully lilting accent," Jenny replied with a smile. "He believes he can speak a lot of languages."

"Actually, I can speak six fluently," Jack assured her.

"Six?" the little American lady gasped.

"Yes," he went on. "French, English, Spanish, Yiddish, Radish and Rubbish." They all laughed at his straight-faced delivery.

"No need to apologise for his funny," the American lady assured them. "I appreciate that sort of humour."

"Poor girl!" Joyce said with an apologetic grimace. "Very sad."

"Tickets, then?" Jack asked again. "Any discount for

being … human?”

“Not really,” she replied, taking his money. “But we might do you a deal if you decide to have a go at parascending tomorrow? My name’s Betty, by the way. And your boatman is Lorenzo.”

“OK, Betty Bytheway, thank you,” Jack said. “Do we have a hoist to lift us down to water level? It *is* quite a way down to the boat, and I might miss if I were to jump.”

“Steps to your right,” Betty explained. “And if you wouldn’t mind taking off your footwear before climbing onto the boat? Just leave them on the jetty under the stepway, they’ll be safe there as no-one else has access.”

-o-

“Anybody fancy a chip butty … again?” Jack asked his friends as they set foot on terra firma once more. The smell of frying chips ambushed his nostrils and, as it had turned midday, he felt the need to assuage his obvious peckishness.

“Count me in!” Stick agreed with glee imprinted on his eager face.

“Girls?” Jack went on.

“Not that hungry, particularly after that enormous breakfast and the bouncy ride in yon yellow flash,” Joyce said with a dismissive frown.

“I completely agree with you, Joyce,” Jenny butted in. “How about if we have a look around these shops? And you two bottomless pits can go and … fill your faces.”

“Not a problem for me,” Jack answered.

“Me neither,” Stick agreed. “I’m starving.”

“But you’re *always* starving, Husband,” Joyce said with a grin. “I’m sure you’ve got worms.”

“Don’t worry about us,” Jack said. “We’ll eat your share.”

“Did you ever go to Heath Common Fair?” Jack asked

his friend through a mouthful of delectable chip butty.

"You mean the one that virtually took over the … common land near … Heath Hall?" Stick grinned.

"No, daft bugger, the common land next door to the Sea of Tranquillity on t'Moon!" Jack replied through a chortle as well as a mouthful of chips.

"Which self-respecting Normantunian – or whatever the collective noun is – would knowingly miss that Easter weekend of fun?" Stick insisted. "Went every year up to my being eighteen. Going to teacher training college was t'onny thing that curtailed that."

"I can still hear t'music and taste t'smells, from hot dogs to t'cordite on t'rifle range to t'waltzers' machinery," Jack added. "You?"

"T'taste o' candyfloss and nougat, and all t'other stuff as med you feel sick when you'd had too much to eat," Stick reminisced with his eyes closed, a look of happy contentedness lodged in his face.

"We allus went as a family – mi mam, me and mi dad," Jack replied. "T'onny problem wi' that was that we wanted to catch a bus just by the Co-op near t'Hark to Mopsey! pub. They used to come all right, but because the fair was popular the buses were always full."

"We lived Church Lane way on, not far from t'grammar school," Stick said. "So, we'd catch t'bus in town. Just joined the queue and waited our turn."

"Didn't the bus company put on extra buses that shuttled from Normanton town centre to Heath Common and back, turning round in Normanton's Market Square?" Jack asked.

"I believe they did," Stick replied. "T'onny time of year that t'company made any money!"

"I remember one year we got to the Mopsey bus stop just as a bus arrived," Jack went on. "I think I was nine. Anyway, as this old bus that had seen better days chugged up, mi dad urged, 'Come on! There's room for us,' and legged it, leaping on t'foot plate at the back as it set off. We couldn't make it, so he went without us. Mi mother called him all the names she could think of – under her breath, of course. She always swore he'd done it to spend some time in yon little pub in that village by the Common. King's Arms, I think it was called."

"Aye," Stick agreed with a snort. "Mi dad always used his gammy leg as an excuse to limp along to that hostelry, ostensibly for a 'sit down'. He allus stank of ale when we caught up with him at 'ome time."

"Like most men that took their families there, I should imagine," Jack said. "I took mi tanner pocket money, which unfortunately didn't go very far, but mi dad wouldn't give me any more. His beer money was meant for just that. Sacrosanct."

"What was your favourite thing about t'owd fair, Jack?" Stick asked after another mouthful.

"It 'ad to be t'coconut shy," he added with a grin. "Not because o' t'coconuts you couldn't possibly win, but because mi dad couldn't even hit 'em. In all t'time I went, I never saw anybody knock one off."

"Probably because they weren't *real* coconuts," Stick said. "Long thin stick with a couple of sloping cups near to t'top, and t'coconuts to be knocked off were med o … wood, weighted at t'bottom end wi' lead. All the coconut 'hair' was stuck on. Nigh on impossible to knock off, even if you were spot on with your shot.

"A chap I once remember – big gorilla of a man – hit the stick so hard with his shot that it broke clean in two. The bloke at the shy tried to say he hadn't won because the coconuts hadn't been hit," he went on. "Gorilla man physically 'insisted' that he was owed two coconuts because there had been two on that shy."

"And did he?" Jack grinned. "Get his just rewards?"

"Too right he did!" Stick explained. "Threatened to take the stall apart if he didn't. The stall owner lost out big style as well, because a lot of people had seen what had happened and refused to visit this shyster's … shies."

"What about *your* favourite then, Stick?" Jack asked, intrigued what it might be.

"I liked a few things really," Stick replied. "Rifle range, waltzers, and sometimes t'ghost train when it came. But my favourite of all was rolling a penny through yon glass screen to try to get it into a slit at the far end. I won only once, and it paid out a load of pennies to the tune of two and a tanner – a lot of money in those days."

"Twelve-and-a-half pence in today's money," Jack said, translating it into present day cash. "Or perhaps a couple of quid in real terms?"

"Still eating and reminiscing, you two?" Joyce's voice interrupted their quiet thoughts.

"Nay," Stick said. "Food's long gone, and mi stomach's being attacked by another dire dose of starvation."

"Me too," Jack agreed. "I don't see how I'm going to survive until dinner in a couple of hours' time."

They both sucked in their cheeks as if they had lost a lot of weight around their jowls from lack of food, causing Joyce and Jenny to snigger at the sight.

"Come on then, you poor things," Joyce mocked. "Shall I call for an ambulance to cart you up the hill back to the hotel, or should we stop for a snack along the way?"

–o–

"And how on earth do I get from here to … up there?" Jack said to Lorenzo with bravado and a liberal sprinkling of trepidation. The parascending uplift yellow canopy billowed enormously in the slipstream from the speeding boat only ten feet above the boat's deck. "I don't have to jump. Do I?"

"You see the 'trapeze' below the chute?" Lorenzo explained. "That is where you sit."

"Daring young man on the flying trapeze, eh?" Stick quipped, eyeing it with more than a little apprehension.

"What happens if the rope snaps?" Jenny asked, not sure whether she wanted to take the risk.

"I tell you a story – true story," Lorenzo offered, a wicked glint in his eye. "One day I take out two married couples to do joint parascend for each couple. The ladies went up first together, and as they reached full height one of the gentlemen offered me one thousand euros to cut the rope. I laughed. He laughed – with his friend. Joke? *You* guess. Five minutes later the rope, she broke, and the ladies end in the sea. Not sure about his reaction."

"What happened to the ladies?" Jenny gasped.

"They die," Lorenzo replied, straight-faced.

Jenny and Joyce gasped in horror, hands clasped to mouths.

"I joke," Lorenzo said as he burst into a guffaw, to be joined immediately by Jack and Stick. "The ladies float down slowly to the sea, and we pick them up quickly, along with the chute. Fortunately, we have the other chute for individual rides and all were happy. The man, he very quiet back to marina. Who take first ride?"

"I'll go first," Jack offered, "and I'll check out all the gubbins while I'm up there."

"Just like Our Jack," Joyce said with a laugh. "Making sure it's all right for the rest of us."

-o-

The breeze strengthened as the yellow boat gathered speed, billowing the chute above Jack's head. The higher he rose, the quieter his surroundings became, painting a picture below him almost as if he were a spectator from another world. The slight swell of the sea magically became as in an undisturbed mill pond, and the breeze freshened only enough to disturb his hair. Wow! What an amazing sight! He could barely see the waving arms of wife and friends in the yellow smudge on the sea below.

What was that off to his right? No, couldn't be! A leaping dolphin and … and … the ephemeral glistening flash of an … Atlantic blue marlin swordfish, his sharp nose ready to joust with all comers.

So much to see and such a fleeting time in which to see it all! Jack could have stayed there all day. It was so peaceful and quiet, he could almost hear his heart beating in his heaving chest.

"I couldn't believe how otherworldly it was up there!" Jack gasped, as he was winched back to the gently swaying landing strip at the back of the boat as it sliced its way through the warm Atlantic waters between the islands of Tenerife and her sister island La Gomera. "And of all things, I saw—"

"An Atlantic marlin swordfish," Jenny butted in.

"How on earth did you know that, Jenny Ingles?" Jack said as he struggled out of his safety harness.

"Lorenzo told us," she replied with a giggle.

"Next please for the stairway to heaven!" Lorenzo called, keeping the boat at an even pace to allow the chute to remain billowy.

"That would be Jenny!" Joyce and Stick chorused.

"She's the brave one among the rest of us," Joyce added. "Then we'll be able to see that it's safe before we decide. I can tell by his face that Stick's not owerly in love with the idea of floating up to heaven yet."

-o-

"Wow! Wow! And double wow!" Stick gasped as the gang made its way up the marine steps from the *Ocean Warrior's* berth. "I think it has to be—"

"Chip butty time?" Jack added enthusiastically, as he shouldered his way towards the only empty table at their usual butty bar.

"What was the sign you were making when you were up there, Jenny?" Jack asked, not sure about the way she had been bringing her arms together repeatedly over her head. "It looked like you were trying to tell us there was a crocodile below."

"I was trying to tell you I could see a hammerhead shark not far from the boat," she explained with a laugh.

"There has been one reported around here very recently," Lorenzo added. "Only a youngster, but even so it is around five metres long."

"Give you a nasty gumming, I think," Jack said, pulling a warning grimace. "Do they live around here, Lorenzo?"

"Probably three or four sightings a year," he replied. "They don't go near the beaches – probably because of the black sand."

"Black sand?" Joyce added. "Sand isn't black. It's … yellow and … sandy."

"Unless an oil tanker flushes out its bilges, which ultimately finds its way onto the sands close by," Stick said.

"The beaches here are black," Lorenzo explained as he was taking his leave of them, "as you can see from the entrance to the marina. It *is* volcanic. The nearest sand-coloured beaches to these islands are on the Western Moroccan coasts, about two hundred miles away."

"Did *you* ever go on any trips while you were at school, Stick?" Jack asked as he munched on his mountainous chip butty. Why was it that the Tenerifean tea cakes were twice the size of those back at home? "At QEGS, I mean? I know about the one we did as eleven-year-olds at Normanton Grammar School, but later on, when you were older?"

"Not really," Stick replied. "We had to pay for anything

like that and mi mam couldn't really afford it, what with four other nippers to cater for. Mi dad were summat of a ne'er-do-well, playing a lot on his gammy leg that wasn't *that* gammy. I found that out later on from talking to mi Uncle Sid's daughter, Joan."

"That'd be your Cousin Joan, then," Joyce added. "She was a lovely lass that married a rotten bugger as never worked. She called him out often about his idleness, earning many a clout from him because of it."

"I didn't know that," Stick said.

"You wouldn't have," Joyce said. "That sort of stuff went on behind closed doors, with bullying cowards always using their fists to shut people up."

"My father was as guilty of that as all the others," Jack joined in quietly, a pained look overtaking his face. "Onny he was more subtle. Niver used his fists, but his bullying body was always in mi mam's face. One time he was having a go at her, and I squeezed between 'em and offered 'im out. I said to him, 'You, me outside, NOW!'"

"What did he do?" Joyce asked, stunned at this.

"He was gobsmacked and backed off," Jack replied. "You see, I was eleven and a lot smaller than him."

"Eleven?" she gasped. "I know you've allus been brave, but ... eleven?"

"And did it stop him?" Stick asked, a new light of respect burning in *his* eyes.

"It did that!" Jack replied. "He wasn't as stupid as you might think. He knew full well I wouldn't always be eleven, and one day he might catch a hammering from a rather large eighteen year old if he continued with those ways. He stopped picking on her – at least while I was about."

-o-

"You were going to tell us about your other trip when you were at Normanton Grammar School," Stick pointed out as they sat at their usual table ready for dinner. "But you were side-tracked, side-lined and side-stepped."

"Story of my life," Jack replied.

"Jack!" Jenny harrumphed, almost indignantly.

"Until I met you, Jenny, I was just off to add," he nipped in swiftly.

"I should think so as well," Joyce joined in. "I was about to say—"

"OK! OK!" he capitulated, throwing his hands in the air in submission.

"Don't dig thi hole any deeper, Jack lad," Stick suggested with a knowing grin, glad it wasn't him in that position. "Anyway, trip? Grammar school? Eighteen?"

"During *my* time there, the school was never inclined to acquire a minibus to take youngsters to matches and sports events and such," Jack went on. "Too expensive, the management always pleaded, which was nonsense really. For away fixtures, they had to hire a coach – usually from Gillards – which can't have been cheap. Any road, when I was in t'Upper Sixth, one Saturday morning, this greeny-coloured, old-looking 'minibus' just … appeared, round the back of school, down towards the old gym."

"No announcement?" Stick asked.

"Nay," Jack replied. "We were never involved wi' t'decisions in yon school. We just had to accept. We weren't over sure about its physical condition or comfort. We were supposed to be 'ard lads that could put up wi' discomfort. Staff's driving capabilities were never a condition. Many of the older ones had never *taken* a driving test, let alone passed one.

"We were studying *King Lear* for A-level English Literature with – now what *was* the teacher's name? – Mr Mason, I believe it was," Jack explained. "He had seen that there was a performance of said Shakespeare play at the Crucible Theatre in Sheffield, which is now a venue for world snooker, I believe. As the ten of us were all eighteen and it was out of school time, we were allowed to have a couple of pints of black velvet before the show."

"Black velvet?" Joyce asked, puzzled at the reference. "What's that?"

"Stick?" Jack said, knowing full well that his friend would have the answer.

"The real black velvet is a half-and-half mixture of Guinness and champagne," Stick explained, having drunk many a one in the Crown in Normanton. "As working lads couldn't – or wouldn't – afford such extravagance, it became a half-and-half pint glass of Guinness and cider."

"Excellent it was, too," Jack added.

"Drinking alcohol? With a teacher's permission?" Jenny asked, incredulous at what she was hearing. "In—?"

"An evening at the end of the week," Jack butted in quickly. "During the interval, we all nipped to the loo and out to the pub next door for another swift one before the second half of the play. I don't think many of us heard the rest of the play, let alone understood it. Black velvets do have a habit of blurring the attention the more you drink."

"A booze-up, in other words," Joyce insisted.

"Nay, come on!" Jack replied. "We were old enough and were causing nobody any harm. The journey back to Normanton from the outskirts of Sheffield in a rattly old minibus was done in very thick fog," he went on. "The forty miles or so, along back roads, took us more than four hours. Sometimes we travelled at walking pace with the door open and one of us sitting in the doorstep well, watching that the front wheels didn't hit the road edge. The teacher's visibility was only just beyond the van's bonnet. It was scary, to say the least."

"What time did you get back to school?" Jenny asked, a look of horror clouding her face.

"About one in the morning," Jack replied. "Fortunately,

it was Saturday – with no sports events."

"Last evening, I'm afraid," Stick observed. "So I, for one, am going to fill up on mi dinner because we probably won't be eating much on the way home tomorrow."

"Something you know that we don't?" Jack asked his pal with a guffaw. "I thought you filled up anyway."

Chapter 21

"Glad to be back?" Jack asked Jenny, as they sat in their tiny indoor-outdoor conservatory, shoulder to shoulder on their discounted wicker settee, with a cup of Yorkshire Tea and a digestive. The day after their return from an extremely enjoyable and satisfying fortnight in the sun was always a bit of an anti-climax, particularly with work only a few hours away.

"Don't move!" she said quietly. "Look at the bird house."

"My goodness," Jack gasped. "Fledging bluetits? We've not seen that before. Isn't it a bit late for them?"

"You never know with bluetits," she replied, a little more knowledgeably than her husband. "I think that's the doorbell."

"I'll get it," Jack offered, squeezing out of the space to amble to the front door.

Realising that Jack was taking an inordinate length of time answering the door, Jenny followed him to find out why.

"And how do I know you are who you say you are?" she heard him ask a young man and a young woman at the door. "You could be anybody."

"Jack?" Jenny asked nonplussed.

"This young man tells me he is Sam, my … son," Jack replied, "and this is his … wife and baby daughter. I don't take it for a moment.”

“Can you remember when you were nine?”Jenny asked the young man, although Jack’s face wore a puzzled frown.

“Yes,” he replied. “My mother was ill in hospital, and you took me into your home to teach me while she was there, even though I wasn’t too keen. I enjoyed that you liked history, and we did a lot about the kings and queens of England, which was good. I knew a lot about all of that and still do.”

“Jack, this young man *is* your son,” Jenny said quite definitely. “No-one else could have known what he has just said. Good to meet you again, Sam. Please come in.”

-o-

“And how did you work all that out?” Jack asked, once his son, daughter-in-law and baby granddaughter had left. “All that stuff about history?”

“When he stayed with us, we had the time to explore the sort of stuff he liked to study,” Jenny explained. “You were at work and I … wasn’t, so we had all the time in the world. He knows an enormous amount of historical data in extreme detail – *Who Wants to be a Millionaire?* type detail.”

“Asperger Syndrome sort of knowledge, I assume?” Jack replied.

“Bit like the young lad I worked with in Heysham High, really,” Jenny added.

“Unbelievable,” Jack gasped. “Why *now*, I wonder? He’s old enough to follow his own mind, obviously.”

“His mother was never mentioned, did you notice?” she replied. “Of course, you did.”

“Perhaps he has grown some sense, especially since he is married to a lovely young lady,” Jack speculated. “And … he has given me another granddaughter to boot. Did they say they were living in the UK permanently now?”

"I don't think they said," she answered. "But they do have our address and phone number, so they can contact us when they want. You looking forward to tomorrow?"

"New school. New routine. Should be excited," he replied. "But … I'm not. Another school populated by another set of teachers that have no idea how to treat youngsters finding difficulty with organisational disfunction. Roll on Christmas, the new millennium, and my fifty-fourth birthday anniversary."

"Don't forget, dear Jack, that JWs don't celebrate either Christmas or birthdays," Jenny reiterated.

"Does that mean I don't get a spice cake either?" he said, a look of utter disappointment inching its way into his eyes.

"I think we might be able to manage that one," she said with a smile. "We should be able to arrange something for the day before."

"I have to say that I'm not concerned about those celebrations, because Christmas and birthdays were always my least favourite times of the year," Jack explained. "I never received anything much, and there was always a problem with mi dad, particularly on Christmas Day."

"Why Christmas Day specifically?" Jenny asked, not sure what his response might be.

"The mix of two opposite emotions for him, I think," Jack began to explain. "His club was open until two in the afternoon – which he liked – and Christmas dinner was at three – which he *didn't* like. It usually meant that the folks he *didn't* like often came for a meal. They were mi Grandma Marion and Granddad Jud. I've a feeling his dislike of them stemmed from the time mi granddad's fist met Dad's face when I was a nipper, and mi grandma's straight talking. He didn't like being called a 'toss-pot ne'er-do-well' by a woman."

"No competition, then," Jenny said squeezing his hand.

Although sunny and warm, the short car drive from Jack's all-important home to a strange and forbidding pile that was established as a grammar school on its present site in 1938 – nineteen years after its original formation elsewhere – didn't fill him with awe.

A typical school establishment of its time, built around two quadrangles with science laboratories on an upper floor, it gloried in its acknowledgement of its dated past. As it cried out to be dragged into the twenty-first century, plans were afoot to update its fraying and frayed infrastructure in the near future.

The school's original library reminded Jack very much of the one he had frequented in his later days at *his* grammar school in Normanton, with its solid oak furniture, wall cladding and dated card-index book-recording system. He didn't know, but he felt that *all* grammar school libraries had been designed by the same venerable grandee of past centuries.

"Good morning, Mr Ingles," a gruff Lancashire accent accosted him as he sat down in the staff room, ready for the morning briefing.

"Good morning, Mr Bawker," Jack replied, acknowledging one of the few teachers he had met on his last visit before the summer holidays.

"Tell me," Mr Bawker asked with a sly grin, "is there any truth in the rumour that you and the headteacher are about to set up a tag-team wrestling duo, following your performance with the two fifth formers last term?"

"Sounds like an excellent idea, Barry," Jack replied with a snort. "May I call you Barry?"

"'Course you may," Barry Bawker agreed.

"Good morning, ladies and gentlemen," the headteacher's authoritative voice quietened the crowded room. "You will be aware that we have no customers today, allowing our first Baker Day of this new academic year to remain at your disposal to make all your arrangements and plans to be put into place for tomorrow's influx of the new Year 7 pupils. I'll keep this meeting brief, but we have one or two organisational matters that need attention…"

'Why am I here?' Jack wondered to himself, as the head's monotonous voice droned on. 'Surely I should have been notified by the powers-that-be that my presence would not be necessary with no children in until tomorrow, or even the day after?'

"Would you like to come across to my office for a cup of tea and a chinwag?" Barry Bawker's voice cut in once the meeting had drawn to its inconclusive finale.

"Certainly would, Barry," Jack agreed eagerly. The first bit of hospitality he had met drew a smile to his face as he followed his 'mentor' from the staff room and across the first quadrangle to one of many offices that had a door that opened onto this green space.

"I've been asked by the head to offer support and advice on the youngsters you will be supporting, and to explain how the school manages their needs. I'm head of one of the year groups, and one of my many tasks is to keep track on their behaviour – or lack of it – in the classes mainly in my year group," Barry began over a pathetically weak cup of coolish tea that obviously came from an inefficient Thermos flask.

"So will I need to report to you regularly then?" Jack asked pointedly.

"Only if there's a need," Barry replied. "I'll give you your pupils and the rest is up to … you. You'll need to keep records, which I won't look at but probably your superiors in the Pupil Referral Service will – if they are still around. If there are no further questions, I don't see the need for you to be here. No doubt your feet will hit the floor running tomorrow with our new Year 7."

"See you then, Barry," Jack said as he headed for the door and his car, which was on the road outside the school's boundary. Ten o'clock. Not too bad a day's work. If only they were all like this.

"Jack?" Jenny shouted as she heard the front door sneck. "Half past ten? Bit early, don't you think?"

"Not needed, Jenny," he replied. "But a cup of Yorkshire Tea is! Kettle on? You?"

"No need for me to be there as courses don't start until Wednesday," she explained, putting the kettle on. "Two days off. How come *you're* not needed?"

"Training day," he replied. "As I am not a fully paid-up member of the school's staff, I'm not needed until tomorrow."

"And what does that mean?" she puzzled. "Either you're a teacher there or you're … not. Surely?"

"I still have mi wages paid by the County Council," Jack replied ower his steaming mug. "I have no idea what will happen if – *when* – the Pupil Referral Service folds for good. We're almost there, but not quite."

-o-

"Mam!" Jessie called as she opened the front door at Jenny and Jack's house in Morecambe. "You there, Mam?"

"In the lounge, if you can find your way," Jenny chortled.

"If you're not careful you are in danger of becoming a female version of Daddy Jack, Mother," Jessie warned with a nod. "He not here?"

"In the garden, love," she replied. "Who's your friend, and I don't mean your baby bump?"

"This is Cheryl," Jessie explained "We met a few weeks ago at a café on Street Lane, North Leeds, where you've probably been when you lived there. She went to Merton Grange round about the same time as we were in

220

the area."

"Well, well, Sweet Pea," Jack's voice crawled in from the kitchen. "It's good to see you. I've a feeling I know your friend's face."

"Oh my God!" Cheryl gasped as she covered the bottom half of her face. "It's Mr Ingles!"

"Cheryl Harrington!" Jack replied. "I *knew* I knew you, and I know that you'd know I knew you."

"Same Mr Ingles," Cheryl laughed. "Not in my wildest dreams did I think I'd meet you again. Wait until I tell my sister, Dawn. She'll be mortified … again."

"Why mortified?" Jenny asked.

"Because she was terrified of him at Merton Grange," Cheryl replied with a giggle.

"*Moi?* Terrified of *moi?*" Jack said, aghast. "Why?"

"Don't know," Cheryl said. "It must have been that uncompromising smiley face that hid a multitude of meanings. Same smiling response to every situation, good or not so good. Some kids couldn't cope with not knowing."

"Anyway, who's for a cuppa and a—?" Jack asked, to be cut off by Jenny.

"We'll be having lunch soon," she explained. "So no nibbles or cups of tea. Will you both be staying over?"

"Some other time, perhaps, Mam," Jessie replied. "Johnny's picking us up at five."

"How are things with you then, Cheryl?" Jack asked, not really sure how or why this was happening. "Obviously still living in Leeds."

"Why would I want to live anywhere else?" she replied with a swagger. "I've always liked it and wouldn't want to live anywhere different. Nothing wrong with Brackenwood Estate."

"Too true, but it wasn't always so," Jack said. "Used to have a less than salubrious reputation, but it picked up more than somewhat during your time. Must have been you.”

“Mum and Dad still live there in the house I was born in,” she explained. “My brother, Billy, and sister, Dawn, still live thereabouts, as do my four daughters. It’s a family thing.”

“There’s nothing wrong with that at all,” Jack interjected with a nod and a knowing smile. “A place for family to interact and be part of something wonderfully close. Ours is disparate now, fortunately and unfortunately. We would *like* to be closer with ours, but circumstance and opportunity have dictated otherwise, eh, Jenny?”

“Would we have it any other way?” she replied. “Yes, we would, but family wishes dictate differently. We are close as a family, but not close knit.”

“Still, who else of us can have holidays in the winter in the warmth of Australia?” Cheryl said with a shrug.

“Probably not us,” Jack replied with a sigh. “For the cost of one air fare to Oz, we could probably have three holidays in the sun in Spain. Not that we could afford three holidays in Spain – you know what I mean.”

“Do you ever get to see other people from your time at Merton Grange?” Cheryl asked, probably knowing what the answer might be.

“I rubbed along with most teachers there, but never socially,” Jack replied firmly. “I would have preferred to have met the youngsters I taught, but we moved away when we were divorced from our respective partners. Shame, as it’s turned out, because the wonderful opportunities promised never materialised.”

“Do you ever think back to times at Merton Grange?” Cheryl asked. “You know, the things we all did and how we were?”

“Did you ever come across a lad called Paul Ridsdale, by any chance?” Jack asked.

"I knew of him, but he wasn't my – our – cup of tea," she replied with a grimace. "Strange lad. Why?"

"I was walking down the corridor one day, during one of my only two free lessons," Jack explained.

"Only two?" she gasped. "Didn't most teachers have at least four?"

"Indeed, they did," he replied, eyes flashing. "But that's a tale for another day. Anyway, as I reached room G6 – you know, the one under the stairs opposite the second set of outside doors – the door to the French teacher's classroom bounced open wildly, almost taking the hinges with it, and who should flounce out but Master Paul Ridsdale himself."

"What did he do?" Cheryl asked, agog to hear more.

"He saw me and stopped in his tracks, a shocked and puzzled look on his face," Jack grinned. "There seemed to be a bit of a battle going on in his head – shall I, shan't I, sort of a deal. Finally, decision made, he yelled with a look and flick of his hand over his shoulder, 'I'm not stopping here wi' that f***ing bitch any longer.' And turning on his heels, he fled at speed out of the outside doors."

"What did you do?" Cheryl asked with more than a touch of humour, knowing of old what his answer might be.

"I carried on walking and said, 'See you tomorrow, Paul,' as I went," Jack guffawed.

He and Cheryl laughed together like old friends enjoying a shared memory.

"It reminded me of an older wag of a colleague in a former school when I was a young shaver of a stripling teacher. Bill Jones was his name, a technical-drawing teacher," Jack reminisced. "There's no such thing nowadays. He was a disciplinarian who never became irate or lost his temper. One day a lad lost *his* temper because Bill had been on at him, threw his books and tools on the floor and bounced out. Bill simply ambled to the door and shouted after his disappearing body up the school's driveway, 'See you tomorrow.'

"A few days later, somebody broke into his cabin classroom and wrote on his blackboard, 'Mr Jones is a twat'. Took nothing; messed nothing up. Bill took great pride in pointing out the next day that the intruder had called him 'Mr Jones'."

"Wow!" Cheryl uttered quietly, in awe of the stack of memories her favourite teacher must have stored in that brain of his. "How on earth do you remember such stuff when I have trouble remembering what's on my shopping list?"

"Unfortunately, my mind is stuffed full of useless knowledge and information gathered over a lifetime of doing insignificant things," Jack replied. "Most of the things from Merton days falls into that category."

"I don't call all that 'useless'," Cheryl contradicted. "I suppose it all depends when you use it and to what purpose."

"My knowledge, lovely lady, would never change the course of human history," Jack replied with an appreciative smile and nod.

"But it might change the way people you have been associated with think about sharing *their* memories," she added.

"My Daddy Jack has always been a person with the deeply held belief that people's opinions and feelings might be changed and made better by talking and sharing," Jessie added. "He has influenced the way my siblings and I, and our cousins, have reacted to things, and they have chosen a different path from the one they *might* have chosen. Not a dictator, more a sharer and helper."

"Dinner's ready, people!" Jenny called from the kitchen diner. "Come quickly, or Daddy Jack might think twice about sharing what is on the table.”

Chapter 22

"You need to be aware that most teachers in this school don't subscribe to *your* thinking on poor behaviour in class," Barry Bawker warned Jack the following day in his office.

"Then why am I here?" Jack asked very pointedly of a man who so obviously knew next to nothing about treating problem youngsters with respect and compassion rather than punishment.

"You tell me," Bawker replied with a shrug.

"If I were to begin with the simplest philosophy," Jack went on, "you obviously wouldn't have a clue about what I was saying. Talk about Stone Age!"

"Now hang on a bit!" the teacher began to protest.

"No, you hang on," Jack returned sharply. "We are not in the dark ages any more, with people who neither understand nor want to try. If such a philosophy as you are peddling is all there is here, there is no chance that youngsters will ever be helped out of the downward spiral they have been forced into. Don't you dare tell me there is nothing that can be done to work with them. Or is it 'behave or be permanently excluded'?"

"Now just a minute!" Mr Bawker went on, becoming indignantly defensive.

"Enough!" Jack barked as he made for the door. "If you want to talk sense and reason, I'll be in Special Needs. I'm not listening to this crap." With that, he clicked the door shut behind him. He couldn't do with folks pontificating on stuff they neither understood nor wanted to discuss rationally.

-o-

"Well now, Jack Ingles, you certainly know how to alienate people," Mrs Hopkinson, the head of Special Needs, said at lunchtime. "How long have you been here? Two hours?"

"I believe in what I am doing – or hoping to do – here," he replied. "Besides, I can't do with Bawkerisms."

"Bawkerisms?" she said, a puzzled crease crossing her brow. "I don't— Got it!" she continued with her hallelujah moment.

"Why is it always that people who don't have the intellect to understand, because they are dodos, always seem to be those in power?" Jack asked. "Present company excepted, of course."

"Can we look forward to you always expressing your opinion so … pointedly?" she said, not sure how to deal with such unusually sharp observations.

"I've always said it as I've seen it," he harrumphed. "Can't do it any other way. I'll give my opinion whenever I'm convinced that I am right."

"Are you *always* right?" she said equally pointedly.

"I won't comment if I'm not sure," he replied. "I'm a Yorkshireman and not given to shyness or indecision."

"That's all right then," Mrs Hopkinson said with a smile. "As long as I know where we stand."

"I've quite often got into trouble with high-ups by giving them advice, too," he explained with a shrug.

"Do they ever *take* your advice?" she asked.

"Rarely," he added. "That's why they don't often resolve anything that's staring them in the face. It's always sensible at least to consider good advice that's perhaps not been recognised before."

"We're in for an interesting time, then, because you'll learn not to offer what they won't even consider," she said finally before she left the room.

"Obviously not the right place to be," Jack muttered as he headed for the staff room and his boiled-egg sandwiches.

-o-

"Not the best school I've ever been in, Jen," Jack said, once he had regaled her with his day's adventure.

"Oh dear," she sighed. "Nothing like making your mark, eh, Our Jack."

"I honestly don't see how you can expect to teach youngsters anything if all you do is mete out punishments," he explained. "Don't worry, my Sweet Pea, I won't be leaving. Can't afford to, but I won't keep mi mouth shut. They have a lot to learn, I'm afraid. Can't do wi' know-nowts as wayn't ask for help when they need it, to t'detriment o' them as need it and want it."

"By the way," Jenny said, "we've been invited around to Joyce and Stick's this evening."

"A social gathering or an eating evening?" Jack asked.

"Jack!" Jenny said.

"What?" he replied, a look of mock innocent surprise growing. "I simply wanted to know whether we would have to eat before going, or before bed."

"You and your belly!" she muttered. "I'm off to get ready."

"But it's onny five o'clock," he complained.

"We need to be round there by six for chilli and rice, followed by one of your favourite afters," Jenny continued.

"Which one?" he asked, metaphorically drooling at the thought.

"Flip a coin and you're bound to be right," she said

228

with a snigger.

"I can't help liking mi vittels," he said defensively. "You'd complain if I *wouldn't* eat!"

"Now, that will *never* happen!" she scoffed.

"What would your view on my favourite afters be, putting aside all my other favourites?" he asked.

"Undoubtedly sherry trifle," she replied, almost without thinking. "Why do you ask?"

"I remember Lee once doing me a trifle – quite a large one, as it happened – for my birthday, because I had wittered on about the ones mi mam used to make," Jack explained. "You know, just how *you* do 'em. Sponge soaked in a modicum of proper Spanish sherry from Jerez. Slices of banana under a thick coating of Bird's custard, topped by thickened double cream and chocolate scrapings to finish off."

"And was her trifle like that?" Jenny asked, intrigued by the concept.

"Not on your Nelly!" Jack answered forcibly, to an unexpected guffaw from Jenny. "She covered the sponge with melted jelly, which, when set, she covered with cream and strawberries. Bearing in mind that it was quite a large one, she complained that I hadn't eaten it all. It was a very large glass bowl, when all said and done.

"And before you ask, no, I did not finish it off," he went on. "Luckily, as it turned out. I had a serial dose of heartburn later in the evening to cap a wonderful birthday – not! I shudder to think what agony I would have suffered had I eaten it all. Lee was never one of life's cooks, I'm afraid."

-o-

"Glad you changed schools and counties, Stick?" Jack said, as they each warmed a tot glass of malt whisky before starting dinner.

"Er, fifty per cent right," Stick replied. "This bottle of malt that you brought is good. Edradour?"

"One of the best around," Jack explained. "Visited the distillery the other year and fell in love with it straight away. They employ onny three folks to do the whiskying, and it's about the smallest in Scotland. In the same visit we did the smallest and the oldest in the same area, followed a day or two later by the highest – Edradour, Glenturret and Dalwhinnie. Edradour and Glenturret are in the Pitlochry area, and Dalwhinnie, at 1164 feet above sea level, is nearly sixty-six miles north."

"I'd love to do that," Stick said after another dram.

Jack raised his glass and said, "I'll drink to that. Slan-je-var."

"What does that mean?" Stick puzzled. "Another of your strange customs?"

"In Gaelic it means 'Good health'," Jack explained. "Spelled 'slainte mhath' but pronounced 'Slan-je-var', or 'Slanj' for short. We must do a tour in the near future. You'd like it."

"Slanj," Jack said as the whisky caressed his lips.

"Slanj," Stick replied as the amber nectar crossed *his* tongue.

"We're visiting the whisky fields of Scotland next year," Stick said with a nod, as Joyce and Jenny entered the room to trundle their men folk into the eating area to enjoy a lovely meal, to be capped by a properly made sherry trifle.

"Oh, yes?" Joyce said. "Who says so? And why Scotland?"

"Well, we've never been, and—" Stick began to explain.

"That whisky been talking to you?" she smiled. "Urging you to come visit?"

"You are *so* intuitive, Joyce," Jenny said with a giggle. "Do I recognise your hand in this, Jack?"

"When was the last time we didn't enjoy one of our

visits, Sweet Pea?" he asked his wife. "Even our distillery tours?"

"Could the fact that I don't drink and you get *my* free dram have anything to do with it, perhaps?" she added quickly.

"We wouldn't want to waste it and, of course, it does give you a chance to drive around this wonderful land," he said with a smile. "Even though I have had the occasional 'mishap' because of my name."

"Mishap?" Joyce puzzled. "How could anyone take exception to 'Jack'?"

"We called in at a kilt shop in Edinburgh one time," he started, having made himself comfortable with a cup of tea. "I asked this huge hairy Scot who was dressed in full regalia, sporting a magnificent full beard and 'tache. He said, 'What's your name, Laddie?'

"I replied 'Ingles', upon which he said, 'Spanish for English, eh? Get out ma shop!','" Jack replied. "We laughed nervously, but for the life of me I had no idea whether he was serious."

"You didn't get a kilt, then?" Stick asked. "What a shame."

"As it turns out, I could have had one of the Lamont tartans," he replied with a superior smile. "Or even – Royal Stewart. How about that? It seems, Mi Lady, that you might have married into royalty."

"How many areas have you visited north of the border?" Stick asked, as he and his buddy demolished what was left of the trifle, each sighing with ecstasy.

"Try – all of 'em!" Jack answered. "Not all in the same year, I hasten to add. Our first B&B was in a lovely house in Blair Atholl, owned and run by a lassie called Linda, whose husband was in forestry and part-time acting. From there we went on to Glencoe, to a little two-up-two-down terraced house on the banks of Loch Leven, opposite the

Eilean Munde – the Isle of Munde. It has often been called Burial Island because many from the area were buried there through the ages, including Alasdair MacDonald, the MacIan or Master of Glencoe, following the Glencoe Massacre of the thirteenth of February 1692.”

“Wow!” Stick gasped in awe at his knowledge. “Massacre? What set that off?”

“On the order of William III, his soldiers, led by Archibald Campbell, killed thirty-eight members of the Clan MacDonald, including their leader – thirty-three men, two women and two children,” Jack explained. “There has been animosity ever since between the MacDonalds and the Campbells.”

“Was there a valid reason why he ordered that dire deed?” Stick asked, puzzled by the politics of the day.

“They refused to pledge allegiance to the new monarchs, William III and Mary II,” Jack added. “Rumour has it that they even tried to steal Alasdair MacDonald’s body at some stage, but I don’t know what truth there is in that.”

“Wasn’t that the B&B where we watched from the back window two pine martens descend from the wooded slopes behind their garden *into* the garden to eat bread and jam sandwiches laid on the table?” Jenny said.

“Gerraway!” Stick scoffed. “You’re ’avin’ us on!”

“She’s not,” Jack said in support of his wife’s observation. “Two of ’em – male and female – took bread and jam sandwiches from the table every day … for breakfast.”

“Bloomin’ ’ummer!” Joyce gasped “You’ll be telling us next that they came in for tea!”

“Well … as you mention it … no, they didn’t,” Jack chortled heartily. “However, it was amazing to think that the same flavoured jam I’d had on mi toast that morning was wending its way through a pine marten’s digestive tract.”

"Glencoe itself is a wonderfully mystical, if frightening, deep valley edged all round by mournful, threatening hills and mountains," Jenny butted in. "It's awesome and awe-inspiring in the extreme."

"What about *your* new school, Jack?" Joyce asked, sensing that all wasn't as it ought to be. "Have you fully rediscovered your earlier exuberance and love of what you do?"

"Nothing's ever the same as it was twenty or so years ago, Our Joyce," he replied with a resigned sigh. "We've had some good yet not-so-good times lately, you know."

"Not feel like trying another job elsewhere?" Stick asked.

"I've always wanted to be a teacher ever since I was seven or eight in Mr Hardwick's class," Jack assured him, "and I've always loved working with nippers. That will never change. Things aren't as good nowadays. Too many regulations to be mindful of, and too many targets to aim for to allow for the freedom and flexibility we allus used to have. Anyway, I've onny six years or so before I pack mi bags and retire – hopefully to the sun, eh, Jen?"

Jenny's face said it all. She would adore spending two weeks or so in the sun in Southern Spain every year, but packing up lock, stock and barrel to live permanently in foreign lands just wouldn't do it for her.

"She's like me," Joyce said, taking her cue from Jenny's expression. "Sun's lovely, but coming home to family and friends is equally exciting and uplifting."

"Six years?" Stick queried. "That means t'same for me then, 'cos we're of an age, thee and me, and although I went to a posher school, t'pension's t'same at t'end on it all. We need to start making plans sooner than later, eh, Joyce?"

"As I've done more years than both of you, I don't intend to go on in a school's library – or a library anywhere else for that matter – beyond age fifty-eight," Joyce informed them with a snort. "Because of my time from seventeen, I will be able to draw my work's pension *then*. So, I will be able to draw my state pension when I'm sixty."

"Wow!" Stick gasped. "I can retire on a fullish pension when I'm sixty, with state pension following five years later. *Then* we can start living. Bring it on!"

-o-

"My office, if you please, Mr Ingles," the head's booming voice greeted Jack as he signed in at reception early on Monday morning.

"It has been brought to my notice that the Pupil Referral Service, which employs you, will no longer exist from today," the head explained. "So from now on, you will be employed by this school."

"How come nobody told me about this?" Jack replied indignantly.

"Probably they considered you weren't important enough," the head snorted. "You are only an insignificant pawn in only a slightly more important organisation. You've not been here long, but I think you might be able to fill adequately a post I have been meaning to set up for some time."

"I suppose you are going to offer me a post I can't refuse, with my 'limited' skills?" Jack sneered, irritated by the head's arrogance.

"You will refuse at your peril!" the head warned.

"You threatening me, Mr Allsop?" Jack snapped back.

"No, Mr Ingles, I am not," the head's reply was swift. "Simply saying that if you don't accept my offer, you will be out of a job."

"And your offer is?" Jack replied.

"I want to set up a withdrawal room where recalcitrant pupils can spend half a term being taught by one person

234

– you – throughout the day," Mr Allsop went on. "*That* room will not be *one* room at all. It will be the whole of the now-defunct caretaker's house that is set apart from all else in this school, down the drive towards the road."

"And who will be responsible for the planning, design and set up of what can only be described as a detached exclusion unit?" Jack replied sharply. "You do realise, of course, that this concept goes against all inclusion principles in education at the moment. Don't you?"

"Irrelevant!" the head blustered. "Anyway, you will be responsible for the planning, along with Mr Bawker as Head of Inclusion."

"If I am being promoted to Head of Inclusion, how much will I be paid to do it?" Jack asked, pushing his lot more than somewhat.

"You're not," Mr Allsop explained baldly. "Mr Bawker is the Head of Inclusion. You will be there to provide the expertise to set up the unit under his direction and guidance."

"But he has neither experience nor expertise in the area," Jack complained sharply. "Nor does he have any idea how to provide what is necessary for such youngsters to succeed. In fact, you may as well pluck some passer-by in from the street."

"That's why you will be there," the head said as a final aside. "Now, you will have to excuse me, I have more important business to attend to." With that, he crossed his office to show Jack out with the parting shot that if he needed anything, he should discuss matters with Mr Bawker, who would consider most requests.

-o-

"Not ecstatic about this new place, Our Jen," Jack said as he caressed his mug of hot tea. "Don't like it at all."

"Why's that, then, My Man?" she asked, not surprised.

Most places weren't up to Jack's standards because his standards were far higher than anyone she knew. "What's different from what happened the other day?"

"For a start off, primary schools are too busy trying to achieve the government of the day's targets – that MPs know nothing about – to allow youngsters and schools the flexibility to diversify in their teaching," he replied, following a tack that Jenny was in danger of losing track of. "And yon secondaries have no idea how to help struggling young 'uns to achieve the goals they don't understand. It was never like this when I started teaching in 1967."

"That's a time I know nothing about you and what you were up to," Jenny said. "You were about to enter your final year when I told you I was pregnant, and…"

"Everything seemed to fall apart between you and me, unfortunately," he said, his voice dropping almost to a whisper. "You see, I thought I had lost you and I wasn't sure I could cope with that. I wasn't at all sure *what* I wanted to do, really."

"But I thought you were dead set on being a teacher?" she gasped, not really knowing what to say.

"I was dead set on having you in my life, Jenny," he butted in. "*That* seemed to have been taken away."

Silence descended along with a sad look into her eyes. She had no idea what to say, so she changed tack. "What did you do when you left college?" she asked quietly snuggling up to him once his mug was empty.

"We finished on the first Friday in July," he began. "The accommodation staff wanted us all out so they could organise cleaning and stuff without interruption. I packed mi stuff in mi case – I didn't have anything of intrinsic value except for mi red-and-grey Dansette record player that mi mam had bought me a year or two before – and I was off to … nowhere."

"You'd nowhere to go?" she said with a shocked gasp.

"Nowhere at all, as in … homeless?"

"I had to get some digs pretty sharpish, but with no money to pay for 'em, it was going to be a bit … nip and tuck," he replied. "Fortunately, I'd seen an advert for someone to teach English and organise outings and stuff for two very different groups of twelve French secondary-school youngsters. That was a saviour for me because it came with B&B accommodation with the lady running the courses, down Burley Road just behind Yorkshire Television. It gave me two weeks' grace to find somewhere more permanent."

"Wow!" she gasped. "It's a good job we found each other when we did."

"Certainly is," he agreed. "Still, that two weeks was an enjoyably steep learning curve for me, because it showed one or two sides to working with youngsters – particularly foreign youngsters – that I wouldn't have experienced otherwise."

"I don't know all these places," Jenny said.

"Kirkstall Abbey?" he suggested. "Just down t'road."

"Been there," she said with a smile, "with—"

"Me!" he replied. "More tea, Vicar?"

Chapter 23

"Do you ever wish we had stayed in Leeds instead of decamping over the border into foreign parts?" Jack said, as he polished off his slice of strawberry flan with real cream from Sainsbury's round the corner. "Do you miss our wonderful house in posh Alwoodley?"

"Yes, to both questions," Jenny replied. "Why do you ask? Not thinking of ditching this here post in that local high school – what's its name?"

"No, I'm not," he said quite firmly, "not even if they were to offer me a headship in t'heart of t'Dales wi' a 'ouse chucked in."

"Glad to hear it," she declared. "I don't think I could cope with the upheaval again. Different matter, perhaps, when we are folks of leisure. Anyway, what did you learn from working with those youngsters?"

"Youngsters? Learn?" he puzzled.

"You know – those from France?" she observed. "Two other sides, you said."

"Oh, yes," he said slowly, collecting his thoughts. "The first group was diabolical. They were brought over by a female teacher who had no concept of discipline. She allowed them to run around the church hall we were using as a base and couldn't seem to care less. I wasn't there to chastise or correct behaviour, but to give them the experience of learning English in England, and to enjoy excursions."

"How did you get to the church hall every day from your digs?" Jenny asked.

"Mrs Butterworth, the lady with whom I was staying, took me in her Alvis car every day," he replied. "The only time I have ever been in one of those.

"Waste of time that first group," Jack harrumphed with a grimace. "But the second group was entirely different. Brought across from Paris by an older male teacher called Jean, with his assistant, Alain, who was training to be an actuary. The children were wonderfully behaved, interested, and loved talking to me in both languages. They thought our outings – which I arranged and organised, incidentally – were the bees'."

"Bees?" Jenny said, not understanding the reference.

"As in 'knees'?" he explained. "Or even 'dog's'?"

"Let's not go there!" she warned him. "I might understand that one. Back to excursions?"

"We did Jorvik in York, and the Shambles, after I'd explained – in French this time – what to expect," he continued. "Another day we did Haworth and the Brontës, including a walk up to Top Withens."

"Top—?" she puzzled.

"It's where *Wuthering Heights* was supposed to have been set, out on the moors," he explained. "A bit on a hike, I have to admit.

"The last evening, Jean and Alain asked me out to the Arndale Centre's bowling alley in Headingley as a thank you for a fabulous week. We were about to start our games when they were struck dumb by a Beatles' record that came over the tannoy – 'All You Need Is Love'."

"Struck dumb?" Jenny asked, not really understanding what he was saying. "Why?"

"Because, *mon petit pigeon anglais*, the first few bars of the song are the intro to the 'Marseillaise', their national anthem," Jack explained with a triumphant grin. "I told them that I had arranged for their national anthem to be played in their honour. They laughed like billy-oh when I told them the real reason a short while later, so as not to burst their self-important bubble too soon."

Jenny laughed loudly at her husband's quip, knowing that he would have played it straight-faced to the full. "You seem at least to have enjoyed that one," she observed, seeing the self-satisfied smile still hanging around his face. "And after that, when all the excitement had returned to Paris?"

"Somehow found a couple in Headingley who wanted to rent out a spare room – shared kitchen, bathroom, etc," he replied. "Unfortunately, for a variety of obvious reasons, it didn't work. Took me a week or two into my first term at Broughton until I found a proper bedsit in Roundhay. Number 36, North Park Avenue. Three pounds three shillings and six pence rent, plus a periodic shilling to slot into the meter for the electric fire."

"Three pounds three and a tanner wasn't bad for a month's rent in such a lovely area," Jenny observed. "Lucky."

"Three pounds three and a tanner *per week*, my naïve little Sweet Pea!" he replied emphatically. "That med a significant dent in mi monthly wage of around sixty pounds, I can tell you!"

"Wow!" she gasped. "I don't know what to say."

"I mostly ate cornflakes for breakfast and beans on toast for tea," he reminisced. "During the winter months I went to bed as soon as I got in from school because I couldn't afford the fire. To try to mek up for it, I had school dinner every day because Mrs Dyer, the school's cook, allus put on a rayt good spread. Holidays were a disappointment, though."

"Disappointment?" she asked. "How come?"

"No school," he replied. "Consequently no school dinners."

"Were there *any* positives during that first year?" she ventured.

"Buses were convenient to get to work," he remarked. "Number 6 from Roundhay Park gates into Leeds. Short walk to City Square to get a Number 1 to school. The terminus was spitting distance from the school's back door."

-o-

Whatever life in schools had dropped at his feet, Jack had mostly enjoyed or, at worst, tolerated. The latter experiences were relatively small island stop-overs between much longer voyages of discovery. During these times, he had felt like adventurers of old exploring hidden lands where lived hitherto unknown peoples. His residential school in Cumbria had been one such place – and his present billet seemed to be following suit.

Jack felt that the only reason why its headteacher, Mr Allsop, had employed him was because of pressure applied from head office in Preston.

Because of his forthrightness and perceived arrogance when starting at a new place, Jack was not a popular addition to any new school. That is, until others became used to his Yorkshireness and his opinions that inevitably turned out to be right. This time, however, he wasn't so sure.

Jack knew that the headteacher was the king in his own castle, and not used to being gainsaid on *any* subject. Unfortunately, as head of this former grammar school, Mr Allsop's perceptions, and by association those of his teachers, were undoubtedly outdated and lacking in foundation.

The teacher responsible for Jack's induction into this

particular edifice of learning was a prize case in point. How could anyone who had spent the last twenty-odd years in this one school have the requisite experience and knowledge to lead modern-day youngsters, with their foibles and issues, into a brighter future? Perhaps he was destined for higher office, and this was a means of gaining experience and knowledge from someone who knew a darned sight more than him!

Over time, Jack disassociated himself from his new 'colleagues', and became more involved with the youngsters in the school, offering support whenever a need became apparent.

-o-

"Mr Ingles?" Year 7 Joseph, with his pal, Alan, asked towards the end of a Friday afternoon in late November.

"Yes, Young Sir. What can I do you for?" Jack replied, once he had dismissed the small group he was working with.

"I've been having a bit of bother wi' mi homework," Joseph replied tentatively. "Do any of the teachers do an after-school homework club to help people like us?"

"Not that I know of," Jack said. "But let me look into it and I'll get back to you as soon as possible. OK? Would you be interested in joining if someone was to start one?"

"Certainly would!" the two chorused.

"And so would at least another ten others that I know of," Alan added as he left the room.

-o-

Over the following weekend, Jack's mind went into overdrive working out how to develop the concept of a homework club: how to set it up, cost implications (both income and outgoings), venue etc. He would obviously have to seek permission from some nebulous person like the deputy or head before it might be pursued. Opening it to the whole school was easy, but the question of limited subject knowledge on his part would definitely arise. Consequently, initially it might be better to open it to lower years in the school. Years 7 and 8 perhaps?

With any new concept, this was the sort of process Jack put himself through to explore all possible avenues before committing to just one probability. With everything settled in his mind, he approached the headteacher.

"No problem with setting up this after-school offering, Mr Ingles," Mr Allsop agreed. "You have to bear in mind, however, that it will be at your own cost, if such implications are obvious. There will be no extra-curricular activity allowance payable to you by the school."

"Expenses?" Jack suggested. "Stationery, for example?"

"Same response from me," he replied. "Now if you'll excuse me?"

Although extra-curricular activities ought to be underwritten by the school, no teacher ever claimed recompense. Jack knew his venture would benefit the children so he would have to find the money himself. *That* would be difficult from his meagre income. He would have to think on that one.

-o-

"You know that homework club you set up several weeks ago, Our Jack?" Jenny asked her husband one evening after dinner. "Is it working all right, funding wise?"

"Yes, I do and … why?" he replied, unsure about her motives for such a specific question.

"Well, I know you'd want it to be successful without committing too much of your own money to its implementation," she explained.

"Because we don't have any spare, and Allsop won't

grant me either an allowance or expenses to make it both legit and recognisable as a real support," Jack replied. "Why do you ask?"

"We were talking today at college about grants available from bona-fide organisations to cover educational initiatives. Joan suggested you might want to have a look at what the National Lottery has to offer. She said that they are always going on about the millions they are pouring into local projects countrywide. So why not your little project? Important, isn't it?"

"Never thought of that," he said with a welcoming grin. "I'll look into it."

Most people would have shrugged off the suggestion, feeling that this little project would be too insignificant to be worthy of further investigation. Jenny knew that Jack didn't think like that. She knew also that he would take the possibility seriously and follow it through, either to fruition or to it being a non-starter. National Lottery, eh? How much and when? Perhaps…?

-o-

Although the front garden of their new detached house in Morecambe was perhaps a good single stride from front door to road, their back garden was much better. In the short time they had been there, Jack had created two paved patios – one by the house and one behind the garage – linked by a path along its side. In this sort of a situation most folks would have laid a lawn that they needed to tend once a week. Not Jack! Not in a million years!

He didn't like lawns because they didn't usually leave enough space for exciting slate paths to lead you on to beautiful flower and shrub plantings. He had always wanted a chuckling waterfall dropping many feet into a deep pool where fish played and water boatmen rowed

244

across its width.

Given the garden's almost microscopic size in real terms, he settled for something on a smaller scale that gave him a similar overall effect. Modern materials, too, obviated the need for rocks and boulders; materials like fibrecrete were much lighter and modern constructional techniques allowed for stunning effects to be created with minimal effort.

To bring *his* fantastic landscaping to life, he had handed over the planting to Jenny, with her creative flair and sense of colour. What fun she was going to have turning those large patches and pockets of soil into living visions of vibrant colour. This garden wasn't big enough for a grandiose conservatory like the one they'd had in their Leeds house; any structure would have been more like a small porch. So, that's what they had done, leaving enough space for Jenny's passion – sunbathing in a lounger by the back French doors.

–o–

"Well, that's come as a bit of a surprise," Jack said, as he opened his mail after his Wednesday in school in early October.

"What is it?" Jenny asked as she placed her tray for afternoon tea on their glass-topped octagonal coffee table. "Tax rebate?"

"Try 'Money from National Lottery' credited with immediate effect," he grinned. "Did not expect that so quickly."

"Into our bank?" she gasped. "How much?"

"It's had to be deposited into the school's account with me as the sole signatory," he replied. "You sitting down, ready?"

"Come on!" she chuntered. "Don't keep me waiting!"

"Only … £20,000," he said with downcast eyes but

more than the slightest smile flickering at his mouth corners.

"You're joking!" Jenny gasped, almost passing out at the shock. "Twenty—?"

"Thousand pounds, for the sole use of my homework club," he said proudly, flicking his thumbs under imaginary trouser bracers as he stood up to grasp his congratulatory mug of Yorkshire Tea. What better way to celebrate than with a mug of tea and a home-baked icing bun?

"What does that mean exactly?" Jenny asked, scratching her scalp.

"It means, my lovely, that I can pay myself the extra two points on my pay scale that I should have had from this school, and have enough in the kitty for everything to do with my club," he replied with satisfaction. "You remember? The allowance that Allsop wouldn't countenance?"

Chapter 24

"Jack! Quick!" Jenny called to her husband as she dropped the telephone onto its cradle. "Jack! It's our Jessie!"

"What about our Jessie?" he said, as he rushed into the lounge from the kitchen-diner and collided with his wife. "Jessie? You were saying…?"

"Come and sit down," she said, pointing to their capacious, brightly coloured settee. "You may need to take a breath."

"Jenny!" he hissed between clenched teeth.

"That was Johnny on the phone," she gushed. "Our Jessie's only gone and delivered a boy, and they've decided to call him … Jack."

"I wonder why that is!" he grinned. "When can we see them?"

"Tomorrow, when they are rested," she replied. "We are very fortunate again that it's the middle of our Easter holidays and we can visit our grandson shortly after his birth. Millie Alice is very excited. Can't wait to see her little brother."

"Fortunately, we won't be babysitting on a regular basis with them living so far away," Jack observed with a sage nod.

"Jack!" Jenny gasped, surprised at his bluntness.

"Just saying," he replied. "I know he's my grandchild,

but so are Millie Alice and any others that ours might produce. One other – unrelated – piece of good news, for me at any rate, is that Allsop is retiring at the end of the coming term, to be replaced by a chap called Banbury. He's from Lancaster but is heading from Greater Manchester, I believe. I wonder if he might be somebody I can work with. Perhaps we might be able to get shut of this divisive attached exclusion unit in the caretaker's old house."

"But I thought it was working quite well?" Jenny puzzled.

"It is – reasonably," Jack replied. "But it's the concept that's all wrong. Why would you want to segregate youngsters from their peers to entrench abnormal behaviour which might become ingrained for the rest of their life?"

"How would you propose to go about things, then?" she asked, genuinely wishing to understand Jack's thinking.

"In the first place, I wouldn't have them out on a limb in some owd cottage," he began. "If they needed to be withdrawn from certain lessons – a certain maths teacher, for example – then the child in question would come to *me* in *my* classroom to do his/her maths, and so on."

"But what if there were half a dozen children from different years and different subjects that needed to come to you at the same time?" Jenny said. "Wouldn't that be impossible?"

"How many years have you known me, my Sweet Pea?" Jack asked her quietly, looking at her intently over his spectacles, that steady look in his unblinking eyes that she knew so well. "Do you *really* think I would find anything to do with teaching … impossible? Really?"

They sat for a while without speaking.

"You've thought it all through, haven't you?" Jenny commented, convinced he had given it a great deal of consideration as he always did. He would never undertake anything, no matter what, unless all his strategies stacked up and had just about fallen into place. Now he was ready.

"Given the appropriate support from the rest of the staff is available, there can be *no* problem with my master plan," he replied with a king-sized grin and a slap of his hands. "We'll have to wait and see what the new head is made of."

-o-

The maternity ward in LGI was busy, with families gathering around, welcoming new arrivals and congratulating doting parents.

"Takes me back to the day *I* was born," Jack declared as he held his new grandson in his arms by Jessie's bed, cradling his head so his long neck wouldn't flop too much.

"The day *you* were born, Daddy Jack?" Jessie gasped. "You can't surely expect us to believe that you actually *remember* that, at an age of no days plus a couple of hours or so? Mam?"

"Don't you believe it, Lass," Jenny assured her daughter. "Your father's memory *is* endless, and I have it on good authority from *his* mam, Florence May."

"How do you mean?" Jessie asked incredulously.

"I can remember mi mam tekking me 'ome on the bus from Wakefield to Normanton under her coyt on one of the coldest days in 1946," Jack explained. "I don't remember actual words and pictures, obviously, but 'feelings' pervaded mi consciousness all the time. Mi mam's mam, Marion Holmes, told me that mi father had denied that I was his child because I had a long neck and I looked nothing like him. The sort of stuff I had to put up wi' from 'im all mi life."

"You're joking! Right?" Jessie said nervously, frowning her disdain of anyone who could treat her wonderfully kind Daddy Jack like that.

249

"I'm afraid not," he replied sadly. "No love lost between your grandfather and me. Little Jack here is obviously my grandson because he has my good looks."

They all laughed at the face Jack pulled as he kissed the top of this nipper's head.

"If he lives to be half as good a man as *my* Daddy Jack, he'll do for me," Jessie said, kissing Jack as he handed back this new charge that he would enjoy watching grow.

"Hello Johnny … and Millie Alice," Jack said as he greeted his son-in-law with a warm heart-felt handshake and a hug and cuddle from his granddaughter. "Not at work today? And you, my not-so-little Sweet Pea, seem to be getting bigger by the minute. Soon I'll have to hire a crane to hold you!"

"Silly Granddaddy Jack," she replied. "You wouldn't be able to get a crane into your pocket. Its beak would be too big."

They all laughed, not sure how what she had said had been meant.

"Annual leave to look after my family," Johnny declared with a grin. "Good to see you both."

"You too," Jenny answered. "It's been lovely to see you all, but I think we've been here long enough. You need time together and to rest, so we're off. Ring us if you need anything, Jessie, or if you need someone to talk to when Johnny and Millie Alice are at work."

"But I don't go to work, Nanny Jenny," the little one insisted.

"Don't you work when you are at school?" Jack replied as they made for the door. "If you don't, I may have to have a little word with your teacher."

"Tell you what," Jack said as they walked out into the watery sunshine. "I—"

"Fancy a bite to eat at Betty's?" Jenny interrupted.

"How did you know—?" Jack gasped in surprise.

"How long have I known you, My Man?" Jenny said, with a cock of the head and the raise of an eyebrow. "Don't forget that I *am* psychic."

-o-

Summer term in any high school was always busy, what with end-of-year assessments, public exams and sports days. Trips out were also a great feature that most children loved to become involved with generally. These trips usually fell into two categories. One type was linked to, and supported, an area of curriculum where teachers had worked towards the visit throughout the year. The other type was tied to the curriculum only loosely and was accepted generally as a day out.

Unfortunately for most, because of accidental happenings in other schools, risk assessments for *every* outing were essential legalities that every event had to go through.

"Mr Allsop not in today?" Jack asked the senior deputy.

"He is not in, full stop, Jack," John replied. "Come to some arrangement with the authority and the head designate over the Easter hols – though I suspect it was a done-deal long before. Consequently, the backside of our new head, Mr Ivor Banbury, is now warming the throne of power."

"Oo you are awful, John Weaver!" Jack minced in his best Dick Emery voice. "But I like you! Is there any chance that I might—?"

He was interrupted by the squeak of a wayward, oil-less door hinge and the grating click of a sticking latch, along with a rasping voice he hadn't heard before. "Dr Ingles, I presume?" the voice said. "Have you got a minute?"

"Certainly, Mr Banbury," he replied as he followed the boss man into his office. "What can I do you for?"

"Good to meet you at last," the head said, beckoning

Jack to a seat in front of an enormous – almost empty – mahogany desk. "I've heard a lot about you."

"Some of it good, I hope," Jack quipped.

"You're bound to ruffle some people's feathers when you are as outspoken and forthright as you are purported to be," Banbury said with a mock grimace and snigger. "From what I have heard, you and I are going to get along just fine. Is there anything you'd like to do to maximise your effect? Just one major thing? We can explore details later."

"I'd like to kick yon detached inclusion unit into touch," Jack replied starkly. "Not in keeping with current philosophy on educational inclusion."

"I couldn't agree more," the head said. "To be replaced by what, though?"

Jack spent just five minutes explaining his master plan, as Mr Banbury hedged into a respectful silence.

"Very interesting," the head said at last. "May we discuss your idea, and any others you might have, by the coming May half term? For implementation at the start of the new academic year in September? As you are no doubt aware, Mr Bawker was elevated to assistant headteacher just before I came, leaving you in charge of Behaviour Management, but second to Mrs Hopkinson in charge in Special Needs."

"Will the allowance I got from the National Lottery that I paid to myself – a matter of two extra points on my salary scale – still stand while I am here?" Jack asked pointedly.

"Indeed, it will," Mr Banbury said. "But only with the proviso that you sign over the rest of the grant to the school. Deal?"

"Let me think about that," Jack said with a grin as he stroked his chin, occasionally tapping his cheek with his forefinger. "Deal!"

"Bit of a surprise, isn't it?" Jenny said, puzzled with what she had heard. "You end one term with a head you don't like and start another with—"

"A new one whom I *do* like," Jack replied as he caressed his mug of hot Yorkshire Tea. His voice faded slowly into the background as the granddaughter clock he had inherited from his granddad chimed the hour, the stew they were having for tea bubbled on the hob and Mr Black, their resident blackbird, sang out his challenge to all other yellow-billed males from their house top.

"You're actually getting paid *officially* the extra salary you awarded to … yourself from the grant *you* secured?" she gasped at Jack's audacity. "*And* you are to become second-in-charge of your department. Things don't get much better than that, surely!"

"Do you know that, pro rata, I am getting the same salary, on the same points scale, as I was in 1972 – getting on for thirty years ago?" Jack pointed out.

"You can't be!" she replied. "You're older and—"

"The key words are 'pro' and 'rata'," he explained slowly. "If I was getting the same now as then, we'd be on the breadline. It's as if we haven't moved forward at all. All down to my own ineptitude in choosing a viable and sustainable employment. Still, not too bad a wage with which to slide towards retirement."

He fell silent for a while, gazing into the ether with his eyes unblinkingly steadfast. Jenny knew very well what that meant: he was thinking – but what was he thinking about? And what would be the next thing he drew from the depths of his bottomless pit of memories?

"Do you know?" he said, finally drawing this particular memory into the sunlight. "For some reason I can't stop thinking about the people who started that unique French course with me in 1964 when I started teacher training at Beckett Park College of Education in Headingley, Leeds. They were Patty Levinson, Kate Taylor, Steve Bateson, Terry Spencer, Dave Kind, Tony Martin, Harry Hammersley – he was in his forties when we started – Clive Tordoff, Ivan Taylor, and a few others. There are so many tales I could tell – that I *need* to tell – both good, not so good, and funny."

"Why do you need to do that, Jack?" Jenny asked. "Is it some sort of catharsis, or do you just *want* to tell them, warts and all?"

"I can't for the life of me explain why, for example, Steve, Terry and Dave decided to change their main course from French to History," he said, ignoring her reasoning, although at some stage he would come back to answer her almost rhetorical question. "The only reason I can come up with is that they found it too hard."

"Have you ever thought that they might have lost interest," she said, "and wanted to try something they found more enjoyable?"

"I knew for a fact that Steve and Terry didn't rate History at all," he replied, scratching his puzzled scalp. "Easy option, I think.

"Kate Taylor, I've got to say, was a female version of me," Jack went on with a smile. "She was outspoken in the extreme. We had a tutor called Mr Basford. And one day, as she was answering his question, you can imagine what she called him; slipped out accidentally, she insisted – but with a smirk. He was incandescent with anger but could do nothing about her 'slip'.

"Clive was a big lad, but lovely with it," Jack's reminiscences took over again. "His dad was a butcher in Pudsey, I believe. Clive was funny. He and I were the ones that ate a very hearty breakfast on our last morning in Arras, Northern France – in a department called Pas-de-Calais – in 1967 at the end of our exchange. This turned all the other lads green, following our group's carousing the night before in Jean's café that we frequented every evening. The proprietor closed his café at nine and invited us into the back room with several other – French – regulars to celebrate. I have to say that we did see off quite a few bottles. Clive and I were the only ones to eat the sandwiches the Ecole Normale staff had provided for us at lunchtime. In fact, our lunch started at ten o'clock on the train to Boulogne to catch the ferry to Folkestone.

"It was a bit of a home-from-home, really," Jack went on. "Arras's nearest city was Lille, which is at the centre of a large coal-mining area – bit like the West Riding, really. Onny not as big."

"Wow!" Jenny gasped as she snuggled her head on his chest. "You haven't half lived, Our Jack. It might be nice to revisit some of these life-changing places together, don't you think?"

"Too right it would!" Jack eulogised. "That last night – or should I say morning – was a corker. Because we had been drinking as if there were no tomorrow, Alain, one of the café owner's friends, decided to give us a lift to our separate digs. He thought he would take three of us at a time, but no, we all – all ten of us – piled into his tiny Citroen 2CV. It was a bit of a squeeze, even when he peeled back the canvas roof fully, and all the windows were opened, with our legs and arms and feet sticking out!

"The engine laboured for all it was worth, but we all made it back to our individual digs in one piece. I shared digs with Tony Martin where, unfortunately, his room was bright and airy and mine was on the roadside, damp-smelling and dark. I could only open the window when I was there, which wasn't very often.

"Good gracious! I've just remembered that somebody had the bright idea of thumbing their way to Paris for a laugh."

"Thumbing?" Jenny asked, not quite sure what he was on about. "Do you mean hitch-hiking, by any chance?"

"Aye, that as well," Jack replied with a hoot. "Tony and me spent two hours on this major road – as all roads were supposed to lead to Paris – with not even a tickle or an acknowledgement. Good job, I suppose, because we didn't have enough money to eat or drink or travel anywhere. It was in the days before credit cards were widely available. We just went back to our digs and had a walk around. Apparently Clive and the others had the same luck."

"I wish we'd been together *then*," Jenny said quietly.

"I've never told anybody this, but I never really let go of you, you know," he assured her. "There was always something at the back of my mind telling me 'One day…' We'd been together as close friends for getting on for thirteen years or so – almost since birth. So how could we not continue as such? We were almost part of the same entity, inseparable, until you caught that 'freedom' bug at university. I really didn't know which way to turn. So, I threw missen into school. That turned out to be my saviour in one respect, and my doom in another. History, my sweet. History."

"I always wanted you, Jack," Jenny replied. "Just seemed to go off the rails a bit and got in with a bad crowd. It was an answer to all my prayers when we met again in Normanton's cemetery."

"It preyed on my mind a lot," Jack said emphatically. "I think I always knew Lee wasn't really for me. The only wrench was losing my son, Sam, when we went our separate ways. But then, to compensate, I got you for thirty-odd years, and three lovely nippers whom I've watched grow with pride."

"Don't forget Joey and Mary, and what you've done for them," she added. "They wouldn't be where they are today had it not been for your intervention."

"Which should have been done by their father, instead of his coo-cooing with his fancy piece, creating another family that will no doubt fail for lack of interest and effort," Jack harrumphed loudly. "No. Our family and extended family are successful because those that mean anything are closely involved and always will be."

Chapter 25

"**D**o we *have* to go to the dentist so often?" Jack complained, as they locked the car on King's Avenue outside Mr Barraclough's threatening practice.

"Yes, we do!" Jenny insisted. "Besides, your appointment is first. I've got one or two shops to pop into, one of which is—"

"The charity shop, by any vague chance?" he grinned, knowing that she loved nothing better than an hour's mooch and browse at her leisure on her own.

"And why not?" she replied quickly. "I know *not* to ask you to browse with me, so I'll see you in half an hour."

A check-up was all *he* needed. No butchery, as with Mr Barraclough's past history, although Jack had found out the year before – the last time he had allowed this dentist access to his mouth – that he was on the verge of retirement. He was preparing to introduce new young blood who were *au fait* with advanced modern practices.

Jack came out of the practice's less-than-welcoming exterior to find Jenny just leaving the neighbouring estate agency.

"'A tick, a tick, a tick a good timin',"" Jack sang as he saw Jenny.

"'Timin' is the thing it's true, good timin' brought me to you'," Jenny joined in. "'Good Timin'" by Jimmy Jones. 1960. Good timing on your part, too, because I rather fancy this house and would like us to buy it." Handing over a brochure from the estate agency, she smiled as she disappeared into the dentist's parlour, along with the flies hovering around the entrance.

Jack tutted and harrumphed quietly, wondering why she had suddenly leapt to such a momentous decision. Was there anything wrong with their newly decorated little home? The very point. Compared with their previous home in North Leeds, this one was tiny. They had always said that it was temporary and, as soon as they were ready to move, they would seek out something … bigger. Could this be the right time, and could this be the right one?

"But we've been in it only a matter of minutes," he muttered to himself. "Surely—"

"Well, what do you think?" Jenny said, tapping him on the shoulder.

"I think you have … been very quick," Jack said, almost jumping out of his skin. "Have you really seen t'owd Butcher Barraclough?"

"Course I have," she protested, a mock hurt look on her face. "But I meant what did you think about the house you have in your hand?"

"'Ome then and a cup of tea?" Jack suggested quickly. "*Then* I will have a look."

-o-

"Looks lovely and it seems to be in the right area – bungalows surrounding," Jack said, his specs perched on the end of his nose. "All rayt for owd folks, if it wasn't for the upstairs. Can I take it you'd like to move, then?"

"Do you like having four-bed detached houses surrounding you, with caged bouncy trampolines in every garden – save Stick and Joyce's – and umpteen noisy kids squealing and squawking?" Jenny urged. "I don't think Joyce and Stick will be long before they move."

"But they've onny been here five minutes!" Jack protested.

"And how long have we been here – six?" Jenny harrumphed. "We've been here five years and you've done a wonderful job bringing it up to standard, Our Jack, but I feel it's time to move on to our perhaps-forever home. Don't forget that our three bedrooms aren't big, and we do have 'children' that have children who don't live anywhere near us. I'd like them to be able to come to us to stay now and again. Wouldn't you?"

"Too right!" Jack agreed eagerly. "And—"

The faint chime of the front doorbell interrupted what he wanted to say, but it stopped just as he reached it. Two shadowy figures cast eerie shapes on the frosted but translucent glass panel at the front door's centre.

"Joyce! Stick!" Jack said with a grin. "We were just talking about you. Lugs burning?"

"Kettle on?" Stick asked.

"That's ma boy," Jack replied with an air punch. "Flick of a switch will set things in motion, I can assure you. Tea and scone it is then. Joyce?"

"Yes please, Jack," she said, rubbing her hands together enthusiastically. "Sharing good news over a cup of Yorkshire Tea and a buttered scone is always the best way."

"Good news?" Jack said as he set the tray on their glass-topped coffee table. "Won the lottery or something?"

"We're moving house," Joyce explained.

"You're dark horses, you two," Jenny declared. "But you've onny been here five minutes. What's up? Too posh for you?"

"Too surrounded by noisy kids, actually," Joyce replied. "Much as I love 'em. And we've onny been here for about four years."

"Southern Spain, then?" Jenny asked.

"A three-bedroomed detached bungalow in Wharton,

actually," Stick said. "Probably about mid-way between my school and here. The most important thing is that it's more countryfied, and quieter and easier for both on us to get to work."

"Funny you should say that, but we are thinking along the same lines, but closer to here," Jack said. "The onny detached four-bed bungalow on an oldish estate. We're off to see it tomorrow."

"Jack?" Jenny puzzled, a slight lilt in her voice. "Have we decided then?"

"Like I said, we'll go and have a look … at least. Eh?" he replied. "Maybe it's not what we want – maybe it is."

"By oldish, do you mean built a long time ago or built for 'older' folks?" Joyce asked with a smile.

"Both, I think," Jenny observed, quite pleased with both options. "Both add up to the same conclusion – peace and quiet. That's what's attractive to us both, eh, Jack?"

"Looking at this brochure, it would seem to be what we want," Jack agreed. "But let's wait until we've been to have a look. Would you like us to come with you to cast our critical eyes ower *your* new place?"

"We'd love you to," Joyce said. "Seeing as we've nobody else to share with. It's always good to have a second opinion – a pair of eyes that might see summat as we might have missed."

"This tea and scones are grand," Stick commented, smacking his lips with joy. "Was your Granddad Jud your natural grandfather? Onny, I never got to meet mine because he was killed in a mining accident down t'pit before I was born. I wish I'd been able to experience some of the closeness with mine as you did with yours."

"He *was* my granddad," Jack replied. "But my step-granddad, I suppose, although I always believed we were blood. My natural grandfather – mi mam's biological dad – was killed in t'Great War, along wi' his three brothers.

His name was Albert, and I believe it was either 1916 or 1917 when mi mam was three or four. So, she never really knew him either. She always said her mam hated Germans."

"She hated … Germans?" Joyce asked. "Was that because—?"

"Her husband, and father to her only daughter, was killed in that war … against Germany, and her son – to Jud Holmes – was killed in t'Second World War," Jack explained. "A common denominator?"

"Germans, by any vague chance?" Stick ventured.

"Spot on," Jack said solemnly. "I don't agree with the commonly held thoughts about the whole German nation that a lot of folks from that era have. The whole race can't be held responsible for the actions of a small minority … can they? I see her point, although I don't share it."

"How's your Valerie these days?" Jenny asked, casting her mind back to that difficult birth at the registry office on *her* wedding day.

"Getting married just before Christmas," Joyce replied with a heart-warming smile. "She's got a lovely young man and they're buying a house in Normanton – Queen Street, I believe. She lives a very independent life as – guess what – a librarian at the local library, which has shut down on Castleford Road and has moved into the centre of the town."

"She was telling us that the other day a nipper had thrown up over a very small shelf of books that had to be burned," Stick said. "A rayt mess, apparently. Nothing worse than the smell of stale sick. Yuk!"

"That reminds me of a tale my mate at college once told me. Dave Kind, it was," Jack reminisced eagerly. "One summer, when he was learning about teaching in a school local to his home before he went to training college, an oldish female teacher used to sit out on playtime duty. Her chair was always in the semi-shade of a large wall and, being an ample lady, she always wore a floppy, voluminous dress. Anyway, this particular day, she was sitting there, legs apart with the dress forming a drooping depression between. Unfortunately, a young nipper rushed up to her, hand in the air and green-faced, saying as he slid to a halt, 'Please Miss – yuk!!' and throwing up in the depression in the dress. This gave her a lovely bowl of aromatic vomit between her thighs."

"Oh my God!" Jenny gipped, her face turning a shade paler. "I can't imagine."

"Children, eh?" Joyce commented, her smile belying her support for Jenny's reaction.

-o-

"I can't believe how quickly we've sold this house!" Jenny gasped, once Jack had finished talking to the estate agent before they went into the supermarket. "Coming up to Christmas nobody believed it possible, especially when nothing much in our area has shifted for over six months."

"You do realise, I suppose, that we got twice as much for it as we paid," Jack pointed out.

"But the mortgage we need to take out will be quite daunting," she replied. "That is, if we can get one for the house we want to buy. But I suppose we will manage, even if you have to sell your body."

"Don't forget that we can use some of the money we have from the sale of the other house in Leeds," Jack declared. "Though it's not nearly enough to cover the quarter of a million that we'll have to shell out for the new one. Plus, don't forget I don't get paid that much, even with the cash I get from mi public exam work."

"It's been a nice house and a godsend really," Jenny said. "Just too … surrounded by children and caged trampolines."

"Do you remember the London terrorist bombings earlier this year?" Jack asked tentatively.

"Tubes and double-decker bus, wasn't it?" Jenny replied. "Why?"

"The bus blast was of special interest for me," Jack explained. "If you remember, I became a GCSE examiner in about 2003 and frequently visited a variety of examination venues."

"Birmingham and—" she said. "London?"

"Indeed," he added. "I would stay overnight at the Jury's Inn in Birmingham, or at the Russell Square Hotel in London. Remember?"

"I do," she agreed. "Not very well paid for the work you had to do."

"True, and that's the reason I packed it in this year, after two years or so. I decided at the end of August just gone that this year was my last do."

"So, where's this leading us, Jack?" Jenny puzzled, not sure what he was about to say, although it was bound to be of importance.

"The bus was blown up on the seventh of July – 7/7 as it has since been called – on Tavistock Square, which is a few yards above Russell Square where I always stayed over." He hesitated for a while, as if gathering his memories of that eventful day.

"Almost exactly an hour later than the tube bombings, where more than twenty innocent people were slaughtered, the bus on Tavistock Square exploded and killed fourteen others," Jack said, sadness and foreboding invading his face. "If it had happened exactly one week before, I would have been where that bus disintegrated. Thursday the thirtieth of June at 9.57 am."

"How come I never knew about this?" Jenny asked, a look of fear and horror growing in her eyes.

"I didn't want to upset you," he said quietly. "Because I

had become a team leader and I had to deal with student appeals after the exams, I had to be in London for an executive meeting. Fortunately, the meeting was brought forward by … exactly one week."

"My God!" she gasped, sitting down with a bump. "I could have lost you!"

Tears began to roll down her cheeks and her shoulders shook with emotion at what might have happened. She flung her arms around him and hung on for dear life.

A life without Jack wasn't even worth thinking about.

Chapter 26

Christmas had never been a wonderful time for Jack as a child. Family gatherings were either few and far between, or his father disrupted or destroyed their very essence with his obduracy or drinking. The only reason he needed to drink at his two favourite WMCs – St John's Working Men's Club, and Garth House Working Men's Club – was familiarity.

On Wakefield Road, at the opposite side of the entrance to Garth Avenue housing estate and facing the Linnet Club, was the Hark to Mopsey! inn. This gave most miners in the immediate area a heavenly drinking triangle. Most would achieve their skinful, as Jack's grandma Marion Holmes used to say, in the two working men's clubs. Jack would often wonder why, but the reason was plain and simple: the membership was limited, and the beer was cheaper. No brainer.

In their new house, the approach to Christmas 2005 should have been a time to celebrate. July of the following year would see Jack reach his first real milestone, following his sixtieth birthday anniversary in January, when he could retire from the job he had always wanted to do. He always had to be precise; from an early age he had insisted that he'd had only *one* birthday. All the rest were merely anniversaries of that initial entry to this world on January the fourth, 1946.

The end of this academic year would see him achieving his thirty-ninth year as a teacher. He could have done forty years had he gone to his sixty-first year, but he had decided long ago that *that* wasn't going to happen. Thirty-nine years was a target that few teachers achieved, and for Jack it was enough.

His children all had young nippers to enjoy. This year, they had all decided it would be best to celebrate their Christmas festivities in their own homes, perhaps making fleeting visits to see Jenny and Jack early in the new year to help celebrate his sixtieth birthday anniversary.

"Jack!" Jenny urged on the first Monday in December. "Jack! You're going to be late. Are you all right?"

Staying in bed when work beckoned had never happened in all the years they had been together. "Jack! Now you're beginning to worry me."

"Give us a hand lass, will you, please?" he said, urging himself to rise. "I can't do it on mi own. I feel so incredibly exhausted. If I can't get up for mi breakfast, I can't go in."

His ungainly wobble downstairs was alarming for her. Having sat him on the settee in his barely used dressing gown, she set about making him a bit of breakfast, only to find when she brought him his tray of goodies that he was fast asleep, sitting up, head back and mouth agape. It would normally have looked funny were it not for the fact that Jack was *never* ill. If he was, he never let on.

"OK. If there's any change, I'll let you know," Jenny said to a disembodied voice as she made to hang up the phone. The click of the handset hitting its cradle disturbed Jack enough for him to squint at the mantlepiece clock before attempting resurrection from his soft, cosy prison.

"Woah, Buster!" she warned him. "Down boy! You're going nowhere. School is not expecting you today, or any day soon, so get used to being here. If you're no better when I get back tonight, I'll make an appointment for you to see Dr Greely later in the week. Now I must away. I'll pop back to see how you are at lunchtime. Your breakfast is in the fridge, if you want it." With that, she was out of the front door and away on the very short drive to college and her day's work.

The moment the front door clicked shut, as if on cue, Jack's eyes closed slowly, leading him into a black world of anonymity and obscurity until his mind drew him slowly back to reality and confusion heralded by a similar click of the front door.

It was midday, and Jenny was back to check on her husband's state. "Jack?" her quiet voice washed over him like a breath of warm air. "Are you all right?"

"Have you forgotten something?" he said, his quietly laboured voice throwing concern at her.

"No, my lovely, I haven't," she explained. "It's midday and I'm back to see how you are. Hungry? Did you eat your … breakfast? Obviously not," she continued, as she looked in the fridge. "Now, what can I get you to eat?"

Jenny turned back to him in the lounge to find he was asleep once again.

She brought downstairs a thin duvet to keep him warm, although the central heating system ensured it wasn't entirely necessary. After a quick cuppa and a morsel to eat, she clicked her way out of the house, checking as she went that not only was he still breathing but that he was still fast on.

–o–

"Caused by a virus, I think," the doctor at their local practice said, once he had checked all necessary vitals. "The technical term for what *you* have developed is Myalgic Encephalo-mylitis – ME for short. The common term is Chronic Fatigue Syndrome."

"Any pills or potions I can take to alleviate it, Dr

Greely?" Jack asked hopefully. "You see, I'm in my last year as a teacher and I really need to get back to work so I can go out with a bang."

"It is more likely, I'm afraid, that you'll leave with a whimper," the doctor replied. "This condition is unpredictable. It might leave you tired but recovered, or it might inhabit you for many months and revisit you at times throughout your life."

"That's quite a prognosis, Dr Greely," Jack said with a forced grin.

"There is no way we can predict what will happen. We have no idea where it came from and no idea where it's going," the doctor said.

"A week off school, then?" Jack asked, more in hope than with any degree of certainty.

"I would say you should be prepared to take at least a month in the first instance," the doctor explained. "Your body is not happy that it's suffering such exhaustion, and it needs to recuperate. Consequently, rest as much as you can. Here's a note until the end of January 2006."

-o-

Jack spent the next few months fighting this unholy disease that he didn't approve of at all. To square matters with his own self-esteem, he got up every morning with Jenny. While she was at work during the morning, he set to slowly and cleaned all the rooms in the house in sequence, one every day of the week. This caused Jenny a certain degree of disquiet – a man suffering from extreme exhaustion, cleaning.

She knew that he was doing it to feel useful and to rationalise not being at work, but she didn't know how far he might be exacerbating his condition. He had poor days and then even worse days, but he forced himself on, not doing an awful lot but cleaning and … sleeping.

Jack had insisted that his children not be informed as, no doubt, they would feel it incumbent upon them to wyther about him and be obliged to visit – regularly. They had their own lives to see to and their children to look after.

Even with this subterfuge, Jessie knew. Although not his biological daughter, she had always had a strong intuitive connection with her Daddy Jack. She knew there was something not as it should be.

She would never broadcast her feelings or interfere, but … she … understood. That was one of the reasons she telephoned regularly rather than visit with Millie Alice and the new nipper, Jack. She had no doubt he – *they* – would draw her into the loop before long.

"So, you would like to go back to work, Mr Ingles?" Dr Greely asked, as they sat in his less-than-cheery consulting room.

"It's now approaching Easter in what I had planned to be my last year as a teacher in school," Jack explained. "I must be back in for my last term. I have such a lot to do with my present group."

"Feeling any better?" the doctor asked, leaning forward in his chair behind his cluttered National Health Service desk. "Tiredness fading?"

"Well, not really, to be honest," Jack replied. "But does it make any difference?"

"I don't think you understand the seriousness of your condition, Mr Ingles," the doctor explained. "If we don't keep an eye on it and do things positively, it could deteriorate and your health with it."

"I *have* at least to give it a try," Jack insisted.

"All right," Dr Greely said, "but it's against my professional advice. You must promise that if it gets worse you will be back to see me straight away."

"It's the school's Easter break coming up next week, so

I'll give it a go the week schools start again after Easter," Jack promised. "I will be back if I can't cope, but I think it'll be all right. Will I be all right to try a few days away in the sun?"

"Too right!" the doctor replied. "It can only be beneficial, but I must advise complete rest while you are away. No water skiing or parascending or water scootering, mind you."

"I couldn't do them, even if I knew what they were," Jack scoffed as he rose to leave. "Thank you for all your help."

The air outside the surgery was fresh and invigorating for a very short time. Oh, to be like he was before *this* struck him down!

There had only ever been two occasions when something unexpected and untoward had brought his house tumbling down about his ears. The first was when he was around twenty-eight years old and a severe dose of shingles took him out of action and circulation for a fortnight. The second was about three years later through an accident to his left Achilles tendon, which had become detached from his calf muscle. That was a killer! Unable to walk, great difficulty sleeping and excruciating pain throughout the day and night. He supposed that he had led a charmed life on the whole; throughout his teaching life, in front of classrooms of snotting and sneezing and coughing nippers, he had caught … nothing.

His mind swam back to the second year at teacher training college when virtually the whole of his hall of residence – some eighty or so people – dropped with a severe bout of flu. Jack was the only one not to develop even a snuffle. Several of his friends believed he had been the cause as he had come through unscathed. Others suggested he should bottle his bodily fluids as a cure-all for when the next pandemic struck.

For once in his professional life, Jack really wasn't looking forward to restarting school. Although on that first morning of the summer term he tried to persuade himself that he was feeling better, his wracked body wouldn't let him believe it.

"I *must* go today!" he muttered, as he struggled to rid himself of the accursedly annoying clinging bedclothes. His usual spring wasn't there. He perched on the edge of the bed, already gasping for air and feeling like his life had closed in on him with a vengeance.

"You really ought to rethink this madness, My Man," Jenny urged. "You won't be able to manage even an hour in yonder hellhole, surely."

"I *have* to do it, no matter what or how I feel," he replied, finally managing to reach the bathroom. "Be rayt."

"I wonder how many times you've persuaded yourself that *that* trite saying of yours is right?" Jenny snorted. "But I know all I say will fall on deaf ears with you. Stubborn, that's you, Jack Ingles."

They were quiet for a moment or two while he shaved. Even that simple action was a struggle. How was he to manage in school until four o'clock? He shuddered at the thought.

"Anyway, I'm taking you in today," Jenny insisted. "You have your favourite social sandwiches – boiled egg – so that should keep you away from intrusive interactions. Find somewhere quiet in the staff room so no-one will disturb you."

"T'smell from mi hard-boiled egg sandwiches will see to that, Sweet Pea," he chortled at the thought. "All rayt. Tha can tek mi and drop mi off and pick me up after school. All rayt?"

"Of course it is," she insisted, nodding vigorously. "Do I need David next door to help you into the car?"

"No need to be so bloomin' sarky!" he complained, not overly keen on her hard humour today when he would normally have burst into a hearty guffaw.

They covered the half mile or so to his school's drive in a brisk seven minutes, where Jenny left him to negotiate his way through the minefield of well-meaning greetings from staff and children alike. Metaphorical slaps on the shoulder were just about to pall as he escaped with a deft sidestep into the gents' toilet and cloakroom on the main corridor, opposite the staff-room entrance.

He leaned heavily against a locked toilet cubicle door, aware of what was happening within. He needed to move himself, but that was easier said than done. Goodness, how he wished he didn't need to spend such a long time in this stiflingly claustrophobic little prison with another inmate locked into the only cell!

His morning disappeared slowly, like dirty water disappearing down a semi-blocked U-bend. My God! What a drag it was.

The only light in that godforsaken dungeon was watching how many teachers made to sit near him at lunchtime, only to realise what he was eating for his snap. No backside even glanced the surface of any chair near to him. The aura surrounding him was warning enough.

Tuesday and Wednesday of that week followed the same path, making him realise that he was sliding steadily downhill and teetering on the edge of a dangerous precipice to physical and mental oblivion.

"It's no good, Jen," Jack warned his wife, as he made to sit at the table for tea. "I can't do it."

"*What* can't you do, love?" she asked carefully, seeing the look of desperation in his eyes.

"I can't continue in this school," he answered almost in a whisper. "I can't carry on. Mi body and mi head won't let me. I'm off to see Dr Greely tomorrow first thing. So would you telephone t'school in t'morning, please?"

-o-

"And physically and mentally, I just can't do it anymore, Dr Greely," Jack gasped, a seriously concerned look of capitulation invading his eyes. That look of giving in had never overcome him before in his entire life.

"I'll not say 'I told you so'," the doctor said. "But … I told you so. Tell me, when are you supposed to retire?"

"End of this July," Jack replied with a hefty sigh. "In about six weeks, give or take."

"Then, I would suggest that you retire *now*," the doctor insisted slowly. "I'll give you a note and I will write to your chief man at County Hall in Preston forthwith, detailing why you can't – and are not to – carry on. Now, go home and try to relax, because your working days are over."

-o-

"All you've lavished on this education system," Jenny said, as they had a cup of Yorkshire Tea and a chocolate Hobnob, "and what have you had in return, particularly from this school?"

"Bugger all, Our Lass. Bugger all," he replied. "Well, they can all kiss my lily-white—"

"You haven't had your biscuit yet," she interrupted quickly, pushing a plate in front of him as he sat in his favourite chair with his feet up. "Still, the rest of your – our – life together begins now."

"Mam! Daddy Jack!" a welcome and very recognisable voice rang out in their huge hallway, which was tall enough to keep a giraffe in comfort. "Guess who's come to see you?"

Millie Alice and her brother, Jack, launched themselves at their granddad, wrapping their arms about his neck to

274

the huge delight of both Jack and Jenny.

"How lovely to see you all," Jack said, hugging his grandchildren as if there were no tomorrow. "Now then, we have some wonderful news to tell you all … and then I think I'll start writing mi memoirs."

Epilogue

Twelve months in the planning, and a further twelve months in the writing, who'd have thought *Jack the Lad*, the first volume of my semi-autobiography, would now have spawned Volume 7, ***Where to Now, Jack?***

That first volume was published in 2016 to rave reviews from a couple of people who thought it was good enough to be classed as 'unputdownable'. The ones that followed were classed as the same by the folks that matter – my real reading public that became hooked on the ordinary antics and adventures of an everyday chap whose life has been 'interesting', to say the least.

His – our – life has been difficult at times, but never impossible. Since marrying Jenny – Denise – it has definitely looked up and taken us to places, both metaphorically and in reality, that have tried us on occasion but have made us happy overall. This I owe to Denise Anne English, and for which I thank her from the bottom of my Yorkshire heart.

I know that I have explained to quite a few people why I chose to call my main character ***Jack Ingles.*** So, for those folks that haven't had that explanation, here it is.

I have always liked the forename, Jack. Had I had a choice in the matter at birth, I think – only think, mind you – that I might have chosen that name. As it was, I was named after an uncle whom I never met, and who died in the Second World War when flying a Lancaster bomber over Germany. That is the only association with that city I had, whereas now I live within a couple of miles of it. What a to-do! A staunch Yorkshireman having an association with a Lancashire city!

I have always been a linguist. At school I learned French, refused the opportunity to learn German, and chose instead to be taught Russian by a Danish male teacher at the girls' high school next to my own boys' grammar in Normanton – a town in the West Riding where the Normans set up a fortified garrison during William the Conqueror's reign. It is in the Doomsday Book as Normantune. I chose French as my main teaching subject at teacher training college so I might learn how to teach eight-year-old nippers how to speak the language.

Why choose to learn Russian at the girls' high school, I hear you ask? I think I'll let you make that link.

Why Ingles for a surname, then? Quite simply, it's the Spanish word for … you've guessed it … English. I am now learning to speak Spanish, so I am able to order a cup of Yorkshire Tea and a chocolate digestive (or a chocolate-covered Hobnob), together with the bill, in any local Spanish café.

I am often asked if this book will be the last in the series. To that I have to say an unequivocal … I have no idea. How would Jack fare in the 2020s? Would he ever change? I don't think so, but who am I to gainsay any chap like this Yorkshire lad who's allus droppin' inta dialek as nobdi compriends or talks any mooer, si thi. And whose answer to any problematic interlude will always be 'Be rayt'.

It's been good fun to be part of Jack's growing up to become an adult in occasionally difficult times, to follow his home-grown philosophies on life in general, and to understand his philosophy on the importance of family. If more of us paid half as much attention to that, the better we would all be, si thi.

There has been a mention that Jack wrote a number of books for the nippers in his family. I should tell the reader that they certainly do exist, having been read by those nippers many times over and now being enjoyed by youngsters worldwide. The author's name on the front cover is always, and always will be, Frank English.

If you enjoy fantasy adventure for children aged from seven to ninety-seven, his website (what on earth is a website – somewhere where spiders hang out?) tells you more.

Ever eager to hear from the readers of his stories, Jack (Frank) can be contacted at

frankenglish6@yahoo.com

Frank English

Born in 1946 in the West Riding of Yorkshire's coal fields around Wakefield, he attended grammar school, where he enjoyed sport rather more than academic work. After three years at teacher training college in Leeds, he became a teacher in 1967. He spent a lot of time during his teaching career entertaining children of all ages, a large part of which was through telling stories, and encouraging them to escape into a world of imagination and wonder. Some of his most disturbed youngsters he found to be very talented poets, for example. He has always had a wicked sense of humour, which has blossomed only during the time he has spent with his wife, Denise. This sense of humour also allowed many youngsters to survive often difficult and brutalising home environments.

In 2006, he retired after almost forty years working in schools with young people who had significantly disrupted lives because of behaviour disorders and poor social adjustment, generally brought about through circumstances beyond their control. At the same time as moving from leafy lane suburban middle-class school teaching in Leeds to residential schooling for emotional and behavioural disturbance in the early 1990s, changed family circumstance provided the spur to achieve ambitions. Supported by his wife, Denise, he achieved a Master's degree in his mid-forties and a PhD at the age of fifty-six, because he had always wanted to do so.

Other adult books he has written:

Jack the Lad	*Published 2016*
Jack	*Published 2016*
Hit the Road Jack	*Published 2017*
Welcome Back Jack	*Published 2017*
All Right Jack?	*Published 2018*
Carry On Jack	*Published 2020*
Hidden Secrets	*Published 2021*

(historical novel set in late Victorian times)

Children's books he has written to date:

Magic Parcel: The Awakening	*Published June 2010*
Magic Parcel: The Gathering Storm	*Published March 2011*
Magic Parcel: A New Dawn	*Published August 2012*
18 Mulberry Road	*Published September 2011*
25 Primrose Walk	*Published January 2013*
Autumn Adventures	*Published September 2013*
Winter Tales	*Published September 2014*
Towards Spring	*Published September 2016*

Books he has written *with* children:

Juniper's Tale	*Published August 2018*
Honey	*Published January 2019*
The Story of Lemuel Pecker	*Published April 2019*
Josephine's Journey	*Published June 2019*
Holly's Prize	*Published April 2020*
Sara's Astonishing Story	*Published May 2020*
Garnett's Grand Getaway	*Published June 2020*
The Boys in Black	*Published June 2020*
The Magic Whistle and the Tiny Bag of Wishes	*Published November 2020*
Half Moon Farm	*Published June 2021*

www.ingramcontent.com/pod-product-compliance
Lightning Source LLC
Chambersburg PA
CBHW060806190726
48285CB00002B/565